JOHN LUTZ

SLAUGHTER

PINNACLE BOOKS
Kensington Publishing Corp.
www.kensingtonbooks.com

PINNACLE BOOKS are published by

Kensington Publishing Corp.
119 West 40th Street
New York, NY 10018

All Kensington titles, imprints, and distributed lines are available at special quantity discounts for bulk purchases for sales promotions, premiums, fund-raising, educational, or institutional use. Special book excerpts or customized printings can also be created to fit specific needs. For details, write or phone the office of the Kensington sales manager: Kensington Publishing Corp., 119 West 40th Street, New York, NY 10018, attn: Sales Department; phone 1-800-221-2647.

This book is a work of fiction. Names, characters, businesses, organizations, places, events, and incidents either are the product of the author's imagination or are used fictitiously. Any resemblance to actual persons, living or dead, events, or locales is entirely coincidental.

ISBN-13: 978-0-7860-2831-3
ISBN-10: 0-7860-2831-9

First printing: September 2015

10 9 8 7 6 5 4 3 2 1

Printed in the United States of America

First electronic edition: September 2015

ISBN-13: 978-0-7860-3798-8
ISBN-10: 0-7860-3798-9

Highest Praise for
John Lutz

"John Lutz knows how to make you shiver."
—Harlan Coben

"Lutz offers up a heart-pounding roller coaster
of a tale."
—Jeffery Deaver

"John Lutz is one of the masters of the police novel."
—Ridley Pearson

"John Lutz is a major talent."
—John Lescroart

"I've been a fan for years."
—T. Jefferson Parker

"John Lutz just keeps getting better and better."
—Tony Hillerman

"Lutz ranks with such vintage masters
of big-city murder
as Lawrence Block and Ed McBain."
—*St. Louis Post-Dispatch*

"Lutz is among the best."
—*San Diego Union*

"Lutz knows how to seize and hold the
reader's imagination."
—*Cleveland Plain Dealer*

"It's easy to see why he's won an Edgar
and two Shamuses."
—*Publishers Weekly*

*For The Aardvarkian, Mr. B, Mr. E,
Ms. El, The Em, Mr. J, Mr. Lucas,
The Soph, The journey.*

ACKNOWLEDGMENTS

The author wishes to acknowledge the invaluable aid of Michaela Hamilton, Dominick Abel, Marilyn Davis, and Barbara Lutz.

PART ONE

Still as they run they look behind,
They hear a voice in every wind,
And snatch a fearful joy.

—THOMAS GRAY, "Ode on a Distant
    Prospect of Eton College"

1

Rose Darling knew she'd begun jogging too late. Unless she lengthened her stride, she'd be caught in Central Park after dark. Not that she hadn't been warned, but hadn't everybody at some time or other been warned not to be in Central Park after dark?

The trouble was, she had a date, and if she turned her daily jog into a track meet with the clock, her long dark hair would become a sweaty, unmanageable mass in the summer heat.

Rose was an attractive woman, tall and athletic, with shapely legs and a graceful way about her. Men would stare at her when she jogged.

Like the guy she was approaching on her left, who had a bicycle upside down so it rested on its seat and handlebars. Was he only pretending to work on his bike, so he could stop and watch her pass? Maybe he'd give her a few seconds, make up his mind, and start after her. He could catch her easily on his bike.

And he did straighten up and give her a direct, leering look from beneath a broad blue sweatband.

She averted her eyes and stared straight ahead as she

jogged past. When she was well beyond him, she risked glancing over her shoulder, half expecting to see him pedaling hard and bearing down on her.

But he was bent over his upside-down bicycle again, busy trying to repair whatever was wrong with it.

Big wuss, I am!

She almost smiled.

Breathing more freely, she adjusted her pace so she did a minimum of bouncing, preserving her hairdo. She continued telling herself to calm down, she'd make it to the Central Park West and 81st Street exit before the sky became dark. She'd be out of the jungle then, into the bright lights and ceaseless motion of the city. Safe.

Safer, anyway. A different sort of jungle.

After about five minutes the trail bent and she looked directly ahead and saw the tall buildings along Central Park West. Their windows were beginning to show lights in uneven patterns, reminding her of a crossword puzzle that was all blanks. Behind the jagged skyline the blue sky had become an endless deepening purple.

Rose looked around her. There was no one in sight.

But she could hear the rushing whisper of the traffic now. Ahead of her.

Getting close. I'll make it out before dark.

That was when she heard the cry. It was sharp and distinct, and quickly over. The cry of a wounded or slain animal? A woman?

It had come from off to the right and slightly ahead of her. There were trees there, and thick foliage. She might have seen some movement, but she couldn't be sure. She kept her senses tuned for another cry.

Rose didn't know the source of the cry, but upon reflection she was sure it hadn't been a bird. There was too much . . . anguish in it.

My imagination again.

She could hear herself breathing hard and fast. Without thinking about it, she'd picked up her pace.

Another movement! Off the trail and near where she'd seen the first.

Someone might be over there hurt. Might need her help.

She'd heard the cry and seen the movement. She could veer off, run over there.

Don't be an idiot! If you really saw anything it was probably a dog or cat. Maybe a squirrel. There were about a thousand of them in the park.

Her legs felt suddenly heavier as she jogged past the spot where, if there was anything in the bushes, predator, human, or otherwise, it would have begun pursuing her.

She speeded up even more.

Tomorrow. I'll jog again in the morning and go over there, make sure I saw nothing important. Make sure nothing happened.

She thought she heard something behind her, and she stole a glance over her shoulder.

No one in sight. Almost dark now.

No one in sight.

But plenty of places for them to hide.

Her jog became a dash.

2

"They won't come near me," Lois Graham said in a puzzled voice. "Not even when I try to feed them popcorn."

She demonstrated by dipping her fingers into a small white bag and tossing backhand several still-warm kernels of popcorn.

"See," she said, as the half dozen or so pigeons gathered around the bench drew back and away from the popcorn and Lois, as if a silent signal had been received. "It's almost as if they know something I don't."

"Maybe they know more than most of us, only in different ways. Too bad they can't talk, like parrots."

"I'm not so sure we can't trust parrots. They have a way of looking at me, as if they know something I should but don't."

Corey smiled. He was a small man, wearing carefully faded jeans and a green polo shirt with the collar turned up in back. He had on a Mets cap, tilted so it made him look a little jaunty. "Haven't you ever noticed pigeons get that way just before sundown?"

"No. But I'll take your word for it. What do you think? Some protective instinct?"

"Sure." The pigeons around them fluttered but went nowhere, as if on cue. "They know it's almost bed-time."

Actually Corey had no idea how pigeons thought. Especially New York pigeons. You didn't notice them for a while, then some days they seemed to be every-where. Dumb birds, skittering around and almost get-ting stepped on or run over, but never quite. He knew they were prey to the peregrine falcons that roosted on some of the tall buildings along Central Park West, al-most directly across from where he and Lois were. Beautiful, deadly creatures. Corey thought it would be great if one of the large falcons swooped in and made off with one of the pigeons. Apropos, though Lois didn't yet know that.

"What's in the bag?" she asked, pointing to the large canvas bag at his feet. It was dark blue with black straps and handles and doubled as a backpack.

"Sweaty clothes and exercise equipment," he lied. "I was working out at the gym before I came here."

"The one on Amsterdam?"

"Seventy-second Street," Corey said, figuring there must be a gym somewhere on Seventy-second. Not that it mattered, unless Lois happened to go to a gym in that neighborhood. Corey hadn't been to a gym in years. There were so many much more interesting things to do without breaking a sweat.

He prodded the bag with the toe of his shoe and glanced around. Shadows were longer and more de-fined. It would be dark soon.

"Why don't you come with me?" he said, picking up the bag, then slinging it over one shoulder by one padded strap.

"Where?"

"Out of the park. It's a dangerous place after dark. Full of predators."

She smiled. "I'm not afraid when I'm with you."

He returned the smile with his own. Ever wonder why that is? He wished sometimes for a victim whose intellect he could respect.

She stood up from the bench, brushed popcorn from her blouse and jeans, and turned to go. The pigeons that had ventured nearer fluttered, cooed, and closed in on the discarded popcorn. It must seem tastier to them now that Lois was leaving.

"This way," Corey said, motioning toward a stand of trees and thick foliage.

"This is the way out," Lois said, starting in another direction.

"I know a better way," Corey said, and folded her hand gently in his.

He thought about the jogger, wondering if she was back on the crowded streets by now, or even home, if she lived nearby. A woman like that would explore every nuance of her pain. It was part of the instinct to attempt escape, or to find some hoped-for measure of mercy in her predator.

He felt Lois squeeze his hand three times, like some kind of secret signal.

He signaled back. There would be plenty of time later for the jogger, if that was what he decided. It would be up to him.

A soft breeze kicked up, breaking the heat and swaying the upper limbs of the trees they were walking toward. Lois shifted her weight and walked alongside him, and he was glad he didn't have to tell her yet that for her there was no way out of the park.

Not that it mattered.

She'd soon find out she was going somewhere much more interesting.

3

It was dawn when Patti LuPone's vibrant voice began imploring Argentina not to cry for her. Frank Quinn lay on his stomach, still half asleep, musing that he could never hear enough of the score from *Evita*. Usually he was awake and out of bed before the CD player's timer turned the bedroom of the brownstone on West Seventy-fifth into Argentina. This morning he clung to sleep, as if for some reason he knew he shouldn't get out of bed. If only he had a note from his mother for his teacher, he thought with a smile. He realized he'd been dreaming about algebra, and his math teacher in school in Brooklyn. He could hear her voice telling him that once he conquered algebra he would have no trouble with geometry. You can always find an angle, Francis.

And that's what he was doing in life, only looking for other people's angles.

"Turn shong off," a voice muttered beside him.

Pearl, lying close with one arm slung over him, her face half buried in her wadded pillow.

"Shong off!"

Quinn worked his way out from beneath her arm, propped himself up on one elbow, and sat on the edge of the bed. With thick fingers he fumbled the digital controls on the combination CD player, clock radio, alarm, phone. Finally he touched the right button and the bedroom was silent except for the background noise of the city outside the brownstone.

"Thanksh," Pearl said into her pillow.

Wearing only Jockey shorts, Quinn stood up, a tall, muscular man in the autumn of life but still strong. His shoulders were sloping and powerful, his hands large and dangling like grappling hooks at the ends of his long arms.

The CD player, clock, radio, alarm, phone beeped.

A phone call.

"Damn!" Pearl said, quite clearly.

Quinn saw on the glowing ID panel that the caller was Police Commissioner Harley Renz.

Quinn didn't like talking with Renz anytime, much less when he was still half asleep.

He picked up the receiver, with trepidation.

"Quinn?"

"It's me," Quinn admitted.

"You still in the sack?"

"Sack. Yes."

"Had breakfast yet?

"No."

"Don't. I got something for you."

Quinn's interest quickened. He and his investigating agency, Quinn & Associates (Q&A), sometimes took on cases on a work-for-hire basis for the NYPD. Renz was a purely political animal, stepping on necks and trading in corruption on his way up the bureaucratic path to the top. If a case had political ramifications and was deemed by Renz to be too hot to handle, he passed it down to Quinn and his detectives. Quinn had worked his way, and Renz had bought and extorted his way, to the higher echelons of the NYPD, before Quinn had gone into business for himself.

"You don't want to get your fingers dirty?" he asked Renz.

Renz laughed. "You're my go-to guy when a case looks like shit that might rub off. I admit it. Our business, you gotta expect some shit."

"I like to limit it."

"And I like to roll in it," Renz said. "I don't mind admitting I'm ambitious. We both know the score. We got things to trade. You take the risk and the media flack, and the money. I come away clean, move up a notch or two, and there's more money for me down the line."

Quinn didn't know how Renz figured that, and didn't want to ask. "What is it that you have," he said, "that you're so afraid will bite you in the ass?"

"Someone is dead," Renz said. "A young woman whose purse contents identify her as Lois Graham. Got an address in SoHo."

"Is that where the body is?" Quinn asked. He heard and felt Pearl stir next to him.

"Nope. Central Park. Near the Eighty-first Street entrance, not far off Central Park West."

"Sexual assault?"

"Maybe."

"That why she was killed?" Women were murdered occasionally in Central Park. So why was Renz calling Quinn about this one?

"The why isn't what bothers me. It's the how."

"So what's the how?"

"You'd have to see it."

Quinn knew Renz was right. Despite the aggravating word games, Quinn would be curious enough to get up and drive to Central Park, even at this early hour.

"I'll be there soon as I can," Quinn said.

"Bring Pearl."

Quinn glanced toward the other side of the king-size bed and saw that Pearl was gone. Pipes rattled and squealed and he heard the shower run. Pearl could shower and dress faster than any woman Quinn had known.

"Try to stop her," he said.

4

After parking the Lincoln illegally near a loading dock on a side street, Quinn propped his NYPD plaque in the windshield, and he and Pearl jogged across Central Park West toward the park.

It wasn't difficult to find the crime scene. White canvas panels were propped on two sides of where Quinn and Pearl assumed the body to lie. Yellow crime scene tape kept gawkers at a distance on the other two sides. A uniform appeared and moved to stop them. Then the young cop recognized Quinn and backed away, pointing needlessly toward the canvas and the knot of uniforms as well as plainclothes cops in suits and ties. Most of the detectives had taken off their suit coats, and their shirts were glued to them so the color of their flesh showed through the damp material.

Quinn and Pearl moved through dappled morning sunlight toward the crime scene. Today showed every indication of becoming another scorcher. Quinn, as usual, wore a coat and tie as if already on the hunt. Pearl, vividly attractive as ever with her dark hair and eyes and generous figure, had on casual navy slacks and a white tunic. A breeze rattled the leaves on the branches above as they moved toward the body, careful to avoid where the CSU techs told them not to step. Renz noticed them and gave a half wave. He was wearing a light tan suit instead of his commissioner's uniform. His increasingly rotund form put to waste the expensive material and expert tailoring.

Doctor Julius Nift, the little necrophiliac (it was rumored) ME, was kneeling by the nude dead woman and looked up and smiled at them. Especially at Pearl, who hated him with a passion.

Renz also smiled, his flesh-padded cheeks almost hiding his eyes, the fat pink of his bull neck spilling over his white shirt collar.

"Meet Lois Graham," Nift said. "Beautiful in death." He rose to his full height, which wasn't much, and expanded his chest. He saw himself as Napoleonic. Quinn thought of him as a banty rooster with a sour disposition.

Lois Graham's clothes were stacked neatly folded off to the side. It took a second look to realize they appeared to have been cut away from her body rather than removed in ordinary fashion. Her pale, still form lay on its back so she seemed to be staring up at the sky with frozen wonder.

"She has some rack on her," Nift commented, doubtless trying to get a rise out of Pearl, who ignored him.

But that wasn't what sickened and angered Quinn. Lois Graham had been eviscerated, her intestines coiled next to her body. And there was something about how she lay. A strange awkwardness. Quinn and Pearl moved closer.

And suddenly understood. The corpse's limbs had

been neatly sawed through at the joints. Her wrists were a quarter of an inch short of her hands. Her arms had been severed at the elbows and shoulders. Same kind of sawing with her legs, at the ankles, knees, and hips. Quinn had assumed her throat had been cut. He saw now that her head had been sawn off and replaced slightly crookedly on the stump of her neck. There was, oddly enough, not a lot of blood.

"The injuries are postmortem," Nift said. "If her heart hadn't stopped first there'd be blood all over the place. But as you can see, there isn't."

"Thank God for that," Pearl said.

"Did the killer have medical knowledge?" Quinn asked.

Nift shook his head. "Some. He isn't a surgeon, but he has a basic knowledge of the human body."

"Med-school dropout?" Pearl asked.

"Doubtful. A med-school student would have done this a bit differently, and with different instruments."

"Still . . ." Quinn said

Nift shook his head. "Not part of the curriculum. Though my guess is that he's done this kind of thing before."

They all glanced at Lois Graham. Her corpse reminded Quinn of a marionette that had been carefully laid out because its strings had been removed. Unlike some of the recently dead they had seen, she didn't look as if she might surprise them by getting up and walking away. Something about the detached but related parts. Then there was the compactly coiled length of intestine. Quinn regarded the incision from her sternum to pubis.

"What do you think made the cuts?" he asked.

Nift shot a look at Renz, who had already asked him some of these questions. Renz said nothing. Nift sighed and knew he'd better answer again. He winked at Pearl, who stood stone-faced.

"Not a surgical tool that I could identify," Nift said. "Some kind of sharp, agile saw with a narrow blade. It cut cleanly through bone and gristle, along with flesh."

"Electrical?"

"You mean battery powered?" Nift smoothed his tie. "I doubt it. Not because a portable saw wouldn't do this. It looks to me that the instrument was sharp enough that an electrical or fuel-powered saw wouldn't have been needed. And I'm sure the cutting was done right here. She wasn't sectioned off like this and then moved here and so neatly reassembled."

"But it's possible?" Pearl said.

"Possible," Nift conceded. "More like the work of a jigsaw in the hands of a reasonably strong man."

"Or woman?" Pearl asked.

Nift shrugged. "I doubt it, but I wouldn't rule it out."

"This was . . . sex to him," Pearl said.

"Understandable," Nift said.

Pearl looked at him as if he were the most loathsome thing on the planet.

"Control's what it's all about," he explained. "That's why victims die such slow deaths."

Pearl said, "It's almost as if she was a doll and he took her apart to see how she worked."

Quinn thought it was exactly like that. "Jigsaw," he said. "Do you really suppose that's how he killed them?"

"That's how I'd do it." Nift winked at Pearl. "If I wanted these same results. Of course, I'm a professional. I'd do a cleaner, neater job." He waved a hand to take in the death scene. "This guy was a butcher, but not one without promise."

"As a surgeon," Pearl said.

Nift smiled at her. "No, as a serial killer."

Renz looked at his watch. "I've got important meetings this morning."

And we don't. Pearl considered Renz and Nift. Control.

"I'll drop by and sign the work-for-hire contract, and pick up some NYPD shields," Quinn said. "Then we'll go look over the victim's apartment."

"Crime scene techs have already been there. No sign of the killer having visited. Nothing unusual. Place neat enough, if you don't count a D-cup bra draped over a chair in the bedroom."

"I'm gonna give you Helen for this one," Renz said. Helen Iman was an NYPD profiler, a six-foot-plus amazon in her forties who looked like a women's basketball coach. She was the only profiler Quinn had much faith in. She talked some of the familiar and obvious profiler-standard yammer, but there was no arguing with her results.

"Does Helen know that?" Quinn asked.

"She does," Renz said. "She'll be by for you to brief her later this morning. Remember, she reports to you and works for me." Renz smiled. "She has a tightrope to walk. Not so unlike yourself."

"Who discovered the body?" Quinn asked.

"Early morning jogger. Health nut like the victim. Name of Rose Darling." Renz glanced again at his gold watch. "I'll fax you what we got when it comes in. Keep the info tight, though. The sooner the media find out, and the more they know, the harder it will be to find this psycho and put him down."

"There's only so much we can do with media," Quinn said. "We can't keep this a secret, unless we pay off Rose Darling and send her away on vacation someplace nobody ever heard of."

"It's the mob that does that kind of thing," Renz said.

Pearl concealed a thin smile. Control.

"Let Rose Darling talk," Renz said. "I run an open shop and play square with the citizens. We just won't mention anything in detail about the manner of death, especially about the dismemberment. And we've got a couple of days before we have to officially ID the body."

"A few facts and an inconclusive story will drive the media wolves crazy. They'll have their fangs out and will be pressing for answers."

"Not to worry," Renz said. "I've got a guy who can handle them."

"Who would that be?" Quinn asked.

"You."

5

Jordan Kray sat in his apartment watching the news on his small flat-screen TV. Although he could easily afford a bigger set, he liked to watch the news small, so he could wrap his mind around it. Understand it. Learn how things work.

He sat in his stocking feet with his knees drawn up sideways. His living room was spacious, with a view of the tree-lined street where he'd moved a year ago, when a well-thought-out financial strategy had brought him a windfall. Moving the money from his victims' accounts to his own had been painful for them but a pleasure for him. He relived their agonies each time he turned the key in his front door.

There were two kinds of people in the world. He was a winner, and the other kind didn't matter. Once they were dead and disinterested, what was theirs became his. Cash, jewelry, valuable antiques . . . it all became negotiable and found its way into his portfolio of ETFs and mutual funds. The devil's own treasure chest for one of his disciples.

He'd stopped off at the kitchenware department of a store on Broadway and bought two identical automatic pop-up toasters—one to use in his kitchen, and one to disassemble so he thoroughly understood how the toasters worked. Did they raise the toasted slices of bread when they had become sufficiently toasted, or was the whole thing all about times? Like it took a certain amount of time to toast bread and that was that. Simple. No thermostat, nothing that Jordan couldn't understand.

But what about the timer? If there was one.

He glanced at the TV screen. People in Arab clothing were throwing rocks at each other, while those not involved in some kind of demonstration cowered and tried to stay safe. This was news?

He shifted his attention to the toaster and used a screwdriver to remove its chrome cover.

There were the heat baffles that were within fractions of an inch of the bread slices. They would probably glow red and stay that way until the bread was sufficiently browned.

But how does the toaster know?

On the TV screen, a battered pickup truck arrived on the scene. Men with what looked like Kalashnikov automatic rifles began jumping out of both sides of the truck's bed as it coasted down the street toward the rock throwers.

The killer glanced at the TV, then returned his attention to the toaster. It appeared that what he thought of as heat baffles were actually spring-loaded devices whose purpose was to isolate the toast so it was kept from touching the heating coils.

Not wanting to be fooled twice, the killer left the

chrome body of the toaster off, and slipped the power cord into a wall socket. He put no bread in, but depressed the toaster's handle.

It took less than a minute for the coils to glow bright red.

The sound of gunfire erupted from the TV, and a woman's breathless voice began talking about "the army and the terrorists."

There were several explosions. The pickup truck that had recently arrived at the scene was now upside down and burning. People were bent over and running, crossing the Arab street to escape gunfire.

The killer unplugged the toaster and let it cool. He had it now. He understood how it worked. How this brand of toaster worked, anyway. It was controlled by a timer rather than by a thermostat to register the temperature that would brown the bread without burning it.

Crowd sounds drifted in from the TV.

There was a soft *sproing!* sound and a spring about an inch long flew out of the toaster and landed on the table. The killer bent over and studied what he could see of the toaster's mechanism. There was no sign of where the spring had come from, but he wasn't worried. He could figure it out later. Or maybe the toaster didn't even need the spring in order to work.

He suspected that more expensive toasters had some kind of thermostat and were controlled by heat rather than time. This one was a cheapy, bought for research rather than jelly or jam. Time now to put it back together.

It didn't want to go back together. At least, not to its previous form. Not for the killer. The chrome cover wouldn't go on straight, and he seemed to have broken the Bakelite handle on the lever that depressed the bread.

He picked up a smaller screwdriver and used it to pry the toaster's cover. He needed only about an eighth of an inch. The sleek chrome body of the toaster still wouldn't quite fit. He pried with the smaller screwdriver.

Yeow!

The damned thing was still hot!

And there was that damned spring, rolling off the table.

He went to the sink and filled a glass with cold water, then sat on a kitchen counter stool and soaked his left hand.

He found himself facing the TV. Someone, a man or woman, was on fire and crawling away from the burning truck.

The truck exploded. The person crawling away was enveloped in flames.

The killer removed his hand from the glass and dried it on a dish towel. His burned fingers didn't look serious enough that he'd need ointment and a Band-Aid. He resumed reassembling the toaster.

A man in neatly pressed pajamas, sitting on the edge of a bed, came on the TV screen and began talking about the benefits of a new pill that helped people get to sleep and wasn't habit-forming. It also sometimes eliminated erectile dysfunction.

The killer remained zeroed in on toaster dysfunction. This time being more careful.

Until he heard a local newscaster's voice say Lois Graham's name.

He put down the toaster and sat watching the flat-screen TV. The newscaster, Tad something, was interviewing a detective the killer was familiar with, a man named Frank Quinn. It took the killer only a few seconds to recognize Quinn, but who could forget the imposing figure? He was a big man, too rugged to be a leading man, but with the kind of honest ugliness that attracted some women.

"We're searching now for whoever killed her," Quinn was saying. No doubt talking about Lois Graham. "It appears that he panicked, probably scared away by someone or some animal. Unfortunately, no one reached her in time to save her."

The killer almost laughed out loud; I guess not, with her insides all over the grass, and the rest of her taken apart like a puzzle.

He was proud of his work.

"There's nothing special about this killer," Quinn was saying.

The killer smiled. You're lying!

"But we would like to warn people again about the park," Quinn continued. "Sometimes such places are scenic and safe during daylight hours, but are much different after dark. Central Park is a great place, but don't go there unless you have to after sundown."

"To Central Park?" Tad the newsman seemed incredulous.

"To any park. Cowardly killers like this are friendly with the night."

Cowardly? The killer's hands balled into fists.

"Unless he moves on," Quinn continued, "we'll catch him. Killers like this are doomed to be apprehended. Experience has taught us that they're not overly bright."

You're lying!

"So entangled in their compulsion that they're not capable of logical reasoning."

You're lying!

"There's nothing much in them but evil."

Lying! If God doesn't want me to do this, why is He letting me? Why is He urging me? Why is He my accomplice?

The camera moved to the handsome newscaster, who absently lifted a hand and smoothed back his hair. "So except for the victim and her family—and our hearts go out to them—would you say there is nothing special about this murder?"

Tell him about the gutting, the disassembly of her parts!

"No," Quinn said, "it's just another squalid homicide, probably done on impulse by a maniac."

Lying! Lying!

Tad the newsman shook his head. "So sad . . ."

Lying!

Quinn was back on camera, looking straight into the lens. "It's a kind of sickness that can overcome even the best of us."

"So this kind of killer is a mental case, silently screaming for help?"

"Usually."

Lie on.

Quinn imagined the killer someplace comfortable, with his feet propped up, watching television.

You'll be sorry.

6

The trees blocked their view. Or the dusk was dark enough that there were reflections in the windows and the glass had turned to mirrors. Windows of the buildings across the street from the park, overlooking the crime scene, didn't yield much help. None of the potential witnesses happened to be looking outside at the time of the murder.

That was their story, anyway.

Fedderman, Sal, and Harold knocked on doors much of the day and were dismayed by how no one would claim to have seen Lois Graham's murder. All three detectives knew that some of them might be withholding evidence. They didn't want to get involved; it might somehow taint them, lead to some crime they'd committed without knowing, suck them into the system and rightly or wrongly list their names forever

These days more than ever, people didn't want their names on a list. Any kind of list.

After lunch, Sal and Harold continued canvassing the neighborhood, while Quinn and Fedderman made a second examination of the victim's apartment. They looked again at a stack of blank paper near the printer. Wouldn't it be nice if her laptop or pad turned up, full of information that could identify her killer?

They poked and peered but found nothing of use in the apartment. It was fashionably but not lavishly furnished. *Eclectic* would describe it.

"One thing," Quinn said. "Wasn't there a carpet in the bedroom?"

Fedderman cupped his chin in his hand and thought. "Yes," he said with certainty. "Not very large, though. More like a throw rug."

They tried to think what else had been here but was now gone. They couldn't identify anything for sure. It was possible some dishes or glasses were missing from a kitchen cabinet.

"Weren't there three chairs instead of two at the kitchen table?" Fedderman asked, pointing to the small drop-leaf table and two wooden chairs that looked as if they'd spent years in classrooms.

"Could have been," Quinn said.

"I remember now because the missing chair didn't look like the others. It was a little larger and had some guy's name carved in it."

"Our killer?" Quinn asked, knowing it wouldn't be so.

"If his name is Hinkley," Fedderman said.

They continued their search. Like last time, they found no evidence that the victim had been under duress, or was being stalked, during the time leading up to her murder. Her purse, found near her body, had held the usual items found in women's purses—wadded tissue, a comb, lipstick, an oversized key ring holding a plastic four-leaf clover that if squeezed became a tiny flashlight, a pair of very dark made-in-Taiwan sunglasses, some old theater and movie ticket stubs. There was a wallet containing two twenty-dollar bills and the usual charge, debit, and ID cards. No driver's license (no surprise, in New York City). A plasticized card proclaimed her membership in a gym. (They all belong to gyms, Quinn thought.) Her keys were missing. The supposition was that after killing Lois, the murderer let himself into her apartment and stole her computer. Obviously, he was afraid something on it might lead to him.

Maybe, Quinn thought, he'd also stolen a throw rug and a wooden chair.

A phone call to a local antique dealer shed some light. The dealer said on the phone he'd have to see the rug in order to give an estimate of its worth. The missing wooden chair, he said, after hearing Quinn's description, if genuine and in good condition, might be worth several thousand dollars.

So the killer had taken the victim's computer and then come back later to move what was valuable and more noticeable. Quinn assumed the killer would have dressed like some sort of workman and simply walked out of the building and to his car or truck with the chair and rolled rug.

But what amazed and angered the detectives was the strong possibility that he had returned and taken away what was valuable in the apartment while they were eating lunch.

After work at Coaxly and Simms, writing ad copy, Rose Darling entered her apartment, closed the door behind her, and fastened all her locks. Since finding that girl the way she was in Central Park, Rose hadn't felt safe. She read everything she could find on the murder. Watched the news.

How could something have happened so close to her? She had passed right by where and when that poor woman was murdered. The fear had pushed her into a run.

She recalled the curious sense of dread she'd felt while jogging there. Some part of her mind must have realized something. Her anxiety had been so real!

She decided she wasn't going to run this evening in the unrelenting heat. And certainly not in the park. She wasn't sure when she'd feel comfortable again while jogging. The thing to do, she decided, was wait until the sicko killer was caught. And killed. (She hoped.) Then she could run again, but on the sidewalks, where people were walking. Then she realized that might be unwise, being the fastest one and drawing everyone's stares.

Everyone's.

She cranked up the air-conditioning, sat down on the sofa, and, using one foot, then the other, worked off her high heels. She could recall her father's cautioning voice from her youth: Don't stick your neck out. Don't make it easier for the bastards.

Never had she believed more in her father's simple wisdom.

She let herself sink back into fatherly philosophy and the welcoming embrace of the sofa cushions.

7

"Lennon was shot there," Sal Vitali said to Harold Mishkin, as they walked along Central Park West toward where they'd parked the unmarked car.

Before them loomed the ornate stone building that occupied an entire block.

"The Russian or the singer?" Harold asked.

Not sure whether Harold was playing dumb, Sal growled simply, "The singer."

Harold's expression of detached mildness didn't change as he made a slight sound that might have meant anything.

They'd finished interviewing Lois Graham's pertinent neighbors, catching some of them after work hours but before dinner. People didn't like to have their meals delayed or interrupted.

The two detectives thought it might be worth talking to the victim's upstairs neighbor again, a guy named Masterson, who had seemed more than a little nervous the first time. But maybe that was because his apartment smelled strongly of weed. He and a busty twenty-three-year-old girl named Mitzy, who'd spent the night with him, swore they'd been in bed all evening the night of the murder. They'd been listening to CDs of Harry Connick Jr. songs. Harold thought that was unlikely, though he himself liked Connick Jr.

Tonight when Masterson ("call me Bat—everyone does") opened his door to them, Mitzy was nowhere to be found.

Bat motioned for Sal and Harold to sit on the sofa, and sat down across from them in a ratty old recliner that creaked beneath his weight. Harold noted that Masterson was a larger man than he'd first thought. Broad and muscular.

"Where's Mitzy this evening?" Sal asked.

Masterson shrugged. Not easy to do in a recliner, but he managed. "At her quilting bee. She belongs to this gang of women who sit around and gossip and make quilts. Give them to people they like or love. I've got so many I don't know what to do with the damned things." He shrugged again, exactly like the first time. "I'd be happy to see a Christmas tie this year."

"You mean between two of the women in the quilting bee?" Harold said.

Masterson looked at Harold the way Sal had. Harold seemed not to notice.

Sal thought Masterson was going to shrug a third time, but he just sat there, as if the brief conversation and two sitting shrugs had been enough to exhaust him. Harold could do that to people.

"Would you like to amend your account of last night in any way?" Harold asked.

Masterson raised his eyebrows in a practiced way, as if he'd had enough of shrugs. "You mean have I thought of anything else?"

Sal and Harold sat still, waiting.

"I remember riding down in the elevator with Lois Graham. She had a bag of popcorn with her. She is—was—an attractive lady. The sort anybody would remember."

"She and you were alone in the elevator?" Sal asked.

"Yes, just the two of us. We both got out at lobby level. I went to pick up my mail at the boxes. She started walking off as soon as she stepped on the sidewalk."

"Did she know Mitzy?" Sal asked, not knowing quite why.

Masterson wasn't thrown by the question. "The two never met that I can remember. I mean, Lois Graham and I didn't really know each other. We were what you'd call nodding acquaintances."

"Then the two of you never dated?"

"Never anything like that. I mean, you saw Mitzy."

"She has a certain glint in her eye," Harold said.

"Well," Sal said, closing his notepad, "we won't arrest her just now as a suspect, but she should see a doctor about that glint."

Bat Masterson and Harold both looked momentarily startled, then relaxed, realizing Sal was joking. Fedderman wandered in from his interview in another unit, saw the smiles and joined in.

The detectives thanked Masterson for his cooperation, then left the building and walked toward their unmarked car, finished after a long day.

As they passed where John Lennon had been shot, two young girls were standing and gawking. One kept snapping photos with her cell phone. The other stared at the sidewalk approximately where Lennon had fallen and seemed about to cry.

"Where the Russian was shot," Sal said dryly.

Harold said, "Yeah, yeah, yeah."

A ragged figure stepped out from the narrow dark space between two buildings and limped toward them. Fedderman moved his unbuttoned white shirt cuff and rested the heel of his hand on his gun in its belt holster.

The man was one of the homeless, in a stained and ripped ancient gray sport coat and incredibly wrinkled baggy jeans. He had a lean face with a long, oft-broken nose, and a deep scar on the side of his jaw. He might have been forty or ninety. The street did that to people. Once they gave up, the street was in charge of time.

He stopped a yard in front of Sal and Harold, so that they had to stop.

"I seen what happened," he said in a voice almost as gravel pan as Sal's. "All of it. Whole thing started with the popcorn."

The two detectives looked at each other.

"What's your name?" Harold asked.

Sal rolled his eyes. He was tired and his feet hurt. He didn't feel like dealing with a nutcase.

"I just go by Spud."

Harold made a show of writing the name in his leather-covered notepad as if it were vitally important. "You understand we're with the police?"

"I knew he was a cop," Spud said, pointing at Sal. "I wasn't so sure about you." Spud used the back of his hand to wipe his nose. "You look like the kind that never played sports as a kid."

"Looks can fool you," Harold said, obviously hurt by Spud's analysis.

"He was a star quarterback at Notre Dame," Sal lied.

Spud looked dubiously at Harold. "That true?"

"I don't give away the plays," Harold said. He hitched his thumbs in his belt so his holstered gun was visible. With his bushy gray mustache and hipshot, slender frame, he was magically changed into an old West gunslinger. "Now what's all this about popcorn?" he asked.

Spud seemed unimpressed. "The woman was sitting on a bench, and for some reason the pigeons didn't like the popcorn she was trying to feed them."

"Maybe it was stale," Harold said. "Some pigeons are particular."

Spud rubbed his bristly chin. It made a lot of noise. "Now, that's how I see it, too. You and me, we think alike."

"Who was the woman feeding popcorn to the pigeons?" Sal asked.

"Don't know her name. Never seen her before. Then this guy came along, and they started talking."

"The girl and the new arrival?"

"The girl and the pigeons," Sal said. Harold could be excruciating.

"Describe him."

"Kinda little guy, wearing faded designer jeans, a pullover shirt with the collar turned up in back. Had on a Mets baseball cap, had one ear inside it, another outside it. That ear stuck straight out and was kinda funny looking."

"Funny looking how?"

"Pointed, it was." He looked thoughtful. "I was drunk once and seen a leprechaun had ears like that."

"Right ear? Left ear?"

"Right one, I'd say. Maybe both of 'em. Hard to know, the way he had his cap tilted."

"Where did the popcorn come from?" Harold asked.

"Hell, I don't know. Woman had it but the pigeons wouldn't touch the popcorn till she stood up to leave. Then a couple of them got close and pecked at it."

"The man?" Sal asked.

Spud wiped his jutting chin again. Harold couldn't decide whether Spud smelled like gin or diesel fuel. "Oh, they musta known each other, or else he was an awful good talker, 'cause they left together. He picked up his bag and off they went."

"Bag?" Sal asked.

"Sure. Big blue bag with a lotta straps."

"Did it look heavy?"

"Not at all."

"Where did they go? Did they leave the park?"

"No. I'm sure of that. I kinda followed them, for some reason."

Sal could guess the reason. If the opportunity arose, Spud could throw a sucker punch, snatch the man's wallet, and run. The man might not be in any position to follow.

"This woman," Sal said. "Do you think you could identify her?"

Spud went into his chin rub again. Smiled the ugliest smile Sal and Harold had ever seen. "You mean her head?"

Spud objected, but Sal and Harold drove him to Q&A and he signed a statement. He wasn't too worried, because he didn't see Sal or Harold or any of these people as real cops. If they were, they wouldn't have been so nice to him. He might even be up on a vagrancy charge.

To Spud, these were play cops, but not cops playing games.

Sal and Harold wrote their own reports, while Quinn and Fedderman drove Spud to the morgue in Quinn's old black Lincoln.

Quinn figured maybe they had something here, but probably not.

"I feel like the mayor," Spud said, leaning back in his plush seat and crossing his arms. "My kingdom's right on the other side of this window."

Quinn wondered what the real mayor would think of that. He drove faster.

Fedderman figured the entire car might have to be fumigated. Quinn didn't seem to mind. The man could prioritize.

Spud, it turned out, was an ex-marine who'd seen the worst of it in Desert Storm. He didn't react when they showed him the morgue photos of Lois Graham. Simply said, "Uh-huh. Same woman. Damned shame."

Quinn said, "You might have seen her with her killer."

Spud raised a bushy gray eyebrow. "Mr. Popcorn?"

"The same."

"Maybe. Didn't get a clear look at him, though. Told you he looked like a gremlin."

"Leprechaun."

"Did I say that? Shoulda said *gremlin*. Leprechauns ain't always bad. Gremlins are the worst. Too curious and up to mischief all the time. No pot of gold involved."

"Some mischief," Quinn said.

"There a reward?"

Quinn stared at his raggedy witness in the backseat where Feds could keep an eye on him. "If you throw a net over him, I'll pay you something out of my own pocket."

"How much?"

"Negotiable. And remember, your testimony wouldn't be much good if we paid you for it."

"Wouldn't make me no difference what brand it was."

Quinn realized they were talking about bottles, not dollars. He gave a half smile. Spud didn't have the ambition and balls to be mayor of what was outside the car. Good for him. "You net this gremlin and we'll talk." He handed Spud his card. "Give me a call and let me know if you learn anything important."

Spud accepted the card and gave a sloppy salute.

They left the morgue and drove him back to the park where he'd first been accosted by Sal and Harold. A street vendor was set up near the 81st Street entrance. Quinn treated Spud to a knish and orange soda. He noticed that the vendor also sold popcorn.

Quinn thought of warning Spud to be careful, especially where he slept.

Then he figured Spud was careful all the time anyway. On the streets, being careful was his life.

The package Quinn found in the mail at Q&A hadn't been delivered by the post office. There was no stamp on it, and Quinn's name and address were printed neatly in black felt tip pen. Oddly, there was a return address, also neatly printed, in the package's upper left hand corner: Return to Jack Kerouac. There was no actual address.

"This Kerouac the writer?" Renz asked, when Quinn called him and described the package.

"Must be," Quinn said. "It was obviously hand delivered."

"So why are you calling me?" Renz said. "Why aren't you out there trying to find whoever put the damned thing in your mail?"

"Three reasons. I wanted you to know about the package before I opened it."

"And?"

"I want you on the phone while I'm opening the package."

"And . . ."

"I want to tell you what I think about in my few seconds left before a bomb goes off."

There was silence on the phone.

Finally Renz spoke. "You really think there might be a small bomb in that package?"

"Could be."

"The department does have a bomb squad. Why don't we let them open the package?"

"I'm not sure the risk justifies all that," Quinn said. "I can examine the package carefully, see what we got, then if need be we can call in the experts."

"That's insane. If that is a bomb, or something that shoots white powder, we have people who know how to— Just a minute, Quinn."

Within about two minutes, Renz was back. "Stay put, Quinn. And don't touch that package. The bomb squad is on the way."

"What's going on, Harley?"

"I just got my mail put on my desk. It contains a package just like the one you described."

Quinn sighed. "Okay, Harley. I guess we'd better treat this for what it is."

"Considering who must have sent the packages. Or maybe hand delivered them himself."

"Probably paid some poor dumb schmuck to deliver them," Quinn said.

"Yeah. Well, you better get outta your building, make sure everybody else does the same. They'll think it's a drill."

"You doing the same?"

"Not right away. If you get anthraxed or blown up, I'll know what to do. One thing, Quinn, in case we don't see each other again. You think the phony return address name on the packages means the real Jack Kerouac? The author?"

"Yeah. But I don't know what that means."

"He wrote *Peyton Place,* didn't he?"

Quinn said, "Good luck, Harley," and hung up.

Half an hour later, the packages were declared safe. Quinn and Renz had each been the recipient of a jigsaw with a charred wooden handle. As they suspected, there was no clue as to who had placed the packages in the mail. Not a very direct clue, anyway.

8

Just looking at it, no one would guess that the building in the West Village had once been a bakery. In the early seventies it had been converted to a three-story apartment building, with a small foyer. In the nineties, the building had been renovated again, and in a major way. Twenty more stories had been added, and the building had become a boutique hotel, serving both guests and residents. Stone had replaced brick on part of the exterior, the foyer had become a legitimate lobby, complete with leather easy chairs and potted plants, and an elevator had been installed. Upstairs, most large rooms had become suites or been subdivided into small rooms. The halls were carpeted in a deep red, and paneled halfway up to cream-colored wallpaper with a subtle rose print.

Emilio Torres, the head of maintenance in the building, lived with his wife, Anna, in a separate, super's apartment below ground level. He could open his door, take two steps forward, climb three steps, and be in the lobby near the elevators. During certain late-night hours one of the elevators stayed in service, while the other was used only by the staff. When that happened, whatever workmen or equipment needed was shuffled between floors, using the other elevator.

The virtually new building was named Off the Road, in a sort of salute to the beat generation of the fifties, and the rates were reasonable—by Manhattan standards.

The West Village was home to artists of all types, some of whom were doing at least okay financially. Off the Road was a success. Units were purchased for ownership or rental, and recently all had become occupied.

Emilio slept well. All of the systems in the building were almost new. Everything worked as it should, and almost everything was designed to make maintenance and upkeep as easy and infrequent as possible.

He wasn't sure what had awakened him at three a.m. At first he thought he must have something to do, and either he or Anna had set the alarm. After all, it was precisely three o'clock.

But he knew it was unlikely that either he or Anna had set the alarm as a reminder of some task.

He felt worry slip away as he felt himself drawn again to sleep. The apartment—the entire building—seemed quiet now. All he could hear was the steady rhythm of Anna breathing.

She stirred and turned away from him, drawing up her knees. Her familiar, gentle snoring comforted him.

Maybe that was what had awoken him. Anna had for some reason cried out in her sleep. Emilio punched his pillow to fluff it up, then rolled onto his stomach and rested the right side of his face on the cool, soft linen.

He might have gone back to sleep. He wasn't sure afterward.

There was a muffled shuffling sound from out in the

lobby. Anna put out an arm so she could reach the lamp on her side of the bed, and switched it on.

She and Emilio lay facing each other, staring puzzled into each other's eyes.

Anna started to say something, but Emilio lifted a hand and put his forefinger to his lips, urging her to be quiet.

Sirens were wailing off in the distance. A lot of them. It took less than a minute for Emilio to be sure they were converging on Off the Road.

His building!

Emilio sprang out of bed and yanked on his pants, which were folded on a nearby chair. He fastened his belt, slid his bare feet into slippers. After cautioning Anna to stay in the apartment, he pulled a wifebeater shirt over his head and went to the door.

He felt the brass doorknob first, to make sure it was cool. Then he was through the door, and up the steps to the lobby.

The smell hit him first. Something burning. Then he saw a thick pall of black smoke clinging to the ceiling. Tenants were running and sometimes tumbling down the fire stairs, pursued by the smoke. A paunchy, white-haired guy, wearing nothing but Jockey shorts, shoved Emilio out of the way, cursed, and ran for the street door. Voices were calling back and forth. At least no one was mindlessly screaming. Not yet.

Though the fire was obviously upstairs, the elevator was at lobby level. As its door slid open, people tried to stream out but were blocked by others. Every few seconds someone was ejected by force out onto the lobby floor.

Finally they managed something like order, and came stumbling out one after the other. The last one out, a woman whose name was Karen and who Emilio thought was a painter, paused at the elevator door and reached back inside before stepping away.

"No!" Emilio cried. "Don't send the elevator back up! Don't use it! You can be trapped in it."

Karen stared at him, comprehended, then stopped the elevator doors from closing and stuffed her purse in the door. The elevator stalled, stopped, and began to ding over and over. It was already filling up with smoke.

Karen, in a blue robe and one blue slipper, stopped running and gripped Emilio by the bicep, squeezing hard.

"Get out, Emilio! There's nothing you can do."

But there was. "Anna!"

"There!" Karen cried, and pointed.

Anna was crossing the lobby toward Emilio. He slipped from Karen's grasp and went to save her. They hugged, but quickly, and he began to lead her through lowering, thickening black smoke toward the street door.

The door hung open, its vacuum sweep dangling and broken.

They were three feet away from it when a huge apparition burst in. A New York fireman in full regalia, boots, slicker, gloves, a hat, and some kind of respiratory mask.

Emilio and Anna jumped back out of the way as several more fireman streamed in and headed for the stairway.

The first one who'd come in stared at Emilio from behind the mask.

"I'm the super," Emilio said.

"Get out for now," said the gruff voice on the other side of the mask's visor. "But don't go away."

"We've got no place to go," Emilio said. "This is home."

"Better leave it before it falls on you," the fireman said.

One of the firemen who'd gone upstairs was back. The one talking with Emilio and Anna went over to him, and the two men started shouting at each other. The big fireman, with the hat that suggested he was in charge, glanced over and noticed Emilio and Anna and waved them toward the street door.

The smoke was thickest where it was backed up at the door, though the door itself had been removed and lay shattered off to the side. Emilio and Anna made their way outside and began coughing. A fireman led them away.

"How did this happen?" Emilio shouted, as if maybe the fireman was at fault.

"Don't know how yet," the fireman said. "But it looks like it started on the upper floors first, then another fire in the basement. On timers, so the fire would move up and down, catch people in a kind of pincer movement of flames."

"Then somebody did this on purpose," Karen said.

"Yes, ma'am. That'd be my guess."

"Whoever did it wanted to kill people."

"Oh, yes, ma'am."

Emilio and Anna had stopped on the street.

The fireman studied the flames for a moment. "Don't waste time, then," he said. "Get some distance between you and the fire." He patted them both on the shoulder. "Go!"

The fire seemed to close in on them, and the smoke thickened, as if the flames wanted to take advantage of the firefighter's departure.

But they both knew the way. Emilio knew these streets.

The acrid smoke made their eyes sting and caused them to water. Their throats felt raw, and every cough hurt.

Squinting so he could see at least partially, Emilio took Anna's hand, and they made their way among shadowy desperate figures, python-like coils of hose, flashing multicolored lights. There was a lot of shouting and cursing. A police car arrived, its siren dying as the vehicle pulled to the curb half a block away, then backed around at a right angle so the car blocked the street. Two uniformed cops got out and redirected traffic even as they jogged toward the intersection.

Emilio and Anna made their way along the far side of the street and sat on the stoop of a building across the street from theirs. Anna produced tissues from somewhere and they dabbed at their eyes.

When they could see better, Emilio looked more carefully at Off the Road. The building was burning fiercely. Flames seemed to show in every window.

Almost at ground level, toward the rear where it wasn't noticeable from the street, there was movement. Emilio knew that a basement window was there; it was small, but it let in light.

Now it was letting someone out. A small figure fleeing the fire. At first Emilio thought he was imagining it. He used a wad of tissue to wipe tears from his eyes. Yes! A woman, judging by her size, was exiting the building via the basement window. Both arms were visible now, a leg crooked sharply at the knee. The figure didn't look so much like a woman now. Something in the way it moved.

It was a small man, wearing a baseball cap crookedly cocked on his head. Outside the window, he glanced around, noticed Emilio staring at him, and trotted, then walked to join the gawkers down the street.

He glanced back again. In the brightness of the street-light and police and FDNY flashing lights, Emilio no-ticed an elfin quality about him. Because of his ear. One large ear stuck straight out from his head and came to a sharp point. He had his head turned so Emilio couldn't see the other ear. The jockey-size man moved away, back among the gawkers. He was so graceful that he almost danced. Within seconds he was invisible.

"Did you see that?" Emilio asked.

Anna shook her head and dabbed at her eyes with her tissue. "I can hardly see my toes," she said. "What was it?"

"I thought I saw somebody, a small man, climb out of a basement window."

"Getting away from the flames," Anna said. "Did he make it?"

"Yes. He seemed to have plenty of time. Seemed . . ."

"What?"

"To know what he was doing. It was very strange, Anna."

She moved to sit nearer to him on the hard concrete step. "This whole night has been very strange."

"There's something else that's strange," Emilio said, staring at the water from the fire hoses running like a small creek toward a storm sewer. "I see them directing their hoses to put water on the lower floors of the building, but not the upper."

"It looks as if the streams of water won't reach that high."

"There are standpipes on the landings of the high floors. All they have to do is carry the hoses up and attach them."

"That's where the fire seems to have started," Anna said. "Maybe they already decided they couldn't save it."

"Maybe." Emilio looked again at the gurgling stream of water hugging the curb. "It seems that for such a big fire, we've seen very little water."

Anna shook her head. "Water, fire, they both ruin things."

Emilio snaked an arm around her and hugged. "Not everything."

9

Seven people were dead. Thirteen more were still hospitalized, most of them the victims of smoke inhalation.

The morning after the Off the Road hotel fire, Quinn and Fedderman stood in the building's ruined basement. Most of the ashes were soaked, and the acrid smell of the fire, which was still smoldering here and there, was enough to sting noses with every breath. There was a lingering, nauseating smell that Quinn recognized from other fires and their aftermaths. He wouldn't eat steak for a while.

An Arson Squad investigator stood near the collapsed stairway, near a blackened furnace that was the origin of the fire. His name was Hertz, like the car rental company, but he wasn't family, or what would he be doing analyzing fires? He was in dark blue uniform except for oversized green rubber boots that came almost up to his knees. He was carrying a clipboard with a thick sheaf of paper, which he now and then jotted on with a stubby yellow pencil. All three men wore yellow hard hats. Hertz's had his name stenciled on it and it looked as if afforded more protection than the helmets on Quinn and Fedderman.

"We don't wanna stay around too long here," he said.

Fedderman glanced around nervously. "This place about to fall?" he asked, obviously trying to stay calm.

Hertz laughed in a way that was a kind of snort that aggravated Quinn.

"I wouldn't be here myself if I thought it was dangerous."

Fedderman looked at him. "You just said "

"We believe in every measure of precaution," Hertz assured him.

Quinn wasn't sure what that meant but let it pass. "You sure the fire was deliberately set?" he asked. Already knowing the answer.

Hertz nodded his helmeted head. "Look at this." He moved over a few steps to his right and pointed at a blackened, half-melted mass. "See that?" He pointed at a charred arc of metal, and something else, a tiny black arrow. "That's the top of a minute hand. This is what's left of a wind-up alarm clock. When it rang, a key rotated and wound some string that pulled two wires together and triggered an incendiary blast." He gestured with his hand. "See how the alligatoring starts here and moves out in all direction? The floor looks that way, too, only on a larger scale. There was some kind of accelerant on it that caught fire and spread flames fast. People wouldn't believe how fast."

Quinn believed. He'd seen the results of fires set by clever arsonists.

"This guy know what he was doing?" Quinn asked.

"Judging by the results, he knew enough."

"I mean, was he a pro?"

"I don't think so. The timing device is jerry-rigged, but good enough to strike a spark. But it doesn't look like the work of a really skilled arsonist. I'd describe this guy as a clumsy but talented amateur." Hertz jutted out his chin and looked out to the side, thinking. "Unless . . ."

"What?" Fedderman asked.

"Unless he was an expert pretending to be an amateur," Quinn said.

Hertz looked at him, obviously miffed that Quinn had been a step ahead of him and had stolen his line.

"Exactly," he said, smiling. "Very good, Captain." As if Quinn were an apt pupil. "But there's also the sabotaging of the coiled fire hoses."

"We didn't know about that."

"When there are fires higher than our ladders and hoses can reach, there are standpipes installed at each landing. Fire hoses are coiled in glass front cases near them. They're usually not long enough to reach very far along the halls, so extension hoses carried up by the FDNY are coupled to them. Improvised steel clamps are used to pinch the standpipe hoses about seven feet from the standpipes, where they couldn't be seen when the hoses were coiled. They backed up the water and the crimped hoses burst under the pressure. It took valuable time to replace them, especially considering that the brass on them had been beaten out of round. Amateur work, but effective."

Quinn understood now why the flames had so fiercely ravaged the building's upper floors. A simple shortage of water.

Hertz grinned in a way that wasn't pleasant. "He's a clever arsonist, our firebug."

"A clever killer," Quinn amended.

Hertz snorted. "That, too."

Something shifted above them, making a loud groan.

"Let's get out of here," Fedderman said. "Before the place falls on us."

No one argued with him.

Back across the street from the burned-out building, the three men removed their helmets and smoothed back sweat-drenched hair.

"You need a shower after each of these inspections?" Quinn asked.

Hertz laughed and emitted his peculiar snort. "That'd be nice. 'Specially for my wife." He looked from Fedderman to Quinn. "So, what's next for you guys?"

"We're going to interview the super," Quinn said. "We'll copy you."

"Vice versa," Hertz said. "Supers know everything in these buildings. See if he's missing any alarm clocks."

He was smiling again, obviously enjoying his work. Quinn liked him for that.

"His wife, Anna, is not to be taken lightly, either," Hertz said. "She's the beauty and the brains."

10

Quinn and Fedderman found out from Hertz that Emilio and his wife Anna were staying temporarily in an apartment that was owned by the proprietor of Off the Road.

They were both home and both looked nervous when Emilio opened the door and invited them in.

"More questions," Emilio said. He was a short, mustachioed man and seemed more tired than annoyed. "I've already told my story more than once to the police."

"We're fussbudgets," Fedderman said.

Anna, a handsome Latin woman with a profile that belonged on a coin, smiled wearily and motioned for them to sit down. Quinn and Fedderman sat in uncomfortable modern wooden chairs of the sort that rigid religions might use to guarantee discomfort during sermons. Anna offered them water.

"We could have used more of that last night," Quinn said.

"Yes," Emilio said. "We found that out too late." He

and his wife sat down side by side on a sagging, stained sofa. It looked as if it would open and become a back-breaking bed. Anna absently reached over and patted Emilio's thigh. Quinn saw that these two were actually in love. And the arson investigator wasn't wrong about her being beautiful. Emilio wasn't going to do any better.

"We read your statement," Quinn said. "You saw someone who might have been the arsonist emerging from a basement window."

Emilio said simply, "Yes," as if testifying in court and a stenographer needed brief words from him rather than images.

Fedderman said, "Would you say he was trying to get away from the scene, or attempting to escape the flames?"

Emilio thought. Shrugged. "It could have been either. The whole thing didn't last that long. He squeezed out of the window, then took off running and disappeared in all the smoke."

"I only caught a slight glimpse of him, if I saw him at all," Anna said. "The smoke, the smell, it played with the senses."

Quinn smiled, wishing she was as helpful as she was beautiful. He focused his attention on Emilio. "Can you give us a description of the man?"

"I would be repeating it once again."

"Yes," Quinn said.

Emilio sighed. "Small man, dressed in black and wearing a blue baseball cap pulled down low. Moved in a very nimble way. One of his ears—his right one, I think—stuck straight out and came to a point at the top. Like he was a . . ."

"Gremlin," Anna said.

"I thought you were going to say *leprechaun*," Fedderman said.

Anna looked puzzled. Shrugged. "I don't know *leprechaun*. I know *gremlin*. They tinker. Break."

"You'd have to be Irish," Quinn said. "What about his other ear?" he asked Emilio.

"I'm not sure. The cap was too large for him, and it might have covered his right ear, held it flat against his head. Hard to say. He moved very fast, like a mirage."

"But you did see him?"

"My husband doesn't see mirages," Anna said.

That seemed definite and final.

Quinn smiled. "Don't worry. That's not what we think. The fire was started by someone who wasn't a mirage, but was very real, using an alarm clock as a timer to set off an incendiary bomb."

"Terrorism?" Anna asked, her dark eyes wide.

"We don't think so. No terrorist group is taking credit, and this wasn't a very skilled bomb maker."

"But the bomb worked," Emilio said.

"That's a good point," Fedderman told him. "But everyone who should know sees this as simple arson, committed by someone clever, but not very knowledgeable about bombs."

"And you can't put a policeman in every building," Anna said.

Fedderman said, "Another good point."

"The neighborhood gossip, who usually starts and ends nowhere, is speaking of him as a firebug," Emilio said.

"That might be part of it," Quinn said. "But it's more

than that. He seems compelled to look inside things, see how they work. Know anyone like that?"

"A lot of people," Emilio said. "But not arsonists."

"There is the off chance that they're not the same person," Quinn said.

"Not much chance of that," Fedderman said.

"'The Gremlin,' some newscasters are calling him," Anna said. "A kind of ghost in the machine, causing trouble."

She apparently believed the single-killer-arsonist theory.

"Gremlins have been known to tinker with electronics or engines and bring down airplanes," Fedderman said.

Quinn looked at him. "Who told you that? The FAA?"

"Harold."

Of course.

"Those media people who tagged the killer the Gremlin," Quinn said. "Was one of those mouthy newscasters Minnie Miner?"

Anna said, "How did you know?"

Quinn wasn't telling.

Minnie Miner had cooperated, and the rapacious little newshound would surely want something in return.

But right now Quinn was trying to keep a lid on things, and *gremlin* was a kinder word than *terrorist*.

"'Gremlin,'" he said. "Very descriptive."

"We wouldn't want it to become a household word," Fedderman said.

"We wouldn't," Quinn said, "but the killer might."

11

"About half an hour before the fire in the Village," Renz said, "there was a similar fire uptown."

It was the next morning, and he and Quinn were in World Famous Diner on Amsterdam, having coffee and doughnuts. Renz had a large red napkin tucked under his chin so as not to get powdered sugar on his Ralph Lauren tie, tan silk suit jacket, or white shirt. Quinn could see the tiny roughness of sugar on the part of the shirt that showed, like lumps of something under a recent snowfall. Probably all the sugar would drop onto Renz's pants when he stood up.

"Coincidence?" he asked Renz.

Renz shook his head, causing sugar to drop from his napkin to somewhere beneath table level. "Diversion. Same arsonist."

"How do we know that?"

"The fire was in a dry cleaners only a few blocks from a firehouse. It didn't get a chance to burn very long before the FDNY arrived in full force and extinguished the flames."

"Start with an incendiary device?" Quinn asked.

"Yesh," Renz said around a mouthful of chocolate-iced doughnut. "Alsho an alarm clock timer. The fire-bug didn't splash a lot of flammable liquid—probably plain old gasoline—around the place. Enough, though, that the blackened clock didn't yield any prints or anything else. It was the same kind of job as down in the Village, only on a smaller scale. Like a warm-up as well as a diversion that would rob the larger conflagration of firefighters and equipment."

"Any casualties?"

"None."

"Same amateur touch?"

"Oh, yes. Almost certainly the same arsonist. It was almost like a practice run."

Quinn sipped from his white coffee mug. "Witnesses?"

"Not of any value. One guy in the building across the street claimed he saw somebody or something running from the fire about an hour before it even began to look like a fire."

Hope moved in Quinn's heart. Not a lot of hope, because he knew how much an eyewitness report from someone glimpsing something from a window across the street was worth.

"He just got a quick look, doesn't know if there's any connection with the fire. But the guy was moving fast, as if trying to get away from the area without drawing a lot of attention to himself."

"You think this witness is worth talking to?" Quinn asked.

"Definitely."

"Small guy?"

Renz stared at him. "Yeah. Somebody else see him?"

"Maybe somebody downtown." Quinn looked into his coffee mug, as if for answers, found only questions. "Anything else your witness notice about the uptown guy?"

"That suggests he was also the Village firebug?" Renz glanced around as if to make sure they wouldn't be overheard. No one else was in the diner except for three teenage girls giggling in a back booth, and a bearded guy at the counter almost embracing a mug of coffee as if he wished it were booze. "There is one thing," Renz said. "The witness said the firebug's ears stuck out."

Quinn was interested. "Both ears?"

"I asked him that question," Renz said. "He told me he doesn't know. Might have been only one ear, pointed as it was."

"Pointed?"

"Yeah. It stuck out and was pointed on top." Renz took a huge bite of doughnut and chewed. "Newswoman called the firebug a gremlin, maybe because of the ears."

"Leprechauns' ears stick out, too," Quinn said. Not actually knowing.

"But they don't plant bombs," Renz said. "They're too busy looking for rainbows and pots of gold." He swallowed masticated doughnut. Quinn could hear his esophagus working to get the doughy mass down.

"If they want to give this guy a tag," Quinn said, "the Gremlin is as good as any."

"I guess," Renz said. "I wonder who thought it up?" He smiled like a croissant.

12

Jordan Kray's twelfth birthday hadn't been mentioned except for the traditional birthday spanking, which was expertly applied to his buttocks and upper thighs with a leather whip. The flesh hadn't been broken but was raised with fiery welts that would sting for hours. He didn't think he'd sleep at all tonight.

His twin brother, Kent, hadn't minded his birthday at all. He was given a Timex watch and allowed to stay up and watch television. Their father had told him it was for work done around the house and small farm, work that was seldom done by Jordan. Kent and Jordan's mother smilingly agreed while she wielded the whip and her husband watched, fondling himself.

It was a fairly normal night for the Krays, while five-year-old Nora slept peacefully in her bed in the far bedroom. Kent had told Jordan he'd heard their mother and father talking about moving Nora in with him and sending Jordan to Nora's shoebox-size room. Alice and Jason—their mother and father—had talked about moving different kinds of equipment into the room with Jordan, but Kent, overhearing this, had no idea what they were planning.

Whipping required exertion, and Alice stopped and stepped back, breathing hard.

"Leave yourself alone and use this for a while," she said, tossing Jason the coiled whip.

Jason obeyed, but didn't whip hard. Jordan knew this wasn't an act of kindness; his father was simply more interested in other things. Kent lay on his stomach, pretending sleep while facing the wall.

Jordan knew his brother was the better looking of the twins. His features were even and he resembled his mother, with her bold features and curly hair. Jordan had small, pinched features, and one of his ears stood straight out like an open car door and was kind of pointed. This, along with his diminutive size even for his age, lent him an elfin quality that would stay with him the rest of his life. The other ear—his left—stuck out a little and wasn't pointed. The midwife who'd delivered the twins had learned from the firstborn, Jordan, who was a few minutes older than his twin, that identical twins weren't alike in every respect. The protruding, pointed ear seemed to become even larger and more pointed after a schoolyard bully held Jordan in a headlock and rubbed the side of his face over and over on concrete. It was decided that Jordan had started the fight.

Kent tried to explain to his mother that the accusers were lying, but Jordan received a harder than usual whipping, and was made to stand in a corner for yelping and waking up Nora.

A week later Jordan tried to change the oil in the car

but confused it with transmission fluid. He enjoyed working on things mechanical, large and small. He had a driving curiosity. Jordan liked to think that anything he took apart he could reassemble. He was as wrong as he was confident, but that didn't stop him from tinkering.

He saved his money and bought a model airplane he had to construct by hand. When it was finished, it looked more like a Russian MIG than the sleek American Saber Jet pictured on the box. When he tried to glide it, the plane looped and then nosed hard into the ground. He would have rebuilt it and tried again, only his father stomped on the plane, laughed, and said he'd thought it was a big bug.

That was how Jordan's childhood went, except for his dreams where he went to hide. Except for his nighttime hours of lying in the silence and thinking until early morning, when he was forced to get up and do his chores before walking down to the road and waiting for the school bus.

Kent sometimes walked with him, but usually had been sent on before Jordan. Nora, too young for school, lay dozing in her crib and was treated like a princess.

Jordan knew she wouldn't always be treated like a princess. Sometimes he found himself looking forward to that and felt guilty.

He was thirteen when he came upon an old *Movie Spotlight* magazine that was mostly pages of beautiful women posed various ways in various skimpy costumes. Some of the women Jordan was familiar with, like Julia Roberts and Meg Ryan. Others were more his friends' grandfathers' age; Sophia Loren and Ava Gardner. Others had names that were only vaguely familiar.

Jordan turned a page and was surprised to see a

photo of a man. Bing Crosby. Jordan knew he had been a singer and a movie star—had been famous for some time. There was a black-and-white photo of Crosby leaning on the fender of a car. A newer photo, in color, had him leaning on a tree and looking straight at the camera. He was, in fact, looking straight at the camera in both photos. In the earlier one, his ears stood straight out, not so unlike Jordan's. In the newer, color photo, his ears were almost flat against his head. Beneath both photos was the caption "Bing's Secret."

Jordan read the accompanying short text. It seemed that Crosby's ears did stick out, but there was this tape that was sticky on both sides that the movie star used when he was in front of the camera. Supposedly, Clark Gable used it, too.

Jordan couldn't help but smile. If famous people used the special tape, he shouldn't be embarrassed by his ears. He could find where the tape was sold and buy a roll.

He stood before the bathroom mirror, holding both ears back with his forefingers.

Yes, it made a difference.

He was almost as handsome as Kent.

He got a role of white adhesive tape from the medicine cabinet, and unrolled about an inch of tape, tore it off the roll, and then doubled it so it was sticky on both sides. He tried it on his right ear.

It worked for a few seconds, then the ear pulled lose and sprang out from his skull.

When he attempted to tear off another piece of tape, the metal and cardboard spool came apart. That and the roll of tape flew from his grasp and clattered to the tile floor.

The door opened. His mother. She looked at him, then at the clutter on the floor.

"What the hell are you doing?" she asked.

Jordan was too surprised and frightened to reply.

She grabbed him by the right ear, squeezing hard, and walked him out of the bathroom. He could feel tears streaming down his cheeks.

His father was standing in the hall, holding a sheet of newspaper—the sports page. "What the hell you catch him doing?" he asked Jordan's mother. "Jerking off again?"

"Who knows or cares?" his mother said. She released his ear and slapped him hard on the left side of his face. His cheek burned.

"What'd he break now?" his father asked. "Was he taking that tape dispenser apart?" He clucked his tongue at Jordan. "You ever see anything you didn't wanna take apart and screw up?"

Jordan knew when not to answer.

His mother shoved him toward the bedroom, scraping his bare elbow against the wall. "I'll take care of him."

Jordan's father studied Jordan's face, which Jordan studied to control, and then shook his head. "You really do need to learn to behave."

"I'll teach him." Another push toward the bedroom. His mother and father's room.

There was motion off to the side, and Kent peeked around the corner. His face paled. "What's goin' on?"

His mother glared at him, and he pulled back and disappeared.

The noise had awakened Nora, who screamed in her crib.

"I'll take care of her," Jordan's mother said, "soon as I'm done with you."

"Don't be too hard on him," Jordan's father said.

She laughed at her husband and looked at him a certain way, until he turned away from her.

13

New York, the present

"Have a nice night, Margaret."

The woman, Margaret, returned the good wishes of the man in the suit and tie who had come out of the office building she had just left. A fellow worker drone, no doubt.

Jordan watched her as she crossed the street at the signal. How could she move that way? The precision of her stride, the rhythmic sway of her hips, the swing of her free arm with its opposite resting lightly on the purse that was supported by a leather strap slung over her shoulder. Why wasn't she like the other women he saw every day? How was she different?

Whatever the answers to those questions, he knew it was fate and not chance that had brought them together. And that would bring them ever closer to each other.

She descended the steps to a subway platform without losing her distinctive rhythmic gait that was almost a dance. He followed her down the narrow concrete steps.

Jordan observed her from farther down the platform. She was looking away from him, idly watching and waiting for the push of cool air and the gleam of lights that meant a subway train was coming. While she was momentarily distracted, he wandered along the platform toward where she was standing. Her hand tightened on her purse strap, as if she wanted to be sure she wouldn't lose her bag in the rush of riders leaving the train, and those traveling in her direction to board.

The train, a dragon of gray metal and reflective glass, roared before them and appeared for a moment that it was going to speed past and keep going. Then, with a screaming of steel on steel, it slowed rapidly and smoothly almost to a halt. It stopped and sat quietly. It was the 1 train, headed downtown, and like everyone on board, it had rules to obey.

Those waiting to board pressed forward. The woman, Margaret, had to assert herself and back up a step so she remained behind the yellow line. One of the pneumatic doors had stopped exactly in front of her and then hissed open. She was one of the first to board as the flow of passengers both ways met and then broke into two distinct lines, moving in opposite directions.

Jordan was near a door in the same car, only farther down the platform. He stepped inside just as the door was about to close.

There were no seats, so he stood with several others in the crowded car, shifting his weight from foot to foot. He could see Margaret seated near the door she had entered.

By the time the train stopped at West 42nd Street, in the theater district, it had taken on more passengers, and Jordan had to crane his neck now and then to catch sight of her.

There she was, standing up and edging toward the door.

He pushed toward her, using his elbows. Someone in the crowded car elbowed him back, but he ignored it. A little pain was a tonic to the system, as his mother had often told him.

He left the subway behind and followed Margaret toward the concrete steps leading to the sidewalk. As she pushed through a black iron revolving gate that looked designed to eat people, she didn't glance back, but he doubted if she'd recognize him anyway. He'd let his hair grow, and it was combed back like dark wings over his ears.

Soon they surfaced into the loud, warm night. The sidewalk was almost as crowded as the subway, and he stayed close behind her.

After a block, she cut down a side street that was a mix of businesses, most of them restaurants, and residences. Some of the old brick and brownstone buildings had been subdivided into apartments. A few of them looked vacant.

Margaret paused in the glare of a streetlight, in front of a dentist's office. She rummaged about in her purse until she found what looked like a key ring, then continued to the stoop of the next building. As she went up the steps, he watched her, mesmerized, listening to the clack of her high heels on the concrete steps. The rhythm and precision of her movements captivated him. The click and clack and sway and roll and rhythm and click and clack had a hypnotic effect on him that he couldn't understand but must.

As she entered the building through an oversized oak door, he resisted a glance to the side.

He walked past her building and continued down the street, but he used his ballpoint pen to write her address on the palm of his left hand.

He pressed hard enough to make the hand bleed.

Margaret Evans stood leaning with her back pressed against the inside of her apartment door to the hall. She knew the man had been following her, picked up on the fact when she'd gotten on the subway and noticed him waiting, then timing his movements as he entered the same subway car before the doors closed and the train moved away.

It wasn't all that unusual in Margaret's life that a man might follow her to see where she was going. Usually they were harmless. Lonely guys killing time and looking for something to do. Dreamers who moved in her wake, waiting for their dreams to come true. With those guys, they were mostly too timid to approach her. Her late aunt Clara had told her more than once that women had little idea of the power they held over men. Men didn't know it either, but were moved by it, sometimes even believing that they were the agents of change.

"You're beautiful and will grow up to be even more beautiful," her aunt had said. "You're special and will have to understand more about men, how one day you are their friend and the next day their goddess."

Clara had been dead for three years now. Margaret wished she'd listened more to what her aunt had said. There was a lot that the pancreatic cancer had cut short, or Margaret would have understood more about what made her special, and more about men. Such as why they sometimes need to destroy their goddesses.

Margaret was sure she'd never before seen the man who'd followed her to her apartment building. And probably he'd never seen her.

But sometimes, as Clara said, it was all in a look, or a certain movement in a certain light. Or . . . who knew what else? A person could glimpse another through a bus window and be in love for life.

Or something like love.

Jordan couldn't get Margaret out of his mind. She was a mystery he had to explore. He pushed her away from his thoughts. There would be time for her. He would make time.

A mist closed in on him as he walked. Soon it became a light drizzle. He walked faster, then turned up his collar and broke into a jog. At the end of the block he turned left and climbed steps to the porch of a white-stone and brownstone building and went inside to a small foyer. A long, narrow stairwell ran to the second floor. Jordan climbed the stairs quickly, then stood before the single door at the top of the steps.

He waited for a count of fifty, then knocked on the door, as instructed. He didn't look up at the camera mounted at a downward angle near the ceiling.

"Come in," a woman's voice said, almost bored.

He opened the door and stepped inside, aware of a

scent of jasmine. The woman was sitting in a chair near the foot of a bed. Something had been done to extend the chair's legs to make them longer. The chair resembled a throne. The tall, lean woman in black leather, seated calmly in the chair, brought to mind royalty and authority.

"Have you behaved yourself since we last met?" she asked.

"No, I have not."

They both smiled.

"Go to my closet and open it," she said. "Hanging on the back of the closet door is a whip. Bring it to me."

Jordan obeyed.

14

Renz dropped by the Q&A office with what he described as new information. He drew a plain brown folder from his recently acquired calfskin attaché case, and plopped it on Quinn's desk in front of Quinn.

"Lab come up with something new?" Quinn asked.

"In a way. Those five women who were among the dead in the Off the Road fire. Two of them were in bathtubs and weren't killed by the flames."

Quinn leaned back in his desk chair, listening to its familiar squeal, and holding a pen lightly level with the thumb and index fingers of both hands, as if taking a measurement. "What? Did they fill the tubs with water so they might submerge holding their breath and wait the fire out?" Quinn had seen this attempted, ten years ago, and recalled that it hadn't worked. The victims who thought they might find enough time to submerge and let the fire rage over and past them had been boiled alive. He experienced a vivid memory with an image that still haunted him. One of the boiled, a woman, hanging halfway out of the bathtub, her hair reduced to white ash, her eye sockets hollowed by the flames.

"You thinking about that Clovis Hotel fire?" Renz asked Quinn, which jolted Quinn. That was exactly the fire that was occupying his mind. Renz, a younger, slightly slimmer Renz, had also been at the Clovis fire.

"I think about it from time to time," Quinn said.

Renz emitted a low, guttural laugh. "Some of those victims, you could stick a fork in 'em and serve 'em at a fancy restaurant. Tell the diners it was gourmet fare. You ever heard of lamb *amirstan*?"

"No," Quinn said, "and I don't want to."

"Well, it doesn't matter," Renz said, leaning forward and sliding about a dozen sheets of paper out onto Quinn's desk blotter. "Helen and a police sketch artist created this."

Quinn looked at a detailed drawing of the suspect in the Off the Road and crosstown dry cleaners fires, keying off the scant eyewitness accounts. Staring back at Quinn from the sketch pad was a man, slender judging by his neck and shoulders, who was quite handsome until a certain something came through. His pinched features were faintly rodent-like. The effect was enhanced by an oversized, pointed right ear that jutted almost straight out from his head. It gave the man a kind of intense feral look, which lent his elfin features a sinister air. He seemed halfway between a leprechaun and a gargoyle. A small, blithe spirit of evil that tinkered and turned mishap into catastrophe. A gremlin.

"DNA samples are still being worked up, but so far blood taken out of the pipes beneath the tub drains provides no conclusive evidence that the Off the Road and Clovis Hotel fires were set by the same person."

Quinn laid the photos and sketch on his desk.

He said, "Something's wrong here."

"I see it," Renz said. "The drainpipes under the bathtubs were clogged with blood. Some of the bathtub victims weren't burned to death or died from smoke inhalation. They were tortured to death while their blood ran down so thick it clogged the drains."

"It looks like the killer did his routine on both hotels." Quinn could imagine the women lying awkwardly in the bathtubs, losing blood and so losing the strength to resist. They probably knew they wouldn't leave the bathtubs alive, but assumed they were going to drown.

When the killer was finished with what he'd come to do, he probably left in a way he'd planned, careful not to be caught in his own trap of flames and smoke. The victims would have been too weak to claw their way up and climb out of the tubs. They probably kept trying harder and harder as the water kept getting hotter and hotter. Each of their attempts to escape would have been more feeble than the previous ones. Then the smells of charring flesh, the hopeless screams. The boiling.

Then silence except for the crackling of the flames.

Quinn looked up from the material on his desk. On the other side of the desk, Renz sat staring at him.

Quinn got up and crossed the office to a cabinet, which he unlocked. He withdrew a bottle of Jameson's and poured two fingers into a couple of on-the-rocks glasses. He didn't add ice or water before carrying the two glasses back to his desk, setting one on the blotting pad, and handing the other glass to Renz.

Renz tossed down most of his drink in a series of gulps.

Quinn sipped his drink slowly, thinking things over.

15

"There was a similar mass murder in Florida about five years ago," Helen the profiler said. She was standing in front of Quinn's desk with her arms crossed, rocking back and forth on her heels. "Two women found dead in their bathtubs, after a fire in a hotel on Pompano Beach. They'd been tortured, then boiled to death. Fire was deliberate, most likely set by the same person who killed the women. Three other people—all men—were killed in the fire. Firebug was never caught."

"The men were collateral damage?"

"Looks that way. Men often are."

Quinn was thinking about that when Jerry Lido came in through the street door. The air stirred with a faint scent of gin. Lido's stained white shirt was unbuttoned and hanging out over wrinkled pants. His eyes seemed focused, though, and he was walking straight. Fedderman, over by the coffeepot, and himself no fashion plate, looked at Lido and said, "You look like something the cat dragged in."

"I fought the cat all the way," Lido said.

Quinn said, "I need you to find out what you can about a hotel fire five years ago in Pompano."

"Sandy Toes Hotel?"

Helen shifted her feet and stood up straighter. She and Quinn looked at each other.

Lido caught the subtle exchange and smiled. He placed a wrinkled yellow envelope on Quinn's desk.

The charred debris in the Sandy Toes photos was surprising. The burn victims' bodies were shriveled black horrors. Breasts had been removed from some of the women. Quinn recalled another case, long ago, involving an urban cannibal who dined on breasts.

He was almost relieved when he saw that here most of the breasts—what was left of them—were lying near the victims' bodies.

None of the male victims of the Sandy Toes Hotel fire seemed to have been tortured, and only one of them, possibly coincidentally, was found burned to death in a bathtub.

They seemed to have simply been in the way.

Collateral damage.

The women, however, were a different story. What was left of them—including their severed breasts— that was too large to fit down a drain was lying in a jumble at the bottoms of the tubs.

Preliminary autopsy reports on the women suggested they were killed and dismembered swiftly. The killer had known he had minimum time.

"He made every second count," Quinn said, leafing through the autopsy sheets, which were complete with photos.

"He must have known he had a way out without being

trapped by the flames or smoke," Fedderman said as the detectives passed around the files with photos.

"Looks like he went from point to point, killing and dismembering the women, then starting or feeding the fires."

"Those women didn't run because they were terrified," Pearl said. She looked angry, but calm.

Quinn, reading further, said, "And with their Achilles tendons sawed through, right above their heels, there was no way they could stand up, or even crawl, out of a bathtub. Then, when the fire reached a certain point, the killer quickly finished his butchery and moved on in search of more victims."

"How did he find them?" Pearl asked. "Look in every bathtub?"

"Listening for screams or calls for help," Harold said. "Bathtubs are where lots of people trapped by fire take refuge. They fill them with water, climb in, and hope for the best."

"And have their pleas answered by a gremlin with knives and saws," Pearl said. "Nightmare stuff."

Helen studied the postmortem report. "A figure of authority heard their calls and appeared, probably a fireman in a slicker and helmet. That's why they didn't run. They thought a rescuer had arrived. One of the first things he did was saw through their Achilles tendons. Then they couldn't stand up or climb out of the tub. He'd have had to waste a move disassembling them as they got weaker and weaker from loss of blood. He probably eviscerated them last and then unwound and stacked their intestines."

"Think of it without the blood," Harold said, "and he sure does neat work."

"Neat enough to be a doctor or a med-school student doing extra homework," Sal said.

"Like a project," Harold said.

Nobody spoke for a moment, thinking that one over.

"Nift says no," Quinn said. "Our killer doesn't possess that level of efficiency."

"And there's no sign of him having used power tools," Fedderman said.

"Our guy wouldn't do that," Helen said. "That would depersonalize it."

"Power tools might be noisy, too," Harold said, and made a buzzing sound with his mouth to demonstrate.

Sal gave him the look, cautioning Harold not to get on a roll.

"The killer in Florida might have used the surf to cover up the sounds," Jerry Lido said with a sideways glance. He'd been working on his computer while the others talked.

"Drowned them out," Harold said.

"And the murder in Florida had an element of cannibalism."

"Dinner is surfed," Harold said.

Sal came within an inch of telling him to shut up.

"Not the same as the murders we're investigating," Sal said with raspy moderation. "The killer six years ago wasn't nearly as proficient with his instruments as our killer."

"Our gremlin tinkers," Fedderman said. "Like he's taking apart a robot to see how it's put together."

"How do we know he tinkers?"

"That's what gremlins do," Helen said. "And he was in a hurry, so he had the victims get in their bathtubs for him to protect themselves from the fire. In a rush, our Gremlin, as if he was on an assembly line doing piecework."

"A sexual thing?" Fedderman asked.

"Gadgetry and efficiency as applied to flesh and bone," Helen said. "We've all known people who've conducted stranger secret sex lives."

Harold looked at her. "We have?"

Pearl said, "Shut up, Harold."

Fedderman said, "I knew a guy with an enormous collection of Barbie dolls, and each one had a—"

"Forget it, Feds," Pearl said.

"You guys," Helen said, "are pathetic."

"But they might be right," Quinn said. "Especially when you put firebugs in the mix."

"The hell with firebugs," Sal grated in his bullfrog voice.

Quinn made an effort not to smile. He liked it when his detectives squabbled. Oysters and pearls.

16

When she studied him through the peephole and then opened her door to his knock, he hardly looked like a threat. A jockey-size man in built-up shoes to make him appear taller. His dark hair was long on the sides and combed back in wings that obviously existed to cover his ears. For all of that he was somehow physically appealing. There was a force about him. A certainty that drew a particular sort of woman.

Men like this, Margaret thought. They somehow know about women like me.

"You're the man who's been following me," she said.

He smiled. "You're the woman who's been observing me following. You've got a lot of nerve, buzzing me in and answering my knock."

"You took a chance coming here, yourself. For all you know, I might have considered you a rapist or burglar and shot you on the spot. I've done it before."

Some of this happened to be true, but the burglar had been her ex-husband, and she'd stabbed him in the shoulder, not shot him. None of that mattered now.

They'd stitched him up, and he was fine. And she'd gotten a restraining order against him.

"I was sure you wouldn't think of me as dangerous," he said.

"Why not?"

"Because I'm not dangerous in any way. I'm sure you can read that in me." He smiled. "You're a good reader of men."

"How would you know?"

"I'm a good reader of women."

"Now you're bullshitting, flattering yourself. That's an ugly thing in a man."

"If that's true, how come you're going to invite me in?"

"Maybe I like absurdly determined men."

"You like men who sense right off how you are."

"Oh? How am I?"

"A good person, but always up for adventure."

Margaret leaned against the doorframe and looked at him for a long time. She had to look down at an angle, but that didn't seem to bother him. The little bastard didn't blink.

"You've got me pegged," she said, realizing too late the sexual connotation.

He pretended not to notice, which helped to keep her in his corner. A real gentleman.

"If you ask me," he said, "the world needs more like you."

"It has more like me."

"But they're rare and hard to find."

"You mean we're rare and hard to find."

He turned that over in his mind. "Yeah, I guess I do."

"Modesty doesn't become you."

"That's okay. I hardly ever become modest."

"Do you know where the Grinder Minder is?" she asked.

"The coffee shop, yeah. Two blocks over. A pleasant walk."

"I'm not crazy enough to invite you in," she said, "but let's take that walk. We can see through the lies, get to know each other better over coffee."

"Learn what makes us tick," he said, smiling. It was an unexpectedly beatific smile that made him, for an instant, look like a mischievous child.

"Sounds like us," she said. She told him to wait a second while she got her purse.

They were one of only two couples in the Grinder Minder. The other couple was older, he with a scraggly gray beard and a bald head, she wearing faded jeans and a colorful tie-dyed T-shirt. There were winding tattoos on the woman's inner wrists and up her forearms to the elbows, probably to disguise needle marks. Or maybe razor scars.

Margaret ordered a venti vanilla latte, and, amazingly, that was what he always drank. Most of the time, anyway. The killer watched Margaret's gaze stay fixed for a few seconds on the other couple.

"Hippies lost in time," he said.

Margaret shrugged. "As long as they're happy."

"Big job," he said, "not trusting anyone over thirty when you're over forty."

"Drugs help," Margaret said.

"We can get some. Pot's easy enough to get now."

"That's why it's less desirable."

"Point taken."

"I'm a month and a half out of rehab," she said.

"Then we won't do drugs. Tell you the truth, I was never big on them. My brother got screwed up on them. High on meth when he drove onto a highway and discovered too late he was on an exit ramp. Van full of teenagers hit him head-on. Three killed, including my brother. Four injured."

"God! That's terrible!"

He shrugged sadly, elaborately, exemplar of all the grief in the world. "You learn to live with it. There's no choice." He forced a smile. "Tell me about you, but nothing sad, please."

She returned his smile and her eyes held his. "First, I think we should introduce ourselves."

He made a big deal out of slapping his cheek, not hard, but loud enough to make the hippie woman glance over. "Good grief, you're right," he said. "I'm Corey."

"Margaret."

"I know."

"How?"

"Your mailbox down in the vestibule."

"Of course! How sneaky of you."

"Observant, I like to think."

"How very you."

"Thanks," he said. "Now tell me about Margaret. Or is it Maggie?"

"Never. Only Margaret."

"So let me into your past, beautiful Margaret."

She sipped her latte deliberately, looking like a woman thinking up something for a parlor game. It occurred to him that she was probably a bigger liar than he was. But certainly less convincing.

"I grew up in Baltimore," she began. "We were poor but didn't know it . . ."

He stopped paying attention, figuring it was probably all a string of lies anyway.

". . . And here I am doing proofreading for an advertising company."

He raised his latte mug in a salute. "You're to be admired, Margaret. Really!"

"Oh, not so much."

"Don't shortchange yourself. You might be pleasantly surprised by what's in your future."

So might you.

He finished his latte and dabbed at his lips with a napkin.

"Should we start back?"

"Back?

"To your apartment. I have to at least show you to your door. Make sure you're safe in this big bad city."

"I suppose that makes sense." And it makes sense to keep you dangling. Anticipation can work wonders.

As they walked through the lowering night he kept slightly off to the side so he could observe the rhythm of her stride. Her high heels abbreviated her steps; the clicking and clacking of her shoes on the hard sidewalk was mesmerizing. Her hips rolled slightly as she walked, her body like a sensuous metronome under perfect, relentless rhythm, meting out precisely the remainder of her life. There was something amazing about it.

The things we don't know until it's too late.

The Gremlin glanced up at the beautiful woman walking alongside him and felt the thrill of possession. Her lithe body kept moving to the rhythm being beaten out by her shoes. He realized he was getting an erection.

Can't have that. Not now, not yet . . .

"You a baseball fan?" he asked.

"The Yankees, when they're the Yankees," she said.

She half stumbled—or pretended to—and found herself leaning against him. He might be a small man but he was hard and muscular. She could feel strength emanating from him like a field of electricity. Did he do sports? Did he work out at a gym? After a few more steps they were holding hands.

They talked baseball for a few minutes and then walked silently until they came to her building. She didn't say anything as they stood by the elevator. The Gremlin glanced around, saw that they were alone.

The elevator arrived, and as the doors opened he saw that it was empty. He kissed Margaret on the cheek. "I'd better go up with you, see you inside so I know you're safe."

She didn't discourage him.

They kissed again in the elevator.

As the elevator door opened on her floor, he heard another door open and close somewhere beneath them. Then descending footsteps. Luck held. Still, no one had seen them.

He waited while she fished her keys from her purse and worked two dead-bolt locks.

The apartment door opened to darkness.

"You mind waiting while I turn on a light?" Margaret asked.

"Of course not. I'll be right here."

As soon as the darkness swallowed her, he crossed the threshold.

She heard him enter and turned, feeling a tingle of alarm.

But when the light came on he was staring at the clock on the table just inside the door. It was an anniversary clock. Its mechanism was beneath a glass dome and revolved a gold filigreed decoration back and forth in a regular circle and a half.

"Does that thing really never need winding?" he asked.

"Once a year," she lied.

"How do they manage that?"

"They?"

"The people who manufacture the clock."

Margaret shrugged. "I don't know. It's got some kind of perpetual motion."

But he knew that was impossible.

Should be impossible.

She was amused by his rapt concentration as he studied the timepiece beneath the small glass dome. He was like a child encountering a new game or puzzle.

"Real gold?" he asked.

"Hardly."

"Gold plated?"

"Not even that."

"It doesn't tick or make a bit of noise, yet it has the correct time. Mind if I look at it closer? See if I can make out how it works?"

She moved farther inside and laid her small brown purse on the sofa.

"Maybe when we get back," she said.

He turned away from the clock, toward her. "Haven't you noticed?" he asked. "We are back."

Margaret ran regularly and worked out religiously at the gym. She was in shape. She'd taken a course in tae kwon do and knew how to hip-toss a man nearly twice her size. No one had taught her how to deal with being fixated by a stare, mesmerized by the glint of a knife blade.

No one had taught her how fear could freeze her insides and make movement impossible.

No one had taught her that she was prey.

17

They sat at their usual assigned places. Jason Kray at the head of the table, next to him, Kent, next to Kent, Jordan. On the other long side of the table, Nora sat next to her mother.

It had been report card day. Even five-year-old Nora, who had recently started kindergarten, had come home after school with a report card. All passing marks, of course. Jordan thought he might be the only one at the table who knew the rest of Nora's class got the same passing marks. His own grades hadn't been so good. Not like his brother Kent's.

Kent had gotten straight A's in his classes, and a note from his adviser saying that he was a pleasure in class. He also earned straight A's for good behavior. Taller than Jordan, but still of average height, he was also going to be a starter on the school basketball team.

His mother had raved when he'd shown up after school and handed the report card to her. She'd passed it to Kent's father, Jason, who merely grunted and took in another glob of collard greens and vinegar on his fork.

"What about your dipshit little brother?" Jason asked.

Kent said nothing. He squirmed in his chair, looked at Jordan, and then looked away. He knew what would happen if he decided to defend Jordan. His father would see that it would never happen again.

Jordan was well aware of his failures as a scholar. It wasn't that he was dumb. He knew that. He simply didn't like studying anything he wasn't interested in. He was curious about how things worked, which seemed to him to have nothing to do with when famous people were born or died, or who was king or queen during what era. How things worked, their inner secrets—that's where the world's real knowledge was to be found. The dates of ancient battles, won or lost, had little to do with it.

"He did the best he could," he heard his mother say. She didn't sound as if she really meant it.

His father grunted again. "Some lessons need learnin' the hard way."

Jordan knew what the hard way was. His mother would wield the whip while his father watched.

Then his father would—

"See that the tractor's in the barn and gassed up," his father was saying. "You got tilling to do tomorrow."

"He's got school," Alice Kray said.

"What's the point? He ain't learnin' anything anyway."

"Still an' all . . ."

"You'll till after school tomorrow," Jason Kray said to Jordan with finality. "That soil needs breaking."

"I can till," Kent said confidentially.

"You got your homework," his mother said. It was a given that Kent was going to college, either because of his grades or his athletic prowess. He could already run high hurdles in near record time and throw a baseball a mile, and now he was concentrating on basketball.

He should easily be in the Olympics, his family figured. If not that, the major leagues, or professional football, after a great college career. Maybe even pro basketball, if he got much taller. One way or another, his assignment was to make the family rich.

"I don't mind tilling," Kent said. He actually liked driving the tractor, listening to the engine roar and watching how the oversized back tires dug into the bare earth while the tiller blades laid open the soil for planting.

"You got other after-school chores tomorrow," his mother said.

All through this conversation, Jordan's mind was elsewhere. He liked to learn; he just didn't like school. And for sure he couldn't run track, or throw a baseball half as far as Kent. But why should he be able to do those things? He was smaller than Kent. His arms were skinny and his legs were bony. He wasn't built to be an athlete, even though he lifted weights in the barn.

It wasn't that he was weak.

He didn't want them to know how strong he was. It seemed to him that if they did know, they'd figure out a way to use it against him.

Nora spilled her juice and began to cry. Strained peas dribbled from her mouth.

"Shut up the rug rat," Jason Kray said. He shoved his chair back so hard it turned over as he stood up and strode into the living room. Jordan and Kent's little sister, Nora, didn't quiet down that easily. She'd have to learn, and was almost old enough to be taught.

Hard lessons, not easily forgotten. That's what this family was about. What all families should be about. Hard lessons, and weathering storms inside and out.

Kent followed his father into the living room. They would sit on opposite ends of the couch and watch a replay of last night's baseball game between the Red Sox and Cleveland Indians.

Jordan, still seated in the kitchen, didn't have to be told to help his mother clear the table. Women's work, according to his father.

As Jordan worked, he became fascinated by the magnifying glass his mother used instead of glasses to help her read. She had magnifiers all over the house, but the biggest one was on the kitchen windowsill, where it was handy for her to use while reading food labels or recipes. She watched her calories and carbohydrates. Jason had told her what would happen if she let herself get fat.

The way she had the magnifier tilted up against the window was interesting to Jordan. He had read in various outdoors magazines how it was possible to start a fire with a magnifying glass. The sunlight and heat streaming through the curved glass could be focused to a tiny flammable dot.

He'd almost started a fire that way once himself. One of the magazines had a story about a guy in Alaska who'd used a single lens from his glasses to start a campfire that kept him and his sled dogs from freezing to death. Jordan didn't know if the story was true, but he saw how such a thing could have happened.

It was fascinating, the way so many things had more than one purpose.

Like a belt that would keep your pants up, or be used for something else altogether.

In the morning, when it was ten minutes past time to get up and start getting dressed for school, Jordan's mother shook his bed as if an earthquake had struck.

"I was you, I'd make sure I wouldn't miss that school bus this mornin'," she said. "You got no room to misbehave."

"Where's everybody?" he asked, though he could hear his father snoring.

"They're sleepin' in. I'm gonna give you a note that says Kent's got a stomachache. You take that to school and give it to his teacher. Or to the principal or somebody in the office."

"Why can't I stay home and sleep in, too?"

"It wouldn't look right, the both of you being sick at the same time."

"I don't know. It seems —"

"Just get up and get dressed afore that school bus arrives at the end of the road. Unless you want more of what you got last night."

"No," Jordan said. "No more." He wasn't sure if it was pain or embarrassment that was making his cheeks flush.

He managed to climb out of bed and stood swaying. His buttocks and the backs of his thighs were on fire, and it seemed that every joint in his body ached.

"Get movin'," his mother said. "A hot shower'll fix

you up. I'll put out some cereal for you, then I'm goin'
back to bed."

Nude, he stumbled toward the bathroom.

The one thing he surely didn't want was to miss
the bus.

He skipped his shower and got dressed in a hurry.
He decided to skip breakfast, too.

His curiosity was nagging. More than nagging. Raging. Instead of eating the bowl of stale Cheerios his
mother had put out for him, he slightly adjusted the magnifying glass on the windowsill, propping it over some
crinkled tissue and wadded newspaper from the trash.

Near the kitchen curtains.

18

He'd drugged her. Margaret was sure of it. But why?

And where . . . ?

She knew where without having to open her eyes. But, hoping against hope, she did open them.

Margaret was in her apartment's bathroom, nude and in the bathtub in lukewarm water. She was on her back, leaning back, her head tilted up for a view of the ceiling and to keep her face dry. She couldn't close her mouth—something was jammed into it. It felt to her probing tongue like a rubber ball. One of those things sadists used to silence their victims.

She inhaled and made noises, not loud and certainly not understandable.

She felt so weak. . . .

Why so weak? Tired? A faint trickling sound was so restful.

Movement on the periphery of her vision . . .

There was Casey—no, Corey—standing above her

near the foot of her bathtub. The warm water—that must be the trickling sound she heard, a faucet running slightly, slowed to a gradual ticking. The warmth of the water felt so good . . . Was this some kind of kinky sexual experience he'd dreamed up?

I don't even know this man!

He moved closer and she saw what looked like a scalpel or some other kind of sharp knife in his right hand. In his left was a U-shaped saw with a whipcord-thin and taut serrated blade strung between its arms.

A jigsaw.

The bathwater turned cool with her knowledge. Margaret remembered her childhood and her father's basement woodworking shop, his various kinds of saws and what they could do. She made another small, animal noise, raising her right hand to plead with Corey—with the Gremlin. She was shocked by the scarlet, almost black color of her arm. And she knew the liquid in the tub wasn't water, it was blood.

My blood.

She knew what he was going to do with the knife. With the saw.

He squatted down next to the bathtub, knowing she was too weak even to splash him with her blood. Holding the scalpel up so she could see it with her dimming eyesight, he smiled and said, "Open wide." Then he laughed and said, "Oh, I'll do that."

There was an icy sensation at the base of her sternum. Then came the pain. Her body arched and rose to meet him. He bent her right arm over the tub, twisting it and pinning it tight against the porcelain. Then he went to work with the jigsaw.

It was all the same pain that shocked her and sent

her whirling toward brilliant white light and the darkness beyond. The relentless rasping of the saw against
bone or sinew seemed the harsh breathing of predators.

Margaret was alive long enough to see him carry her
arm over to the shower stall and gently lay it inside to
be rinsed off before he studied and reconstructed her.

It was easy, when he was finished with Margaret,
for the Gremlin to leave her apartment building without being seen. A stocky man in dark clothes—Jordan
didn't even know for sure he was a doorman—went
halfway to the corner to hail a cab for some people who
might not even have come from Margaret's building.

To be on the safe side, Jordan waited for the stocky
doorman (if that's what he was) to work his way toward
the corner again to hail another taxi. When the man's
back was turned, Jordan simply slipped outside without being seen and walked away. He was wearing a
stocking cap beneath a Yankees cap, keeping his ears
flat against his skull and unnoticeable.

As he walked away he knew the doorman might be
watching, but he wouldn't know where Jordan had
come from. As small as Jordan was, the man might
even mistake him for a woman or child. For good
measure, Jordan stuffed his hands in his pockets and
skipped a couple of steps. Serial killers didn't play
hopscotch.

When he turned the corner, he felt safe.

He continued to walk, relaxed now, replaying in his
mind Margaret's miseries and final moments. Her
grasping at life and her inexorable slide into death. Her
eyes. Yes, her eyes. They'd fixed on his and the primal

understanding was there. This was a shared experience, all but the last brief fractions of seconds, when he, in doom and shadow, turned away from the void as she could not.

That was his power, and it was monumental.

19

The private road, more a long driveway, actually, ran straight from the Kray house to the county road. The driveway was dirt, the road blacktop. Jordan stood alone at the T of the private drive and county road, a math book stuck under his arm, his hands in his pants pocket.

Not being obvious about it, he was gazing across the patchwork of farmland where corn, beans, and potatoes were grown. The morning was beginning to heat up beneath a brilliant sun in a cloudless sky. Jordan was watching the house, made small by distance, a neat white geometrical shape among the pattern of fallow and green fields.

Movement caught Jordan's attention, and he shielded his eyes from the sun with his flattened hand, like a frozen military salute. The bus was coming to pick him up at the T and, making three other stops along the way, drive him and some of the area's other students to Robert F. Kennedy School.

Right now, the bus was a small yellow dot crawling in his direction along the perfectly straight, perfectly flat county road. Jordan's view was a mosaic of straight lines and ninety-degree angles.

He looked back toward the distant house and his heartbeat quickened. He was sure there was a barely visible curl of dark smoke rising from the house.

It's working!

He squinted again at the bright morning sun, his friend and accomplice.

Jordan moved out where he could be seen as the bus grew larger. He knew there would be half a dozen kids on the bus, and he wanted to board fast, so no one would look off in the direction of the house. A glance back informed him that the smoke was rising darker and more visible. He knew it wasn't rising as fast and high as it might, because the morning was still.

The bus became larger faster, and then it was very near. Air brakes hissed and the yellow pneumatic doors folded open. Jordan got in fast, flashed his student pass even though the bus driver knew him, and moved quickly down the aisle. He flung himself into a seat halfway back, and saw that the driver, a man he knew only as Ben, was watching him in the big rearview mirror, waiting to make sure he was seated. Ben waited before driving away, making Jordan nervous enough to notice that his right arm was trembling. He willed it to be still, and it became still.

"Nobody else this morning?" the driver called.

"Sleepin' in," Jordan answered.

"Lucky them," Ben the driver said. The diesel engine growled and clattered and the bus moved away.

Jordan could smell burning. He was sure it was the

bus's exhaust and not the house. Not from this distance.

The driver caught his eye in the oversized mirror. "How're your mom and dad?" he called in a loud voice.

"They're good," Jordan said.

As the bus picked up speed, it rattled and roared and became too loud to talk over. Jordan chanced a glance off to the side. There was now what appeared to be a dark cloud looming behind the Kray house. It could have passed for a rain cloud, but he knew it was smoke.

Jordan thought about his mother and father, his sister, and his brother, Kent. He was pleased that he felt no stab of conscience. No regret. None of them, including even Nora, deserved his regret. Bad things in this world simply happened. Everyone tried to make sure they happened to somebody else. Jordan had been taught early on that was how the world worked. And it had to be worked. Losers had to learn to become winners, small fish to survive long enough to become big fish.

He settled back in his seat, excited inside, calm outside. They had taught him how to wear a mask.

The other kids, not long out of their beds, were sleepy and bored and as quiet as Jordan. Ben the driver began mindlessly humming a tune. Jordan couldn't place it at first, but soon realized it was from the movie *The Bridge on the River Kwai.*

Then Rollie Conrad, the fat kid who made top grades, yelled, "Hey! Fire!" He was out of his seat and pointing. "Look! Fire! Fire!"

Everyone in the bus crossed the aisle or swiveled to look in the direction Rollie was pointing.

"Fire!" Rollie yelled again, this time louder and spraying spittle.

"We see it," an older girl named Mary Ann said calmly. She made a face and wiped her mouth with the back of her hand.

Jordan knew it was time to pretend.

"Oh, no! That's my house! My mom and dad—everybody—they're in there sleeping!"

"The other kids are in there with your folks?" the driver asked.

"Yes, yes! I said everybody! My whole family!"

The driver said, "Jesus H. Christ!" and brought the bus to a near stop that caused two of the passengers to fall on the floor. "Everybody back in your seat! Now!"

Ben slowed the bus even more, looking for a place to pull to the side where he wouldn't go off the shoulder or block the road. Then he thought, what the hell? The bus might be the only vehicle for a couple of miles!

He stopped the bus, though it was blocking half of the road, and got his brand-new cell phone. No connection. He remembered the phone company hadn't put the towers up yet. He was too far from any major population center to make a phone call. Too far from anywhere.

A dead zone.

The driver looked at his passengers. A boy named Wally Clark appeared old enough, skinny and fast enough.

"Know where the Johnston farm is?" the driver asked.

Wally was on his feet, getting the idea.

"You run there, Wally. Fast as you can. Get them to use their phone, get some firefighting equipment out here."

"Yes, sir," Wally said as the doors hissed open.

Jordan stood, gripping the seatback in front of him hard with both hands, whitening his knuckles. "Let me go," he pleaded.

"No, no!" the driver said. Obviously imagining what the poor kid might see or hear. "You don't wanna go there, son."

Jordan couldn't remember when anyone had called him son.

He slumped back down in the seat, glimpsing Wally running along the road in the direction of the Johnston farm, the closest phone. Wally's heels were kicking up dust that hung in the air behind him. He was making good time at a pace made to seem slow by distance.

Jordan looked toward the house and saw orange glowing here and there through the thick black smoke. The house was blazing. He knew it would take forever for the volunteer fire department to reach the fire. Then their equipment would be inadequate. And how much water could they bring?

He lowered his head so his face was enveloped by his arms, and sobbed.

"Stay where you are, kids!" Ben the driver yelled.

The bus was hot inside and out, and smelled like fuel. Everyone on board was slick with sweat. Jordan's eyes stung from it and his nose was running. One of the girls was crying.

Jordan counted to ten and then raised his head. Through the bus window he could see Ben the driver running toward the burning house, limping clumsily under the weight of a brass fire extinguisher jouncing in his right hand. Wally, head down and arms pumping, was pulling away from him at an angle, toward the Johnstons and their phone.

Jordan got off the bus and followed Ben.

When they got closer to the house, he saw that a spark or burning tree limb had set the barn roof on fire. Some of the animals were sure to die.

Forget the barn.

He made it to the house.

There were two . . . somethings . . . just inside the porch door, curled and blackened. No one else seemed to have made it that far.

Jordan didn't hesitate. Holding his breath, he made a fast tour of the burning house. He could feel the heat coming up through the soles of his shoes.

Now he had seen them, all of them . . .

A powerful hand gripped Jordan's shoulder and squeezed. It was Ben the bus driver, stopping him, pulling him close, closer. Jordan could hear him breathing. Or was he crying?

Ben dragged him outside, and then Jordan found his balance and was walking on his own. Ben pointed, and immediately Jordan knew what he meant. Unhindered by each other, they began to run.

That was when the propane tank alongside the house exploded.

20

Quinn and Pearl stood alongside Nift the ME and watched him explore with his instruments what was left of Margaret Evans. Where she had been eviscerated and her intestines neatly coiled, her breasts had been severed and laid aside.

Reaching so he could probe something in her abdominal cavity, Nift had to stretch and for a second looked as if he might fall across the corpse.

He shook his head, smiled. "Some set of jugs she has—had," he remarked.

Pearl looked at him as if he were last week's spoiled meat. She thought that someday without warning she would kick the little prick, hard in the ribs. Maybe the head.

Renz came in. He'd been out in the hall, talking to one of his detectives. Quinn and Pearl both wondered if Renz was sharing information as generously as they'd agreed. Renz, playing his customary parallel game.

He walked over to Quinn and Pearl, careful not to step near the nude dead woman's oddly disjointed body on the bedroom floor. "Our guy?" he asked, looking at Nift for confirmation.

"No doubt about it," Nift said.

Renz went over and looked in at the bathroom without entering. He stayed that way about half a minute, then backed away awkwardly, but without touching the doorframe and obscuring any fingerprints.

"Killed her and let her bleed out in the bathtub," Renz said, "then dismembered her in the tub, washed most of the blood down the drain, and moved her in here piece by piece, where he more or less put her back together."

"Naughty Gremlin," Nift said.

"He was reasonably neat," Pearl said, noting that there wasn't much blood on the bedroom carpet.

"Unreasonably neat," Quinn said.

Pearl was thinking how closely, and horrifyingly, the dead woman resembled a ventriloquist's dummy.

If I sat her on my knee, would she tell me who killed her?

Renz said, "You might want to talk to the super. Name's Bud Peltz. His is the apartment right off the foyer. He told one of the uniforms he got a good look at the killer as he was running away."

Quinn was surprised by this stroke of luck.

"Don't get too excited," Renz said. "The uniform—his name is Bill Toth—says Peltz's story doesn't ring true."

"He say why not?"

"It set off an alarm behind his right ear."

"That should play well in court."

Fedderman showed up. He looked tired and was

wearing a gray suit that appeared clean but was amazingly wrinkled, as if it had been scrubbed and rubbed over rocks. The narrow end of his tie extended half an inch beneath the wide end. It didn't matter as long as he kept his suit coat buttoned, which he never did.

Everyone glanced at him, but no one said anything as they let him walk around and take in the crime scene.

"Our gremlin," he said.

"Nasty gremlin," Nift said.

Pearl said, "Why don't you shut up? Or at least think of something else to say."

Nift grinned at having gotten under her skin. "Baaad gremlin."

Quinn was sure he heard Pearl's teeth gnash. He thought about her going with him and Fedderman to talk to Peltz the super, then decided it would be better if she talked with Toth, the uniformed cop who'd been one of the first on the scene. They could get together later and see what fit and what didn't.

Pearl didn't object to the plan. Anything to get away from Nift.

Bud Peltz was a tall, thin man with a bushy, droopy gray mustache that looked a lot like Harold Mishkin's. The rest of him looked nothing like Harold. The super had handsome Latin features and a muscular leanness about him. Dark, direct brown eyes, and large, callused hands.

His street-level apartment was small and tidy. It was well furnished, but would have looked larger and more comfortable without such a clash of colors. He invited them to sit on the flower-pattern sofa, which they did. Springs sang softly beneath them. Fedderman had his notepad out and a short yellow pencil tucked behind his right ear. Peltz sat on some kind of woven basket chair that creaked beneath his weight. A large-screen TV sat muted in a corner near what looked like a door to the kitchen. It was showing an old Carole Lombard movie from the forties. Quinn found himself wondering if anyone had actually been watching the TV when he'd knocked on the door. Maybe Lombard was still known and popular in some quarters. Who was famous, who wasn't . . . it was hard to gauge such things.

A slender, remarkably attractive young woman entered the living room and switched the TV off. She was wearing shorts, and had a ballet dancer's shapely, muscular legs.

"My wife, Maria," Peltz said.

Quinn and Fedderman didn't say anything. Peltz was uneasy, as if he should have to explain his ancestry. He hated that feeling. But a visit from the police . . .

Quinn wondered if these two were not long out of Mexico.

Peltz said, "My mother's maiden name was Rodriguez."

"And mine's was Perez," Maria Peltz said.

Quinn smiled. He didn't want to know too much about these two. "The great melting pot. It's a pleasure to meet you, Mrs. Peltz."

When she returned his smile she was even more beautiful. Quinn guessed she was about half the age of Bud Peltz, who looked to be in his late forties.

"We met when I was working for a contractor in Mexico," Peltz said. He directed his attention to his wife. "They're here to listen to my account I gave to Officer Toth."

"Ah, yes, your account."

A look passed between Peltz and his wife. Something in hot-blooded Maria's eyes. She seemed angry, but at the same time amused.

"Can I get you gentlemen something to drink?" she asked.

Quinn declined, wondering how many times he'd heard that line in the movies or on crap television.

"Ice water would be good," Fedderman said.

Quinn relented and seconded Fedderman's request, and Maria glided gracefully into the kitchen. He noticed that she hadn't offered her husband a glass of water. People in hell . . .

Toth had a good eye, or ear, for a cop. A good gut, really. That was where cops got their hunches. There was something out of tune between Bud Peltz and his wife. Would his statement contain the same discord?

"I'm going outside to shop," Maria said. "I slept through everything last night, so I have nothing to relate. Not even dreams. I've already talked with Officer Toth. But if you need me . . ."

"No, no," Quinn said. "Go right ahead. If we need a statement from you we can get it later."

Fedderman glanced at him, surprised.

Maria said good-bye to them, not including her husband. Quinn might have imagined it, but he thought he heard those shapely thighs brush together as she walked.

"A beautiful woman," he said, when Maria was gone.

Bud Peltz seemed unmoved by Quinn's observation. "Everyone says so, and it's true. But you get used to how your wife looks."

Is this guy nuts?

Quinn stood up. Peltz started to stand also, but Quinn raised a hand palm out and motioned for him to sit back down in the creaky basket chair.

Peltz sat.

"Your account," Quinn said, "is a load of bullshit."

Peltz sat quietly for a few seconds, staring at the floor.

Then he sighed.

"All right," he said. "Let's go upstairs."

21

The door to Margaret Evans's second-floor apartment was still unlocked, but there was a roll of yellow crime scene tape leaning against the doorjamb, and an NYPD sticker that had to be peeled off before the door could be opened. Quinn and Fedderman were ready to enter, but Bud Peltz ushered them to the next door, leading to the apartment directly adjacent to the scene of the murder. The detectives were curious about what Peltz had in mind.

The apartment next to Margaret Evans's was vacant and unfurnished. There were clean rectangles on the otherwise bare off-white walls where picture frames or similar objects had hung. A dead geranium sat in a green plastic pot on the living room windowsill.

Peltz led them toward the hall to the rear of the apartment, then into a bedroom. Their footfalls on the bare wood floor carried a faint echo.

They entered a bedroom with a window overlooking a side street. The room was completely bare except for a stained double mattress leaning against the window. It blocked enough light so that it was dim in the room.

Quinn flipped a wall switch that turned on an overhead fixture. Nothing changed, only became more visible.

"You need to turn the light out," Peltz said.

Quinn did, making the room dim again. He was getting an idea of where this might be going.

Peltz went to a door, unlocked it with a skeleton key, and opened it. The door led nowhere but to an empty closet. Even the bar where clothes could be hung had been removed. The closet had an empty twelve-inch wooden shelf above and behind the clothes bar. Peltz tilted the shelf, removed it, and a narrow lance of light penetrated the dimness. Behind where the shelf had been, at its precise level, was a one-inch-round peephole.

Quinn stepped into the closet, peered through the hole, and saw two paramedics putting parts of Margaret Evans into a body bag.

"I saw what he did," Bud Peltz said in a tremulous voice. "I couldn't help her. When I started looking, she was already dead. There was nothing I could do to save her."

"So you watched," Fedderman said.

"I—I couldn't look away."

"You could have called us," Fedderman said. "We could have caught the bastard. Stopped him from doing this." Fedderman's voice rose in anger. This voyeur scumbag had watched and done nothing.

Peltz raised both shoulders in a helpless shrug. "I told you, she was already dead. And I . . . Well, I admit, I was afraid to leave and get to a phone."

"Did you have your cell phone?" Quinn asked.

"Yes, but he might have heard, would have killed me."

"Not much doubt of that," Quinn said, modulating his voice. He wanted to get on this guy's side, become his confidant, learn what he knew. "I won't condemn you for looking through a peephole, Mr. Peltz. You're not the only man who's ever done that."

Peltz's entire body was quaking. "I'm so damned ashamed. And Maria might leave me."

"Did you tell her what you saw?"

"Not everything. I didn't want to talk about some of the things the killer did. Didn't want to think about them."

"It isn't easy," Quinn commiserated.

Fedderman still wanted to toss Peltz out the second-story window, but he knew what Quinn was doing. Getting on Peltz's good side so he could mine him for information.

Then maybe they could toss him out a window.

"I saw what he did with his jigsaw," Peltz said. He looked as if he might break down and start sobbing any second. "Poor Maggie . . ."

Maggie?

"We need to know," Quinn said. "Did you and Maggie—Margaret—have a relationship?"

"We were friends."

"With benefits?"

"You mean did we have sex?"

"Yes. By any definition."

"Twice. Three times."

"Idiot!" Fedderman said softly, thinking of Maria Peltz.

"But it didn't mean anything serious. Not to either of us."

"Of course not," Quinn said. "A woman like that, and

a man like yourself . . . hell, things like that are hard to avoid." He gave Fedderman a stern look so he'd be quiet. "They're like ripples in a lake. Left alone, they disappear and it's as if they never happened."

"That's what I wanted," Peltz said. "That's where we were at. The ripples were disappearing and there would have been smooth sailing except for—what happened."

"One thing, Mr. Peltz. And I hope you won't object to my asking this, but did you ever take photographs through that peephole?"

"Oh, God no! I swear!"

"Video?" Fedderman asked.

"Not that, either. And believe me, I could have. The bedroom was bright enough. Margaret liked it with a light on."

Quinn tried not to show his disappointment. It would have been more than convenient to have the Gremlin's photograph. His likeness on video or as a still would go a long way toward finding him.

"So you got a good look at him."

"Yes. Though a lot of the time his back was turned toward me."

Fedderman had his note pad out. "Can you describe him?"

"A small man, but very muscular."

"Hair?"

"Black. Maybe brown. He wore it kind of long in back and on the sides, combed back over his ears."

"Eye color?

Peltz shook his head. "Sorry. I can't recall."

"He have his clothes off?"

"Yeah. Everything. I guess so he wouldn't get blood

on his clothes he couldn't wash off." Peltz began shaking again. "Margaret was nude, too."

"Any identifying marks on either of them?" Fedderman looked up from his note pad. "Like tattoos or scars."

"No. Not that I saw."

"Is there anything in particular that we didn't ask about? Anything. Even if it seems unimportant to you, but for some reason stuck in your mind."

Peltz pressed his fingertips into his temples to make a show of thinking. "The way he moved, maybe. He was quick and kind of hopped. And his body hair. It was dark, and he had a lot of it." He shook his head. "God! Poor Margaret."

"Sounds like she was attacked by some kind of animal," Fedderman said.

Peltz said, "No. But there was something about him . . ."

"Like a leprechaun?"

"No."

"A gremlin?"

"Yeah!" He looked momentarily confused. "However a gremlin's supposed to look."

"You're sure Margaret was dead when you first saw her last night through the peephole?" Quinn asked.

The shaking got worse. There were tears now, and Peltz's voice cracked. "Her head was detached."

Quinn made an effort to keep calm. To at least appear calm. He was the one assigned to find and stop this monster.

"No one could blame you for being upset," he said to Peltz.

"Jesus save me! Horrible as it was, I couldn't look away."

"We understand," Quinn said. "Anyone would react as you did. Even old cops like us."

Fedderman glared at him.

Quinn almost felt guilty about the anger he experienced on learning that Peltz was merely a voyeur and didn't photograph or video Margaret or her killer.

He started toward the door. "If you think of anything else, Mr. Peltz . . ."

"Of course. I'll let you know."

"They'll want your statement down at the precinct house."

Peltz seemed annoyed. "Another statement? I thought that's what this was. Why so many statements?"

"C'mon, Mr. Peltz, you watch cop shows on TV."

"Yeah. You want to see if I contradict myself, then it'll be my ass."

"It's been our experience," Quinn said, "that people who don't contradict themselves are usually lying."

They were silent as they left the building. Out on the sun-warmed sidewalk, Peltz stopped as if his batteries had suddenly run down.

"We going back to my apartment?"

"No," Quinn said. "We'll let you face your wife by yourself."

"All that stuff about the peephole in the closet, will it be on the news?"

"Most likely."

"Do you photograph well?" Fedderman asked.

Peltz looked angry enough to attack Fedderman. Even took a step toward him. Fedderman didn't back up.

"Now, now," Quinn said, moving between them.

"It's all your fault," Peltz said, still zeroed in on Fedderman. "You're supposed to catch dangerous psychos like that, keep them from killing."

"You've got a point there," Quinn said.

That seemed to calm Peltz. He closed his eyes, took a deep breath, and opened them. "Okay, I'm sorry. I guess I got lost in my own anger, in those images of Margaret. I couldn't look away."

"You told us that," Fedderman said.

Peltz looked mournfully at him. "I'd like to think you believe me."

Fedderman turned and walked toward the car.

When Quinn had gotten in on the driver's side and slammed the car door closed, he lowered the window to let out some of the heat. Peltz bent down and said, "Why's your partner got such a hard-on for me?"

"It's that part about you wanting to be believed. He mostly doesn't believe anyone." Quinn smiled. "I'm pretty much the same way."

Peltz looked enraged, his temper barely in check. "Bad cop, bad cop," he said in disgust. He crossed his arms and stood unmoving as a rock.

Quinn said, "I'm sorry you feel that way."

Quinn started the car and turned the air-conditioning on high. He didn't drive away immediately, though. After a minute or so, he goosed the Lincoln and made the tires squeal. He wanted to be sure Bud Peltz saw them leave.

"Something not ring true to you?" Fedderman asked.

"Yeah, but I'm not sure if it matters, except to Maria Peltz."

"You think Peltz might be abusing her?"

"Or she him," Quinn said.

"He's got a temper," Fedderman said, watching Peltz move toward his apartment like a condemned man, "but he controls it."

"Let's hope his wife controls hers," Quinn said. "That woman reminds me of a stick of dynamite."

Fedderman said, "Notice we're both more concerned that she's going to do him serious harm, rather than the other way around?"

Quinn said, "That oughta tell us something."

PART TWO

This is the very ecstasy of love,
Whose violent property fordoes itself
And leads the will to desperate
 undertakings.

—SHAKESPEARE, *Hamlet*

22

As Jordan Kray watched, the propane explosion obliterated the only house he'd ever lived in. Shingles and wooden splinters flew. Chimney bricks and large sections of the house became airborne and arced away from the fiery explosion in all directions. No one could live through the blast and the inferno.

They were dead. His family was dead.

For a moment he saw a flame-shrouded dark figure that might have been his mother running, flailing her arms. Or he might have imagined it. She was dead when he saw her; she had to be.

Another figure, that he knew wasn't a mirage, was hurrying toward him, still absently lugging the fire extinguisher. Ben the bus driver, lucky to be alive. Ben was forty pounds overweight, most of it in his gut, and could run only so fast. But despite his slowness afoot, his fear had helped to propel him outside the radius of death caused by the propane blast.

Also outside the reach of the explosion, Jordan

found himself wondering about the effects of what he'd done.

Was he detached? Already? No. He definitely wasn't detached. And he wasn't horrified or in shock. Maybe he should be both those things. Instead he was being observant and reasonable. Analytical and curious.

He was aware that others might assume that his calm silence was a symptom of shock. Well, let them.

What he'd planned had worked. He was proud of that but knew he mustn't let anyone realize it. He put on his mental mask. Its expression was one of disbelief and disorientation rather than accomplishment.

What would the house look like later, inside its burning walls? How would the walls and what was left of the wiring and plumbing look? There was a steel I beam running the length of the basement. Would it be melted? Or would it withstand heat and explosion long enough to prevent the house from collapsing into the basement? And what about the heating vents? Had the flames found them to be an easy route through the rest of the house?

The firefighting books Jordan had read in the library were accurate and useful. The precautions, when read and interpreted from a different point of view, provided instructions from hell.

The bus was far enough onto the road shoulder to make room for a fire engine, a red-light-festooned chief's car, and several pickup trucks. What there was of the local fire department. The lead vehicles had their lights flashing. None of them sounded a siren. There was no point. The firefighters could see for miles and it was just them and the fire that was drawing them like a magnet.

Ben and Jordan returned to the bus. Ben, looking at the kids in the rearview mirror, fastened the emergency brake and said, "We might as well watch what happens from here and stay outta the way." He opened the bus's front and rear doors, then switched off the engine and air conditioner. In the sweltering heat and silence, several of the kids raised the bus's side windows. A welcome breeze played down the aisle.

Jordan hadn't counted on this. It was his tragedy and he wanted to see it close up. Nobody saw him dash out through the bus's rear door and run across the tilled field toward the burning house until it was too late. Then everyone pointed and yelled. Ben the bus driver said, "You all stay put now," and struggled out of his seat and left the bus.

One of the volunteer firemen noticed Jordan approaching and jogged out to intercept him. Jordan changed the angle of his approach to the burning ruin that had been his family home.

The fireman was in good physical shape and closed in on Jordan while Ben kept him from retreating. They both tackled him and brought him down, knocking the breath from him.

"It's okay," Ben kept repeating. "It's okay, Jordan."

Both men were breathing hard. Jordan tried to talk but was too winded.

"The kid's family was in that house," Ben said

The firefighter coughed and spat off to the side. Said, "I know. He's one of the Krays. I seen him around." He patted Jordan's shoulder."

All three of them lay quiet for a few minutes, working to breathe.

"How many of your family were inside, Jordan?"

"All of them, I think. Everyone but me."

"Shit!" said the fireman.

Ben rested a hand on Jordan's shoulder and kneaded his flesh, as if a good massage was what was needed by someone who'd just lost his entire family.

"You okay, Jordan?"

"Yes. I want to get closer and look."

"Look at what?"

"My mom and dad, Nora my sister, Kent my brother . . ."

"You can't help them now," the firefighter said. "They're in a better place." He looked up at Ben and the other firefighter who'd come over to stand by them. "He tried to save them. Even with the fire."

"Jesus!" the other firefighter said.

Jordan looked from one to the other. What better place were they talking about?

That was when Jordan suddenly recognized the first firefighter. Riley something. He was a deacon at the church Jordan and his family had attended exactly twice, before his mom and dad had declared themselves atheists.

"A brave lad," the second firefighter said.

"Couldn't keep him on the bus," Ben said. "Not after he realized his family's house was on fire."

"Brave is right!" Riley said. "Inspiring!"

23

New York, the present

Charlie Vinson, on the first week of his new job, seemed to be doing well. He'd established his position as supervisor without obviously angering anyone or making any enemies. At least it seemed that way to Charlie. It wasn't easy to make cold call sales, even for a well-established firm like Medlinger Management. Not only had they successfully managed their clients' investments for twelve years; a year ago they had expanded and moved operations to their present high-end address in the financial district.

With the new offices had come the necessity of more employees and someone to supervise them. So they sent out a corporate headhunter, who had accomplished something of a coup by luring Charlie Vinson away from McCaskill and Cotter Enterprises. Charlie harbored the very pleasant feeling that everyone involved was going to be happy with the move.

He didn't think anyone from the firm was still around, among those who, like Charlie, were standing and waiting patiently for an elevator. There was no conversation as the knot of half a dozen people grew to over a dozen. Everyone stood silently with their heads slightly tilted back so they could watch the digital numbers above the elevator doors indicate that two of the four elevators were on the rise.

"Mr. Vinson. Room for one more."

He looked over to the far elevator and saw its light glowing above the door. Charlie moved toward the elevator to see who'd called to him. People were still filing in beneath the glowing green light.

He was surprised to see Della Tanner, one of the salespeople, among those already crowded into the elevator. She was young—still in her twenties—unapologetically ambitious, and attractive, if you liked large-breasted blond women with perfect features. Charlie did.

"Come on!" she said, smiling, and leaned forward to press a button that was out of his field of vision.

She was pressing the right button. The door remained open long enough for Charlie to elbow his way inside. He saw that the lobby button on the brushed aluminum console was glowing, along with half a dozen other numbered lights. The Blenheim Building was emptying out, like a lot of other office buildings in the area.

"Thanks, Della," he said, returning her smile.

He and Della, pressed together between several large men, could barely move as the elevator began its descent. Charlie decided it wasn't so bad being crushed into Della.

The elevator didn't go far. It dropped smoothly from the Medlinger floor, forty-four, toward the next floor down. It stopped at forty-three, and one of the half dozen people waiting there somehow managed to wedge their way into it, mashing Charlie and Della farther toward the back of the car. Someone had forgotten to use deodorant. Someone else was wearing very strong lilac-scented perfume or cologne.

"Push lobby, please," a woman said politely.

But there was no need. Almost every light on the console was glowing. Even "LL" for Lower Level, which was beneath the lobby. People shifted slightly, but no one said anything. The woman who'd asked to go to the lobby must have seen the glowing button.

The door slid open, and a small man in a blue—or was it dark green?—uniform looked into the packed elevator and smiled. He was wearing a blue baseball cap. He said, "I'll wait for the next one."

This was not the place to have a conversation. Della and Charlie both knew they would converse, or at least exchange pleasantries, after they'd reached the lobby. Charlie wondered if Della lived anywhere near the Blenheim Building. Della noticed a wedding ring on Charlie's finger and wondered how much that mattered. Maybe Mr. Vinson—Charlie—drove into the city, or took a train, or stayed here during the week and went home to a dull suburban life on weekends.

No one in the elevator spoke. Charlie tucked in his chin and looked down at Della. She was staring straight ahead and wearing the slightest of smiles.

A hand snaked out and pressed the glowing Lobby button for good measure. The door closed, and there was silence as everyone waited for the elevator to continue its descent.

The elevator door had no sooner closed than it re-opened. A small blond woman huffed up to it. A smaller figure was also waiting at the elevators—a super or maintenance man or some such. He turned away.

"Are you with Medlinger Management?" the woman asked him. "I'm looking for my husband, Charles Vinson. This is his first day at work here and I wondered—"

But the little man had spun on his heel and was swiftly walking away. The woman was left with an obscure image of him hopping and running as he reached the door to the stairs. There was a kind of faint but definite elfin quality about him.

Charlie hadn't been paying attention and hadn't heard his wife, Emma, address the small man. And, truth be told, he and Della were looking at each other in that way again.

Ah, well . . . The blond woman gave up on the elevator and pushed one of the down buttons for another. Then she gave up on that and walked toward the stairs.

Emma would walk up a floor and try an elevator that hadn't yet taken on so many passengers. It was possible that Charlie was down in the lobby, waiting for her. She tried to call him on his cell phone, but apparently it was turned off. Or he'd let the battery run down. They both were distracted these days, he because of the new job, and she because she was pregnant and hadn't yet told her husband. She smiled in anticipation, absently stroking her stomach. Wherever Charlie was, he was soon to discover that their luck had changed in more ways than one.

Everyone on the elevator was silent, but a few people exchanged glances as a rushing, ticking sound began.

The ticks became louder and closer together, but the elevator's descent was smooth.

Charlie Vinson looked at Della, who returned his stare with a puzzled one of her own.

Something was wrong here.

The packed-in elevator passengers milled, moving against each other where that was possible. Someone's breath was coming too harsh and fast. There were gasps, and whimpers, and the beginnings of curses and questions and complaints and pleadings.

The elevator picked up speed during its forty-three-floor drop.

It took a few seconds for confusion to become comprehension, but everyone had time to scream.

There were no stops along the way. The crowded elevator was doing close to a hundred miles per hour when it crashed into the basement.

Among those rushing to see if there were any survivors was a nondescript small man in a gray or green uniform. Or was it light blue? Was it actually a uniform? The man wore a blue or black baseball cap. The cap's bill was cocked at a sharp angle, and his hair, which was dark brown or black, was worn long and combed back in wings over his ears.

He was later reported to have been seen in the building's basement earlier that day. The building wasn't new, and had been undergoing renovations. Workmen came and went without anyone becoming curious. This man was assumed to be with building maintenance, or a tradesman of some sort, because he was carrying a toolbox.

If he was the same man.

There was a dull thud from a distance, not enough to startle Emma Vinson, or to make her stumble in the carpeted hall.

When she took the stairs and reached the higher bank of elevators, the digital floor indicator mounted above its doors was flashing that the elevators were temporarily out of service.

Emma suddenly felt nauseated. She bent over, clutching her stomach with both hands, and slid down the wall to sit leaning with her back against it and her knees drawn up.

Her future had taken a sudden lurch and somehow changed. She knew it but wasn't sure why.

She was terrified to speculate.

24

Within ten minutes the block was closed at both intersections, and police and emergency vehicles were inside the cordon, parked at forty-five-degree angles to the curb. The crowd and uniformed police officers were mostly out on the street. The uniforms provided a corridor for victim after victim to be brought out of the Blenheim Building on gurneys by paramedics and loaded into ambulances. All of the gurneys contained fully zipped body bags.

Quinn, who had rushed to the scene as soon as Renz called him on his cell, saw Renz's black limo parking outside the cordon. Quinn found himself wondering if Renz would someday mount fender flags on the limo. City or state pennants that proclaimed who was in the car.

A tall man in a black business suit, whom Quinn recognized as an NYPD lieutenant and Renz ally, approached Renz and reached him when Quinn did, just after Renz had ducked under the yellow tape. The lieutenant was the only one showing a shield, fastened to his suit coat pocket. They exchanged glances, and Renz looked at the lieutenant, whose name was Willington, and said, "What've we got?"

Willington stepped back out of the path of stretchers and body bags. He had a solemn, hatchet face that Quinn thought made him look a lot like General MacArthur in old newsreels. Quinn and Renz also moved back out of the way.

"What we've got," Willington said, "is a runaway elevator. Dropped over forty floors and crashed in the basement."

"Passengers?" Renz asked.

"You mean casualties?"

"Victims."

"Twelve, and still counting. They're . . . tangled together. Dead. The inside of the elevator is like something out of a bad dream."

"Any survivors?"

"Only one, so far. A guy named Vinson. Both legs and an arm broken—and who knows what else? He's at Roosevelt St. Luke's, being operated on for a head injury."

"Only one survivor?"

"So far."

"I thought you said—"

"Commissioner," Willington said, "over forty stories, packed into an elevator. Those people instantly became meat."

Quinn was surprised to see an experienced cop like Willington looking queasy.

Renz must have noticed it, too. "It's okay, Lieu. We'll just do our jobs."

Willington gave a half salute to Renz, then to Quinn, and walked away toward the Blenheim Building entrance, presumably to do his job.

Quinn followed him. Taking the stairs down to the building's basement. There was a horrible smell that he recognized. As he got closer to where uniforms and paramedics were busy around an elevator, the scene was bathed in bright light from portable battery units set on tripods. A faint buzzing sound got louder as Quinn approached the ruined elevator. He'd assumed it was the lights buzzing; now he saw that flies were swarming. Now and then someone with a clipboard or a rolled-up newspaper would swat them away. The tone and volume of the constant droning didn't change. The odor clinging to the area indicated why. Blood had been spilled, sphincters had released, bladders had burst.

If this isn't hell, it must be a lot like it.

Using ID furnished by the NYPD, Quinn moved even closer.

He decided to skip lunch.

Sal and Harold spent hours talking to witnesses to the Blenheim Building elevator disaster. They could furnish only peripheral statements. The lone survivor in the elevator, Charles Vinson, who had been there on the first day of his new job in the building, did help. When he regained consciousness in his hospital bed, he described a man who'd tried to get on the elevator on the forty-fourth floor but decided it was too crowded.

Vinson was in traction and wrapped with so much tape he might as well have been mummified. Harold found it hard to comprehend that they were interviewing an actual live human being.

Except for the eyes. Vinson's eyes, which were all too human. They never ceased moving, and they were horrified, haunted. Harold and Sal knew the man would be haunted for the rest of his life.

The eyes darted from Harold to Sal to Harold. Pleading. "My wife . . ."

"She's okay, sir," Sal grated.

"Emma," Harold said, knowing the mention of the wife's name would soothe Vinson. "Emma's right outside, waiting for us to be done talking with you."

"She might have been in that damned elevator."

"But she wasn't," Sal said. He started to pat Vinson's bandaged shoulder, then thought he'd better not.

"Can she come in?"

"Not at this point," Sal said. "But we'll be leaving in a few minutes."

"Whaddya want to know from me?" Vinson asked.

"Whatever you know about what happened."

The dark eyes, sunken in gauze peepholes, darted. "Elevator took a dive."

"Why?" Harold asked simply.

"Dunno. Maybe it was too crowded. Weighed too much."

"Elevators are always overcrowded," Sal said. "They usually don't turn into dive-bombers."

"How far did we drop?" Vinson asked.

"Forty-three floors." Harold said.

"Oh, good God!"

"Where did you get in the elevator?"

"Forty-fourth floor. It was already crowded. People getting off work, I guess."

"More than usual?"

"I don't know. This is my first day at work."

"Some luck," Harold said.

Vinson said, "Luckier than some others."

"All the others," Sal said.

Vinson didn't understand at first. Then he did, and the world behind his dark and wounded eyes changed forever.

"How many dead?" Vinson asked.

"We think it's fifteen," Harold said. "It's still . . . hard to get an exact count."

"Can I see my wife now?"

"We're about done," Sal said. "People on the scene downstairs said they and others realized what had happened and rushed to the elevator to see if they could help in rescue attempts."

"That's how I got here. I can't believe I'm the only lucky one."

You only hope you're going to live, Harold thought, looking at the mass of taped gauze, stained here and there with blood. The doctors had told Harold and Sal that pressure was building in Vinson's brain. They were going to operate within minutes. He had about a forty percent chance of survival. At least, Harold thought, he seems to be thinking okay for now.

What does his wife know?

"See anything we oughta know?" Sal asked.

"Not that I can—"

"Little guy in a gray or green outfit with a baseball cap?"

Light glimmered in Vinson's sunken dark eyes. "Yeah, I did see a guy something like that. When they got the elevator doors open, lots of people had gone to the basement, rushed over to help. One of them looked like the guy you described. I saw him when we got on the elevator, too. He said he'd wait for the next one."

"Were his ears pointed?" Harold asked.

Vinson said, "Who are we talking about here? Dr. Spock?"

"Maybe the maintenance guy. Somebody like that."

"Might have been, for all I know. I never before laid eyes on the man except outside the elevator, and I don't remember anything about his ears. Don't recall much about him, actually. I remember a lot of people looking, leaning in for a closer look and then backing away. They must have seen what a mess the inside of the elevator was and it made them . . . Made them wanna be someplace else. Anyplace."

"Little guy stay or leave?" Sal asked.

"I'm not sure. He seemed . . ."

"What?"

"Not like the others. I mean, he was concerned, but also looked calm and . . ." Vinson sought the desired word. Found it: "Curious."

"Calm and curious."

"Something like that. We're talking about a four- or five-second look, more like a glance, then he was gone."

"Gone where?"

"You'd have to ask him. If he works for maintenance in the building or someplace close, maybe you can find him."

"Would you recognize him if you saw him again?" Harold asked.

"I think so. Yeah. I could. That's because he was the only one who didn't look as if he'd had a walk-on in a slasher movie."

"We'll put our sketch artist to work," Sal said.

"Is that when I say to make the nose a little longer, and the eyes meaner and closer together?"

"Something like that," Harold said.

The man behind the gauze might have smiled. "I always wanted to do that."

The door to the hall opened and a uniformed nurse bustled in. Her name tag said she was Juanita. She was holding some rubber tubing and a small tray on which sat a surgical syringe, what looked like a stethoscope but probably wasn't, some white pills, and half a glass of water on a white napkin. She was followed by a tall, handsome man in green scrubs.

"I'm Doctor Weiss," the man in scrubs said. "How we feeling?"

"Are you hurt, too?" Vinson asked.

Weiss said, "Glad to see you're well enough to be a smart ass."

"I hope that doesn't mean I'm going to get the dull needle."

"Of course it does."

"Can my wife come in?"

"Shortly."

The nurse, smiling, made a motion with both hands as if scooping everyone other than herself and the doctor out of the room.

As Sal and Harold left, Juanita bent over Vinson and set to work. Dr. Weiss followed the two detectives out into the hall.

"How is he doing?" Sal asked, as they moved far enough away from the door to Vinson's room not to be overheard.

"It's still a forty percent chance that he'll make it," Dr. Weiss said.

"So nothing's changed?"

"I'm afraid not. Have you learned anything from talking to him?"

"Maybe. We're gonna have him work with a police sketch artist."

"That can't be until after the operation," Dr. Weiss said.

Here was a complication. "Are you sure, Doctor? We can have a sketch artist here in fifteen minutes."

"Absolutely not. The nurse is preparing him for surgery, and the OR is set up and ready."

"What kind of operation?"

"An urgent one."

"I mean, what kind of doctor are you?"

"I'm a neurosurgeon," Dr. Weiss said.

A nurse Sal and Harold hadn't seen before passed in the hall with Emma Vinson. Emma looked miserable and had obviously been crying.

"What's all that about?" Harold asked.

Dr. Weiss said, "They're going to say good-bye."

"Christ!" Sal said.

Dr. Weiss looked thoughtful. "We could use His help."

On the way down in the elevator, Harold kept softly repeating, "We're hard-boiled cops, we're hard-boiled cops . . ."

Sal said, "Keep telling yourself that, Harold."

"What are you telling yourself, Sal?"

"Forty percent. How it's so much better than nothing."

"Especially if it's your forty percent," Harold said.

25

The killer slept late but still got up to sit in on the news on television. Some of the news, anyway. Most of it was just above the level of gossip related by beautiful blondes who for the most part were smarter than he was. Certainly more well-informed.

He had to admit he admired *Minnie Miner ASAP.* Minnie, a small and dynamic African American woman, was more interested in the story than the news. Not that she was the only journalist/entertainer who worked that way. But she was the best at fitting things together so everything seemed newsworthy. She skillfully blended mayhem and murder with fashion and gossip. She was obviously fascinated by the Gremlin. She'd heard the survivor of what she called "The Elevator Nightmare" mention on another talk/news show that a police sketch artist was going to use what evidence the law possessed to create the Gremlin's likeness. Though small, he was also distinctive. If the sketch was close, chances are someone would recognize him.

If it wasn't close enough, it might send the investigation off in the wrong direction.

* * *

The Gremlin laughed out loud. He was sure no one had gotten a good enough look at him—or indeed any look at all—so far in his New York adventures.

He didn't think it unlikely that Minnie Miner would cooperate with the police in trying to manipulate the public, but she was in over her head with this one. He not only wasn't worried, but he was anxious to see this "likeness" of him. It should help to put a picture in people's minds that looked little like him. It should be a help to him, having all those wannabes swarming the police with their worthless confessions.

He settled back in his tan leather sofa to watch the rest of *Minnie Miner ASAP.* It was a phone-call or tweet-in program. Maybe someday he'd give Minnie a call or a tweet. Or maybe he'd even surprise her and meet her personally. People still did that, didn't they?

When he tired of watching television, the killer removed robe and slippers and ran a hot bath. He shampooed his hair with a product that gave it body, then pleasured himself with images of Margaret Evans.

After a while, the images were replaced by mental snapshots of an elevator packed with dark blood, red meat, glistening white bone, and expressions of horror. It was something that the great painter of Hades, Hieronymus Bosch, would be proud of, and see as among his best work.

Wouldn't it be something, the killer thought, standing up and showering down, if that was what people saw when they opened their doors on Halloween?

Better stock up on those treats.

After dressing in designer jeans, a Yankees T-shirt, and soft-soled leather moccasins, the Gremlin unpacked the blue gym bag in which he kept his knives, tape, and various other instruments of his obsession, and replaced them with half a dozen books on the subject of elevators. Their history, variations, uses, and safety features. He'd bought the books at the Strand bookstore, where aisle after aisle was packed with used books covering everything fictional or factual. He paid cash so there would be no charge record of the purchase.

He had learned virtually everything about elevators, from their invention to their present state. They got progressively safer, but still, there were occasional accidents. And there was human error in construction, installation, usage, performance.

When the bag contained the books, along with a few other contents, he saturated them with bleach. Then he carried the bag out to the deserted hall and to the chute to the building's basement compactor.

He fancied that he heard it hit bottom. Even heard the sound of the compactor's harsh welcome. Trash pickup was scheduled for tomorrow.

So much for incriminating books, or bag. Other evidence the killer wiped clean and placed in cabinets, drawers, or toolbox.

Soon everything was where it might reasonably be found, or not found at all because it could be easily replaced. The killer could always buy another, different color bag, different rope, cigarettes of another brand. Different knives.

Helen the profiler could have taken the elevator up eleven floors to the rehab-center gym, but decided instead to take the stairs. She told herself it was because the building was cool and she needed the exercise. Sure.

Charlie Vinson was using an aluminum walker to get around, but his therapist said he'd soon be graduating to a cane. He'd come through the operations better than anyone would have thought, since what looked like serious injury in the MRI images turned out to be congested blood.

He was on a treadmill, wearing knee-length shorts, an untucked sleeveless shirt, and worn-out-looking jogging shoes. The outpatient rehab center was in a brick and stone building that also housed apartments and a corner deli. The exercise room was on the eleventh floor. On the tenth was a rooftop garden area with small, decorative Japanese maples in huge concrete pots. Beyond the pots, bright red geraniums lined the roof. There were a few webbed chairs. Sometimes, when it wasn't so hot and the roof garden was in the shade of taller buildings, it was pleasant to sit outside.

It was ninety in the shade this afternoon, and no one at rehab was sitting in the garden. In the bright light streaming through the window, a shapely woman in tights was bicycling to nowhere. Helen was pretty sure it was Emma Vinson, Charlie's wife. An attractive Asian woman was on a nearby stationary bike, pedaling almost as fast as Emma Vinson but seemingly with less effort. She looked over now and then at Emma, as if she'd like to challenge her to a race.

Emma didn't look up as Helen walked over to Charlie Vinson. She might have been taken for an instructor, with her six-foot-plus frame and muscular legs.

She was wearing a lightweight green dress today that somehow made her look even taller.

Helen got closer and could hear the rasping breathing emitted by Vinson. They had an appointment to meet with a police sketch artist today. She hoped he hadn't forgotten.

When she was only a few feet away she glanced at the complex instrument cluster on the treadmill, and saw that several wires ran to Charlie Vinson's ears, and to what looked like a blood pressure cuff on his left arm. What appeared to be the treadmill's odometer read 1,055 miles.

Pointing to it, Helen, who wasn't the athlete she appeared to be, said "If I'm going that far, I'm taking the bus."

"That's the past week," Vinson said.

"Impressive," Helen said. "All your miles?"

"Well, no."

Vinson smiled and pressed a button on the treadmill, and the thing slowed down. He slowed with it, and didn't step off until it had come to a complete stop.

"I didn't forget," he said breathlessly, "about our appointment with the sketch guy."

"He's on his way. I thought he'd already be here."

The elevator door opened and Richard Warfield, the sketch artist, stepped out. He was a small man holding a cardboard contraption with three steaming paper cups. A broad strap across his right shoulder supported a leather attaché case. It was the scent of doughnuts that commanded attention.

"Since I was taking the elevator up," he said, "I thought I'd stop and get us something from that place around the corner."

Vinson looked at Helen with a superior half smile. "You took the stairs."

"You know me," Helen said, though he didn't. "An athlete."

"You certainly look like one," a woman's voice said.

Emma Vinson, Charlie's wife, had dismounted her bicycle and come over to them.

"How have you been, Mrs. Vinson?"

"Okay. Compared to how I could be."

"Charlie looks like he's well on the road to recovery."

"The road's a steep hill sometimes," Vinson said. "The leg's not all the way back. Arm's almost there, though. I'm a tough guy, except for when I'm not." He leaned over and kissed his wife's cheek. "Helen's taking me to see the sketch artist," he said.

"You don't have to go far to see him," Helen said. She put a hand on Richard's shoulder. She looked as if she might dribble him. "This is Richard Warfield, our best sketch artist."

"She's being polite," Richard said. Helen thought that in the bright light he looked about twelve years old.

She said, "Richard's modest."

"Well, I am that."

Everyone took a cup of coffee except for Emma, who said water wasn't on her diet, and coffee was almost a hundred percent water.

Helen said, "What do you do for . . . liquid?"

Emma smiled. "It's everywhere, in everything we eat. We're even mostly composed of liquids."

"So I've heard," Helen said. Somehow without burning her tongue, she finished her coffee, crumpled the paper cup, and tossed it halfway across the room into a wastebasket.

"I thought so," Emma said. "Basketball."

"I could have kicked it in, too," Helen said, hoping she hadn't used up the next six months of good luck.

"I'd like to be there," Emma said.

Helen looked at her. "In the wastebasket?"

"No. To see Richard do his work."

"Your husband will be doing most of the work," Richard said.

Half a dozen women entered the room and dispersed to various exercise machines. Seeing who could laugh the loudest seemed to be part of their regimen. They wore exercise outfits of various colors and fashion, all of it designed to make them look thinner.

"They look like starving cheerleaders," Emma Vinson said, in a tone somewhere between jeering and jealous. "'Specially the ones with those boobs."

Her husband, Charlie, seemed to view the exercisers in a different light altogether. He was leaning forward on his aluminum walker, and the expression on his face was so fixated it was almost comical. Helen wondered if there had been breast augmentation going on here.

Helen and company had come here to observe Charlie Vinson and hear what he had to say. They wanted to know how certain he seemed, or if there were any contradictions in whatever he said in conversation. While he was searching his memory to recall how someone looked, something he heard might bob to the surface of his thoughts.

"I have a department car in front of the building," Helen said. "We can drive over to Q&A and get Richard set up. The air-conditioning's been repaired, so it will be cooler there, and Quinn might have something to add."

"Quinn has been wonderful through all this," Emma said.

"Black Chevy," Helen said, "parked near the corner."

Everyone filed into the elevator, including Charlie Vinson. Excluding Helen. Vinson used his aluminum walker to help create standing room.

Helen stayed back.

"Are you taking the stairs?" Emma asked in disbelief.

"I'd prefer it," Helen said. "That athlete thing. Builds endurance in the legs."

Charlie Vinson, leaning on his walker, smiled at her. "We've got to learn to face our fears, Helen."

Helen said, "Why?"

26

After the brief drive to Q&A it didn't take Richard Warfield, the sketch artist, long to get set up. Quinn sat back and watched.

Warfield borrowed a small card table and two chairs. He placed the chairs so two people sitting in them would be directly across from each other. Then he removed two small laptop computers from his leather attaché case. He placed the two computers in the center of the table, their screens facing away from each other.

The two people in the chairs would be facing each other. Warfield and Charlie Vinson would be looking at identical screens.

"So this is what sketch artists have come to," Vinson said, understanding how this process was going to work. Warfield could not only get information from Vinson about what the perpetrator looked like; he could also watch Vinson on PIP react as the likeness on the screen before him took shape and went from pixel to person.

"This and a stylus are much more effective than a

sketch pad and pencil, or a lot of false mustaches," Helen said.

"It takes the same sort of talent and expertise," Warfield said.

Helen could see that it would. She'd observed Warfield work several times and been impressed.

"I'll use the stylus directly on my screen," Warfield said. "And I'll use it much as I'd use charcoal or pencil on a sketch pad." He peered around his up tilted laptop screen. "I might ask you to do some basic drawing to get across what you're trying to describe."

"I can't draw anything but water," Vinson said.

"That's okay. The process will concern your memory rather than any artistic talent. And mostly, I'll be responding to your descriptions. I'll fill in when I think you've been too light, but other than that, it's your show. Then we'll discuss what we have and hone and sharpen the likenesses." He glanced around. "Is everybody comfortable?"

Everyone said that they were. No one switched chairs or positions. The only change was that two people asked for bottled water, which was supplied.

Warfield booted up and adjusted both computers. Their monitors showed blank backgrounds.

Warfield picked up his stylus and held it lightly, as he would a piece of chalk, or a flute he was about to play.

"Remember," he said to Vinson, "what will be happening on my screen will be happening on yours. Much of what I say will be determined by the software. Don't use your stylus unless I tell you." He touched stylus to screen. "Ready?"

Vinson said that he was.

Warfield said, "We'll begin with a perfect oval."

Vinson watched a black line appear on his TV screen.

"Now I'm going to make it more egg-shaped."

Before Warfield, the oval on the monitor became slightly smaller at the bottom. More like a real egg. But a perfect egg.

"That about right?" Warfield asked.

Vinson, knowing the figure was to be the basic shape of the killer's head, said, "Maybe a little smaller at the base."

"Okay. Pointed chin?"

"Yes!" Vinson said. "Now that you mention it. Definitely pointed. One of his ears was pointed, too."

"One of his ears?" Quinn asked.

"Yeah. The right one, I think. It looked like he'd done some boxing. Or he mighta been injured or something when he was a kid. Like some bigger kid had him in a headlock and messed up the ear. Broke the cartilage.

"What about his left ear?"

"Nothing. I don't recall exactly, though. He did have hair long on the sides, so maybe it was covered."

"Show us."

Vinson did some crude sketching, then Warfield neatened it up.

"Somebody said he was wearing a baseball cap." Quinn said.

"Might have been, but I don't recall it. He was just some little guy in a hurry to get downstairs, trying to get on the elevator."

Warfield played with the keyboard, mouse, and stylus. The shape on Vinson's monitor changed slightly.

Then he gave the subject longer hair on the sides, and a pointed cauliflower ear, and it underwent a definite alteration.

"That it?" Warfield asked Vinson.

"We're getting there. The hair on the sides was still a little longer, like wings."

The digital image on Warfield's computer changed again. The face on the monitor was looking more familiar. Still, there should be a definite click of recognition. That hadn't happened yet.

Vinson was getting a better idea of how this was going to work. It was going to be a grueling job. Already his back was getting sore from sitting leaning forward in concentration.

"I do feel like there are things swimming just beyond my thoughts, but I can't get to them," Vinson said, looking at Quinn.

"That's okay. Memory's like that."

"What about his nose?" Warfield asked Vinson.

"Long and pointed." No hesitation there.

"Like Pinocchio's?"

"Good Lord, no. The guy wasn't a freak."

Quinn thought, Not on the outside.

Warfield sketched in a smaller nose. "That it?"

"Not quite. There was a little hump in his nose. Know what I mean?"

Warfield brandished his stylus. "Like so?"

"No. Not quite that big."

Warfield made minor adjustments.

"No, no, no, better, better, too much—that's it! Now, can you make the eyes closer together?"

"Sure." Warfield accommodated. He seemed to be having fun now.

"Perfecto!" Vinson said.

"Eye color?" Quinn asked.

Vinson shook his head. "Sorry, Lieutenant."

"It's Captain."

"Sure."

Quinn smiled. Civilian, actually.

"Did he have any facial hair?" Warfield asked.

"Like a mustache or beard?" Vinson asked.

"Or anything else," Quinn said.

"Not as I can recall, Cap'n."

Cap'n.

Was Vinson messing with him? Quinn stared at the man, detecting no irony. So Vinson wasn't another Harold.

"Tattoos, warts, scars, anything noticeable?" Warfield asked Vinson.

"He had a chin with a line in it."

"Vertical?"

"Up and down."

"Cleft chin?" Helen asked.

"Yeah, that's it."

"What was he wearing?" Quinn asked.

"Like I said a couple dozen times, he mighta had on some sort of work outfit. Green, gray, blue. One of those colors that changes a little according to what color room they're in."

"What color are the forty-third-floor walls and carpet?"

"By the elevators?"

"Yes."

"Tell you the truth, I'd be guessing," Vinson said.

That, Quinn thought, probably was the truth.

Warfield did a little touching up. Then he stood and finished with a flourish. Quinn thought he might kick his chair away like a rock star to share and express his enthusiasm, but he merely stepped back.

"Not a spittin' image," Vinson said, "but I don't think anybody could do it better. It captures the essence."

"You an art critic?" Harold asked seriously.

Quinn knew it was one of those seemingly unrelated questions that Harold sometimes asked, and sometimes led somewhere the other detectives hadn't known existed. Harold's World.

"In my spare time," Vinson said.

It turned out that Vinson had a blog, Splatter Chatter, that specialized in cubism and the impressionist masters. He gave everyone his card, on which was his blog's web address and a tiny portrait of van Gogh with his ear bandaged.

All of this, Quinn thought, was apropos of nothing.

Maybe.

27

A slightly hungover Lido arrived the next morning at Q&A and situated himself at the main computer. He had the air of a man who was at home and alone—his world, his house, his investigation.

Quinn walked over and Lido acknowledged his presence with a languid wave. Two of the computer's monitors were flashing head shots of males, one of which might be a match with the digital likeness of the suspect. It could happen any moment, suddenly. Or not at all. It was asking a lot of facial recognition software to match a photograph with a police artist's sketch.

"Any luck?" Quinn asked.

Lido shot him a glance. "Not so far. It would be nice if we had a photo to match with a photo. Or, better yet, fingerprints."

"In a dreamworld," Quinn said.

Lido said, "Isn't that where we are?"

"Sounds like a question that could lead to one of those existentialist arguments heard in dorm rooms around the world."

"Dorm rooms, did you say?"

"Around the world," Quinn affirmed.

"I been there," Lido said, "and it's not so great."

The shrill first ten notes of "One Hundred Bottles of Beer on the Wall" suddenly sounded from the computer

The frenetic movement on the monitor adjacent to the one that displayed only the artist's and witness's still, digital image of the suspect suddenly became motionless. It was as if that entire wall had ceased swaying.

Lido leaned forward. Quinn stepped forward. Attentions were riveted on the monitor.

Lido went to a split screen. The sketch of the suspect was next to a black-and-white newspaper photo of a scrawny teenage boy. Quinn wouldn't say the sketch and photo were like a young and older image of the same person. Still, there was a strong resemblance. Even the cleft chins.

"This isn't a mug shot," Quinn said. "That's what I was expecting."

"If we had that," Lido said, "we'd probably also have fingerprints we might match."

Both men stared hard at the photos.

"What's that behind him?" Lido asked, motioning toward the near image.

"Where the height chart should be?" Quinn moved closer. "Looks like a stairway. Inside somewhere, judging by the light and shadow."

"No, that. It looks like a double exposure, or a shot taken with a cheap camera in incredibly bad light."

Quinn saw what he meant. On the broad landing before the stairs, several people showed as shadowy forms in the background. A woman in a long dress. Two men, one of whom had his arm around the shoulders of the other. One of them was wearing a white shirt and dark tie. The upper body of another man, without a tie, was visible descending the steps. They were like ghosts.

"Could be the inside of a public building," Lido said.

"Courthouse?"

"That would be nice. If our gremlin was messed up with the law, there should be an ID and photo of him somewhere. An account of the case—if there was a case."

"I'll narrow the parameters," Lido said.

"What will that do?"

"We'll be looking for a bigger needle in a smaller haystack."

Pearl and Helen entered the office, letting in warm air with the hiss of the street door. Both women slowed down when they saw Quinn and Lido in the rear of the office, at Lido's computer setup.

"We got something?" Pearl asked.

"Maybe," Quinn said.

Helen moved closer, then bent at the waist to get a clearer view.

"Tell you the truth," she said, "they don't look all that much alike. I know Mr. Sketch, but who's the other guy?"

"Maybe the Gremlin."

"No, I mean who is he?"

"We were hoping he'd be a match with Mr. Sketch," Quinn said.

Pearl said, "Good luck with that."

"If we get him ID'd we might find a long sheet on him."

"If the images match closely enough," Pearl said.

Helen had moved very close to one of the monitors. "Can you zoom in on the other guy?"

"Other guy?"

"The one most obviously not Mr. Sketch."

"Sure," Lido said.

As Lido worked the computer like a mad scientist, the figure in the photo became larger and lost more definition. "All I can tell is he looks young," Lido said.

"That's lettering, there in the lower right," Helen said. She pointed. "I think it's a name."

"I'll zoom in on it," Lido said, "but it's gonna break up pretty soon."

Helen reached into her purse and put on a pink pair of glasses. No one had seen her in glasses before.

She removed the glasses and stood up straight. "That's okay, I got it."

"The photographer's name?" Lido asked.

"No, it's not a photo credit. It's the kid's name in newspaper print: Jordan Kray."

Lido pressed save and then ran printouts of what was on the monitor. Then he went to work with his computer, immersing himself again in his private digital world. Someday Lido might stay there, Quinn thought. Might even be trapped there in geek land, with all the other brilliant geeks who wear mismatched socks but can work complex equations in their heads.

"There's no Jordan Kray that fits the characteristics we're looking for," Lido said, after a while.

"He doesn't even have a Web page?" Fedderman asked. He had come in with Harold's partner, Sal. They'd held their silence while Lido was working.

Fedderman's wife, Penny, had been coaching him on the computer while trying to create a Web site. She had convinced him that everyone other than the Feddermans had a Web site, and that he was a natural. Already he had a tendency to store information on a cloud someplace that he could never access.

"The guy's a troglodyte," Fedderman said.

"Something like that," Lido said.

They stared again at the blown-up digital image. Under Lido's coaxing it was larger now, in sharper definition. The photo was obviously one of a young male teenager. Or maybe he wasn't even in his teens.

"That's a newspaper photo, so let's find out which paper," Quinn said.

"Small-town rag," Fedderman said. "Maybe a give-away. And not recent. You can tell by the print under the photo."

"You mean the font," Harold said knowledgeably. "That's how they started calling front-page news in the early twenties. In newspaper slang, 'big font' meant big news. Since it was always on the first page, 'font-page news' gradually became front-page news."

"Is any of that true, Harold?" Sal asked.

"Should be."

"Get the enhanced sketch in circulation," Quinn said, marveling as he often did that his bickering team of detectives could solve anything. What accounted for their success? Unconventional thinking, maybe. "Let's follow it up with the photograph of the kid. Send both images out to the media, then hit the neighborhoods and shops where the victims lived or worked. Do it on foot, face-to-face, so you can see what reaction you get when they first lay eyes on the photo."

"We need to find out more on that photo," Sal said.

"More on the kid," Harold said.

"It amounts to the same thing, Harold," Sal rasped in his annoyed tone. Sometimes Harold could be intolerable.

"Don't be negative," Harold said.

There! Negative. Photography. Was Harold joking, or making fun of Sal? Or making Sal the joke? Or was Harold just plain dumb? Or so dumb he was smart?

"I'll drive the unmarked," Sal rasped, "and I'll control the air conditioner. Think of me as the captain of the ship."

Harold said, "Font news."

28

Iowa, 1998

For the next several years, after his family's destruction, Jordan stayed with the Millman family, who had a farm a mile west of the Krays' house that had burned.

He went to school on the yellow bus as before, but the other kids tended not to talk to him. No one made fun of him; they simply didn't seem to know quite what to make of him. A kid like Jordan, their classmate, an actual hero. Nobody knew how to approach or talk to him. A kid who in truth had been thought of as something of a dork had miraculously become "awesome."

Jordan enjoyed his celebrity status—at least some of it. But after a while he became withdrawn and quiet. He would look around the bus sometimes at his schoolmates and wonder how something that had nothing directly to do with their lives could strike them as so great a tragedy that they seldom knew what to say to him. He thought it shouldn't be such a problem. Even the nitwits they saw on TV news were always yammering about "getting on with" their lives.

The Millmans were a nice enough family. The father, Will, had died three years ago in an auto accident. His wife, only slightly injured, became "The Widow Julia." Their son Bill, also injured, was a little younger than Jordan. He seemed to look up to Jordan, who, while older, was considerably smaller.

At times Bill would follow Jordan to the burned, partially collapsed hulk of what had been the Krays' home. The burned smell was still strong, but Jordan was used to it and didn't mind. He would stand at the edge of the ruin and point things out to Bill. Teacher-to-student mode: "See how the kitchen floor caved in first? That's because the appliances were so heavy. And the fire almost melted part of the house's main beam, running the length of the structure. That's a steel I beam that held up the entire weight of the house," Jordan told Bill, "but look how it's bent. Like it's squishy rubber instead of steel. See over there, where the electrical service was run in and mounted on that wall? That metal box hanging on the wall is full of circuit breakers."

While Jordan talked, Bill listened carefully about electric current and circuit breakers. Then they covered the subject of smoke alarms. What kinds there were and how sometimes they worked but sometimes didn't. Jordan explained about the sprinkler system, and how it was kept dry by air pressure unless one piece of metal melted faster than another, which completed a circuit and triggered an alarm and an indoor cloudburst.

Bill Millman thought that if someone walked in or listened to them, it would sound as if Jordan was trying to sell him the ruined house.

What Jordan never talked about was the short time

he'd spent after entering the burning house. Before the propane explosion.

Jordan had learned a great deal observing the fire that morning, not the least of which was how a burned body looked. Kent, he thought.

Jordan only had to move a few feet to find what must be his mother's body. Interesting how the blackened corpse might have worked when alive, the bone and muscle and tendon receiving instructions from the brain. Human bodies were simply large gadgets, Jordan realized. Parts working in conjunction with each other.

How fascinating.

Especially women's parts.

The widow Julia liked to cook. Bill and Jordan liked to eat. Bill became tall and lean, an outfielder on the school baseball team. He was disciplined for using the janitor's tools to peel a baseball like an onion, unwinding what was inside. He never told anyone that Jordan had ruined the baseball, curious about how and why it behaved as it did when it met the bat.

The two boys grew apart. Bill became immersed in baseball, and Jordan, more and move aloof, discovered reading. It was rumored that the Cincinnati Reds were going to send a scout to assess Bill's talent. Bill shagged fly balls and spent extra hours in the batting cage, but the scout never showed up.

Toward the end of that season, a batted ball shattered Bill's kneecap. He managed to adapt well to an artificial knee, but that was the end of baseball or any other active sport.

Bill did, however, learn to walk with the knee so well that unless you knew about the injury, you'd think it was just fine.

Then Bill got into the habit of spending time in the park, hitting fly balls to slightly younger, more nimble outfielders. Now and then Bill would even break into a run to field a ball that was thrown back in.

Not a long run, but it was amazing the way Bill could get around with the man-made knee.

Jordan sometimes watched from the shadows on summer nights when Bill would sit with the widow Julia in the porch glider. With every gentle rock the glider would squeal as if in ecstasy. Jordan mentioned a few times that it would be no trouble to oil the glider's steel rockers. A couple of drops would do the trick. But Bill told him to leave them alone, he kind of liked the sound. He told Jordan it was more pleasant to listen to than the crickets. Jordan wondered if Bill had ever taken apart a cricket.

Jordan took to playing solitaire by the light of a yellow bulb, while Bill and the widow Julia rocked. Occasionally Bill would get up and go inside to the kitchen to get a couple of Budweiser beers and bring them outside. He never brought a bottle out for Jordan.

Jordan got into the habit of ignoring the squeaking sound of the glider. But when the squeaking stopped, he would wait to watch Bill clomp across the porch, then with the slam of the screen door reappear a few minutes later with the two bottles of beer.

Then one warm night the squeaking stopped. The boots clomped across the dark porch, and there were lighter, trailing footfalls.

Then the night was quiet except for insect noises.

* * *

That night the screen door never slammed, and the glider didn't resume its squealing.

Early the next morning, routine set in again. It was the weekend, and Jordan and Bill had turnips to harvest before the sun got high.

The widow Julia gave little indication that last night had been different for her and Bill. But occasionally their eyes would meet, then quickly look away. There were small, sly smiles.

When the turnip harvesting was done, Julia put biscuits in the oven, brewed a pot of coffee, and scrambled some eggs. Everyone behaved in precariously normal fashion. Jordan sat back in his spoked wooden chair and watched Julia move about the kitchen. She was barefoot and wearing a faded blue robe with its sash pulled tight around her narrow waist. Something about her feet with their painted red nails held his attention.

Jordan and Bill both watched as she bent low with her knees locked to check the biscuits she'd placed in the oven.

Bill shoved his chair back and stood up to help Julia. It didn't look as if it hurt him to stand, but it was obvious he was slowed down.

He stretched and got some mugs and plates down from a cabinet, and Jordan observed how well he moved without his cane. Jordan didn't know what artificial knees were made of—some kind of composite material, he imagined. The human knee was complicated. There must be lots of moving parts.

Jordan wondered how they worked.

29

The concrete saw roared and screamed simultaneously. Dan Snyder, who'd been a worker for SBL Property Management for fifteen years, knew how to use the earsplitting tool to section off concrete better than anyone at SBL. He kept a deceptively loose grip on the saw, using its weight to maintain stability, his arms to guide rather than apply pressure. Let the saw do most of the work.

He'd learned to ignore the noise.

Snyder knew some older workers at SBL whose hearing had been affected by the noises of destruction and construction. He did wear earplugs, though he didn't think they'd make much difference. Already he was asking people to repeat themselves. He was particularly deaf at parties, or wherever a crowd gathered.

Letting people know your hearing was fading wasn't the best way to stay employed by SBL Properties. Snyder was faking understanding more and more. Definitely there were safety issues, but dealing with them was better than unemployment.

Snyder was a big man who, when working, wore wifebeater shirts to show off his muscles, not because of an ego thing, but so he would continue to look physically competent well into his forties. Fifties, in his line of work, might be too much to expect.

He enjoyed working hard, creating change. Like here at the Taggart Building. It remained mostly offices, with retail at first-floor and lobby levels. The arched entrance had been redesigned and would be decorated with inlaid marble. Wide, shallow steps would ascend on a graceful curve, leading to the lobby entrance. What wouldn't be darkly tinted glass in the entrance would be veined marble.

That was what Snyder was working on now, removing concrete that would be replaced by marble. The experts who would install the decorative marble were craftsmen of a different sort, using mallets and chisels. Their art was woven in with history. They cut stone with an eye to infinity.

SBL didn't build or rehab structures that wouldn't last. Most of the work Snyder had been doing for the past fifteen years was still around, and visible, if you knew where to look.

The Taggart Building was projected to be one of the tallest structures on Manhattan's West Side. Right now it wasn't all that impressive. It was stripped of most of its outer shell, and its extended skeletal presence was already taller than most buildings on the block. That basic framework would be strengthened and built upon, and within weeks a bold brick and stone structure would take form.

At present, the only thing taller in this part of town was the steel crane looming twenty feet above the Taggart Building's thirty-fifth floor. That would soon change.

Over the years, Snyder had developed a proprietary attitude toward New York. His city. It didn't hurt, either, to trade remarks with passing women, unless Snyder's wife, Claudia, somehow found out about it.

Claudia never actually snooped. At least, Snyder didn't think so. He'd never caught her at it, and he gave her the benefit of the doubt. Yet she had a way of somehow knowing things.

Maybe that was the reason why she'd been so uneasy this morning. She'd had a premonition, she said, and she'd asked Snyder to be particularly careful today.

Snyder dutifully told her he'd be more careful than usual, and kissed her good-bye.

In truth he wasn't much for premonitions, but women did sometimes seem to have some mysterious source of information. On average, they found out things well before men did. It was as if they had their own secret Internet.

In this crazy world, it was possible.

Seated in a booth in their favorite diner, Quinn and Pearl were enjoying breakfast—eggs Benedict for her, over hard with hash for him—when Quinn's cell phone chimed. He wrestled the phone out of his pants pocket and saw that the caller was Renz.

"It's Renz," he mouthed to Pearl, just before accepting the call. Then, "Morning, Harley."

"You anywhere near a TV?" Renz asked.

"We're having breakfast at the White Flame over on Broadway."

"The place with the great blintzes?"

"I thought that was something the German army did," Quinn said. "But this place has got a TV behind the counter. It's showing Martha Stewart reruns right now."

"Have them put it on New York One," Renz said.

Quinn glanced at his watch. Oh no! "Minnie Miner?"

"ASAP," Renz said. "You know the media types. They have to be fed if you want to keep them on your side. Newshounds like Minnie Miner need meat thrown to them now and then, so they can have a bone to gnaw on. Keeps them happy and quiet for a while."

As soon as he broke the connection with Renz, Quinn asked Ozzie the counterman if he minded tuning the TV to *Minnie Miner ASAP.*

"This is part of your work?" Ozzie asked. He was an athletically built black man who strongly resembled the former Cardinals baseball shortstop genius, the real Ozzie Smith. His legal name was Ozzie Graves, but that wasn't very glamorous, and when some gullible customer thought Ozzie behind the counter was the genuine Ozzie, who could play baseball and do backflips, all at the same time, Ozzie Graves simply rolled with it.

"Why do you ask?" Quinn said.

"We ain't got a lot of Minnie Miner fans here," Ozzie said.

"Subject them to her for a little while," Quinn said, "or I'll tell everyone your real name."

Ozzie went "Ummm," which he always did when he was thinking.

"This about those murdered women and that Gremlin nutcase?" he asked.

"We're trying to find that out," Quinn said.

"Okay, then. Long as you let me autograph some baseballs. I can sign them Ossie Snith—keep it legal."

"Of course, as long as the photos are genuine."

"Today we're going to interview a real serial killer," Minnie Miner was saying on television. "He might be able to shed some light on this subject—if he wants to, of course. We don't twist arms on this show—that's how we get so many interesting guests and—hopefully—we learn something." She glanced at the simple set. Two green easy chairs flanked a small table with a stack of half a dozen books on it. There was a low coffee table in front of the sofa. It could be reached by all the guests. The cordless phone was on the table between the chairs. There was a worn, trashy look to some of the set, though it all came across nicely on TV.

The *Minnie Miner ASAP* news show was actually mostly a call-in radio show, but plenty of interesting guests had learned of it by first watching it on television. Minnie always had a phone number and e-mail address superimposed on the bottom of the screen. The Gremlin had at first vowed only to talk on the phone, but the lure of TV, of all those eyeballs trained on you, was for many almost irresistible.

Not yet, the Gremlin told himself. When the time came, there would be plenty of cameras aimed at him.

Almost, but not quite yet.

Minnie was standing by the table when the phone made a weird swishing sound, like a sword or large knife splitting the air. She grinned—an attractive black woman with mischievous eyes, a great shape, and a big smile—and raised her forefinger to her pursed lips in a request for silence.

And the audience was silent.

The phone made the weird sound again. She looked at the audience, gave them an even bigger smile, and lifted the receiver with both anxious hands.

Smiling yet wider, the phone pressed to her ear, she nodded over and over, as if trying to shake off her smile.

This was great. This was wonderful! She mouthed the word "Gremlin" several times, her sparkling dark eyes scanning the audience, then spoke into the receiver, as obsequious and happy as if she'd gotten an interview with the Queen of England.

She was talking to a killer.

30

Quinn, watching *Minnie Miner ASAP*, was amazed by the smattering of applause from the studio audience as Minnie introduced the killer, referring to him simply as "the Gremlin." That's what Minnie's audience was trained to do, so it was automatic even though the applause sign didn't light up.

Minnie, wearing a mauve pants suit and with her hair slicked back, looked dignified and important. She was seated in her usual armchair she used when interviewing guests. In the matching armchair sat a black cardboard cutout of a man with an oval head and no features.

"First of all," Minnie said into her handheld microphone, "I'm glad you had the courage to call."

"Let's not waste time talking about that."

"Do you object to me referring to you that way—the Gremlin?"

"If you can hear a shrug on the phone, you just did," the Gremlin said. His voice was male and strong, not what one might expect from a man described as resembling a destructive elf or leprechaun.

"And why did you want to talk with me, personally, rather than another journalist?"

"I'm interested in reaching your audience through you."

"And the reason for that?"

"I don't mind tales being told about me, as long as they're based at least in part on the truth."

"Do you think lies have been told?"

"You might call them selective editing. I call them lies."

"Such as?" Minnie asked. She looked knowingly at the cardboard cutout, then at the audience. They were all going to get a glimpse into the hell that was the killer's mind. This was journalism at its best.

"That I'm angry, violent, and vicious," the Gremlin said, "and trying to get back at someone. Or that I'm on some kind of crusade. Or that I'm seriously mentally unbalanced."

"Are you saying you're none of those things?"

For several seconds there was only the sound of heavy breathing. Then what might have been a whimper. "I'm wondering how you get into the club they call the human race."

Minnie looked wonderingly at her studio audience. "Is that what this is about? Are we going to hear about an unhappy childhood? Because that's what all killers say." Suddenly Minnie was angry. "Because if that's it, we—that's me and my audience and the huge audience out there—aren't buying any of those bananas."

"I'm not selling bananas. Or anything else. I'm just looking for the truth. For someone who won't lie to me."

"Well. You found her. The language spoken here is the liberating, sometimes uncomfortable truth."

"It wasn't my fault those people died."

"Which people?"

"The women who rejected me. The men who betrayed me."

"Did you even know those people?"

"I knew all of them, because they're all the same."

"Like the people in the fire, and in the elevator?"

"All the same."

"But why did you kill them?"

"So I might better understand them."

"Are you saying that's why you killed all those people in the elevator—so you could better understand them?"

"Not the people. The elevator." Another pause. "The people, too, though."

Minnie locked gazes with the audience, made a face, shook her head. "That's so . . . sick."

"You shouldn't say those things about me."

"I promised I'd tell you the truth."

"That didn't mean anything."

"It most certainly did."

"How do you make your living?" Minnie asked. "Do you have a job?"

"Of course I do. Robbing from the rich and giving to myself. And I enjoy the agony and acquiescence my profession entails."

"Robbing the dead. You must know how perverse that is. You need help."

"You mean someone to hold their finger on the knots while I pull them tight?"

"I can give you some names and phone numbers," Minnie said.

"I can't trust you."

"You can, you can."

"Are you trying to keep me on the line long enough so the police can trace my call?"

"Of course not."

"See?"

Quinn heard the click as the killer hung up, then watched Minnie do the same.

Ten minutes later, Renz called. "It was a drugstore throwaway phone," he told Quinn. "The call originated someplace in midtown west of Broadway. Even if we could find the phone, or what's left of it after it's been stomped on, it wouldn't help us."

"We can't be sure of that."

"Sure we can," Renz said. "I can tell stories two different ways, then later on I can take my pick. Fall back on the one that's the best fit. No one remembers what other people say, anyway."

"Cops do," Quinn said.

"Not if they don't remember they've forgotten something."

Quinn said, "I'll grant you that. And they—we— also overlook things."

"Not us. Not cops."

"Even cops."

"But how would we know?"

"We'd find out," Quinn said. "Eventually."

31

Betty Lincoln and Macy Adams looked like Broadway dancers. Both of them, from time to time, had come close. They were wearing tight designer jeans, pullover tops, and flat-soled, comfortable-looking shoes. Not shoes to dance in, but to give their feet a rest. Betty and Macy waited patiently for their shrimp salads and iced tea. Each woman was small, with a tight body, flat abdomen, large muscular buttocks and calves. Betty was blond and had a turned-up nose. Macy had dark hair and a Mediterranean profile. They moved with a kind of grace and power that drew the eye, even when they simply crossed the Liner Diner to the booths beyond the counter.

Sitting toward the back of the diner suited them. There were windows there, and they didn't have complete privacy, but it would do. Students from the nearby Theatre Arts Academy hung out at the Liner Diner, and neither Betty or Macy wanted to be seen. Especially Macy. Betty had made the second cattle call. Macy knew by the casting director's piercing look that she wasn't going to make it.

They would find out officially after lunch.

Two other dancers, and Darby Keen, hot new star out of the TV world, walked up and stood outside talking, near the front window of the diner. Betty and Macy sat still, unnoticed, while the other two dancers entered and found a booth near the entrance, to the side and out of sight and earshot.

"At least we won't have to listen to Keen brag about himself," Macy said.

Betty didn't comment. She thought Darby Keen was a beautiful piece of work. Couldn't sing. Couldn't dance. But what the hell, he was a draw. And more than once, when she was onstage with the other dancers, he'd given her a certain look.

"What do you think of the playwright?" Macy asked.

The writer of *Other People's Honey,* Seth Mander, was still in his thirties, tall and blond, with sloe blue eyes that turned Betty on. Betty thought she and Seth would make a good pair. Even if he was part of the process that might deny her the job, she was still prepared to like him.

Perhaps more than like him.

"Betty?"

"Seth is beyond cute."

"And talented," Macy said. "*Other People's Honey* is a seriously good play."

"With lousy choreography."

"You noticed?"

"It'll sprain or break a few ankles," Betty said.

Both women laughed.

Then Macy felt suddenly glum. She'd be glad to risk a sprain, if only her luck would change and she could be a member of the cast that was shaping up for *Other*

People's Honey. Nobody really knew where hit musicals came from—they either did or didn't have the magic. It looked, sounded, felt like *Other People's Honey* was going to be a hit.

But Macy knew it wasn't going to happen for her. Not this time, and maybe never. Enough rejection taught you how to recognize it when it was still on the way. She could see it in the posture and faces of the ones who were judging hopefuls for *Other People's Honey.* The money gods who held fate in their hands. Macy, in her heart, was already defeated. All that was needed was for it to be made official.

Macy wanted to know, wanted the suspense to end. Or was not knowing a kind of masochistic pleasure? After all, if you didn't know you were a failure, it wasn't yet an established fact in the minds of others.

And in your own mind.

The verdict would be suspended for another hour or more, after the tryouts for voice. Macy didn't worry about that. She didn't even pretend to be able to sing. She was a dancer, and not just a chorus line dancer. She knew she was unique, and could carry a show.

Yet something in her doubted, and it seemed impossible to change that.

She knew what she needed. A new love. And luck with a new luster. The first would be easier than the last. She could fall in love—or something like love—easier than she should.

There was a flurry of activity up near the front of the diner. The background traffic noise was louder, then softer. Someone had entered. Others had stood up.

Darby Keen, sleek and muscular in jeans and a T-shirt (he certainly looked like he could dance), entered the diner. And right behind him, Seth Mander, his straight blond hair mussed by the breeze and dangling over one eye. He was wearing dress slacks, loosened tie, and scuffed moccasins. Betty stared at him, transfixed.

Hands were shaken, backs were slapped. The dancers in the front booth were standing up. Everyone was standing. Some were congratulating themselves.

"They've seen us," Macy said.

Betty forced herself to raise her head and look.

My God! They're coming back here!

32

Little Louie, as his fellow workers called Louis Farrato, was working the jackhammer today, breaking up already cracked concrete in front of the Taggart Building, the area that was to become the driveway of a portico. Louie, who was a few inches over six feet tall and built like an NFL linebacker, handled the jackhammer like a toy. He was following a yellow chalk line, where a concrete saw would neaten and emphasize the driveway, where it was projected it would encircle a fountain.

It took skill to use a jackhammer, alternating heavy and light touches, and it was a tool that had to be guided carefully. That was why Louie so diligently followed the curved yellow chalk line.

Louie had paused in his work with the other hard hats as the women they'd heard were Broadway dancers crossed the street and entered the Liner Diner. On a scale of one through ten, they were all tens, on the basis of their bodies alone. The little blond one they called Betty was particularly appealing to Louie. For whatever reason, he preferred small women. His wife, Madge, was only a little over five feet tall.

Not that she wasn't a fireball. More of one than the blond dancer, actually.

Thinking of Madge, Louie smiled.

Which was why he almost missed seeing the guy in the battered yellow hard hat.

At first Louie thought he was looking at a kid roaming through the debris of the building. Then he saw that the guy had the bearing if not the stature of a man. He had on faded jeans and a tan shirt with a tie and was carrying a clipboard.

Louie looked around, and didn't see Jack Feldman, the job foreman, or anybody else. Then he realized everyone was on lunch break. He hadn't worn his wristwatch today because he didn't want it subjected to the jackhammer vibrations.

He leaned the jackhammer at an easy angle against a pile of debris. Then he pulled a handkerchief stuffed in a back pocket and used it to wipe sweat from his face and the back of his neck.

Louie put on his own hard hat, with the company logo on it, and made his way toward the little guy.

He could see, as he drew closer, that the man was smaller and older than he'd seemed from across the jumble of debris, and the steel stacked near where the crane was systematically lifting it to be eased into position. Those involved in this delicate operation worked while the others were at lunch or otherwise off-site. Everything was done with extreme care. People had died working with high steel. People Louie had known. But he figured the pay warranted the risk, so here he was.

The crane, affixed to the twentieth floor, was preparing to lift a steel beam that looked small from this angle, up to where it would straighten its long, jointed arm and steel would be fixed to steel with rivets. The welders would follow close behind, making all but permanent what the riveters had done. And another piece of an empire's giant toy would be fitted in place.

Some of the other workers were coming back to work now, after leaving the Liner Diner. The Broadway-star types were hanging around in front of the diner, the women casually bending and doing light exercises, well aware they were being watched.

The little guy in the hard hat looked over at Louie, looked back at his clipboard, and made a check mark. Then back at Louie. He smiled and said, "Safety."

Louie noticed a line of faded black letters on the scuffed and dented yellow hard hat. So the twerp was here in some official capacity.

"I think we're up to code here," Louie said, though he had no idea. This guy, in washed-out jeans and a tan shirt with a tie, looked like management to him. A dress shirt and tie and a clipboard could add up to trouble.

"You want me to call the boss over for you?" Louie asked. Pass-the-buck time.

The little guy looked up at him, smiling. "I already talked with him. Give me a few minutes and I'll get outta your hair."

"Okay." Louie gave a little wave and started back to where he'd left the jackhammer, along with half a sandwich from his lunch bag. Pastrami and mustard, with just the right amount of horseradish. He wondered, could any of those Broadway babes with the boobs and swinging behinds put together a pastrami sandwich like his wife Madge could?

He doubted it.

As he picked his way toward where he'd broken off work, he noticed the guy with the hard hat and clipboard over where the street had been torn up. He was making his way through piles of debris, stepping carefully, still making notations on his clipboard.

Louie heard his name called.

He looked over and saw Feldman, his boss, standing across the intersection, near the Liner Diner.

Feldman saw that he had Louie's attention and waved him over.

Jack Feldman was a reasonable guy, but when he was mad he was a son of a bitch. Mistakes couldn't be made here. There were few second chances, and no third. Louie had no idea what Feldman wanted. He started walking toward Feldman. There was a large lump in Louie's throat, but he couldn't figure out if he'd screwed up, or if Feldman was simply going to ask for a progress report on the removal of the portico concrete. Louie couldn't think of any reason why he should endure an ass-chewing. He told himself that maybe he was going to get a promotion, and smiled at that one.

The sun had moved enough so that there was a stark shadow lying across the intersection where the Liner Diner was located. Louie realized the shadow was from the crane.

Feldman was standing in the shadow, which extended from the diner to beyond Louie.

Louie found it a few degrees cooler in the shadow of the crane, and walked toward Feldman, who stood with his fists on his hips, watching Louie.

There was a sharp, cracking sound from overhead.

Lightning strike was Louie's first, alarmed thought. But the sky was a cloudless blue.

When Louie lowered his vision he saw that Jack Feldman was for some reason sitting on the pavement, as if he'd fallen. He was waving and pointing at the sky. Maybe he had been struck by lightning. Louie could feel his own hair standing on end.

Then he noticed there was something different about the deeply shadowed path on which he stood, leading toward Feldman and beyond. The shadow of the crane.

It was moving.

Feldman was struggling to get to his feet, where he had instinctively dived to the ground at the loud noise. Disoriented, he ran to his right, then back left, toward the crane's looming shadow. The long shadow was moving in a greater arc now, back and forth, like a gigantic scythe trying to break free from whatever held it high.

Feldman waved his arms at Louie. He was shouting something Louie couldn't understand.

Louie didn't stop, didn't think, running toward Feldman.

There was another loud *crack!* from above as the huge crane pulled away from its moorings. Somewhere a woman was screaming.

Louie put his head down and ran harder.

33

Betty and Macy had left the diner and were about to cross the street to walk beneath the scaffolding where the Taggart Building was being transformed to its larger, more useful self. In the bright sunlight outside the diner, they absently paused to do some stretching and bending after sitting so long. They, like the other dancers, were well aware of the staring eyes of the hard hats across the street. They were prepared for the shouts, whistles, and occasional lewd suggestions. Sometimes smiles were exchanged across the street, but for the most part the construction workers were ignored. They might as well have been calling to the dancers from another dimension.

"If those guys would ever learn their manners—" Betty, who had just been referred to as "the bouncy blond beauty," began. That was when what sounded like a lightning strike came from above. The shouting from across the street stopped, then became louder. Desperate.

Betty heard a woman scream nearby. There was a subtle change in light and shadow, in the movement of air. She felt Macy grip her shoulder and squeeze it hard enough to hurt.

As he ran toward Feldman, some part of Louie's mind grasped what was happening around them. It wouldn't be the first time a construction crane had fallen in Manhattan, but it might be the worst.

He was closing on Feldman when something like the dark shadow of a raven's wing crossed the ground around them. Louie lowered his head and hunkered down as he ran, prepared to hit Feldman hard enough to carry them both out of harm's way. Feldman was like a football player who'd forgotten to signal for a fair catch and was about to pay for it.

He turned away just before contact, and 260 pounds of Louie slammed into Feldman's hip. Louie heard the deafening crash of the crane, felt the ground tilt beneath him so that for a few seconds he and Feldman were airborne.

Before he hit the ground again, Louie was sure his collarbone was broken from hitting Feldman. He knew, too, all in a split second, that he had more injury coming when the two of them landed and slid, with Feldman on top.

Louie thought they might both live, though, as long as more falling debris didn't hit them.

He was thinking of Madge as consciousness left him.

Quinn said, "What the hell was that?"

Fedderman raised his eyebrows. "Earthquake?"

They were at Q&A, Quinn at his desk, waiting for

Pearl to call and say where she wanted to meet for lunch, Fedderman in a chair over by the coffee brewer, going over case notes.

Quinn walked over and looked out a window at West 79th Street. He could hear sirens now, but they were from the south, and not close.

He went outside and stood on the concrete stoop, looking around. No sign of smoke. The sirens were slightly louder, and there were more of them.

Quinn went back inside and called Renz at One Police Plaza, and was told that Renz couldn't be reached right now.

"Is he dead?" Quinn asked the duty sergeant.

"Not to my knowledge."

"Then he can be reached. Is this Sergeant Ed Rutler?"

"It is. And who might I be talking to?"

"Captain Frank Quinn. How are you, Ed?"

"Still locomoting, Cap'n. Sorry I didn't recognize your voice."

"I'm smoking fewer cigars, Ed. I felt and heard a big boom, and now I hear sirens. What's going on?"

"We're still trying to figure it out. Could be a building collapse. The Taggart Building, that they been screwing around with for months. But it's too early in the game to know."

"Any dead or injured?"

"Not as many as you'd think, is what I hear. They're saying one of those big construction cranes let go and fell about twenty floors, but it's too early to confirm. I hope that's what happened. Fewer killed and injured than there'd be in a building collapse."

"Probably, Ed." Then, "I got confirmation now in a TV news crawl. It's the Taggart Building, all right. A big crane fell. It did bring down some of the building with it."

"Jeez! Casualties?"

"Still counting, Ed. The building was unoccupied at the time, but there were some people killed or injured by the crane itself. And there were people in the vicinity of the building that were too close and got hit by falling debris. I've deduced a lot of that from early reports and what I could see on television They're still fitting it all together. You know how it goes."

Ed did.

Harley Renz called then and got patched through. Sergeant Rutler knew it wasn't going to become a conference call and said his good-byes.

Renz listened while Quinn brought him up to speed with what he knew, mostly gleaned from what he'd seen on TV and what Sergeant Rutler had said.

Renz didn't have anything solid to contribute, even though he'd been among the first to reach the site after the crane fell. Now he was running around, probably in full dress uniform, trying to leave a lasting impression that he was in charge.

A sigh came over the phone. "It isn't pretty here, Quinn."

"Does it look like a crime scene?"

"The way things are these days, I'd have to say yes."

"Has the crane been examined?"

"Not yet. But it doesn't seem there's anything wrong with it. There was an operator in the crane when it fell. Or until just before. We're still interrogating him. We'll keep you informed, Quinn."

"Do that, Harley. This is almost surely part of the Gremlin case."

"Fire, an elevator, a crane, what's this madman thinking?"

"They're all different," Quinn said. "In most ways, they're just like the rest of us. That's why they're difficult to recognize."

"That's why we have you on the case, Quinn. You're just like the rest of us, only different."

"Those are important differences," Quinn said.

Renz said, "That's what all you guys say."

34

The killer sat in his favorite armchair, with a view of nighttime Manhattan out the window that was slightly to his left. He liked to enjoy the spectacular view, shifting eyes and interest back and forth between that and big-screen TV news coverage of the crane collapse. He was in his stocking feet, legs extended and ankles crossed, sipping two fingers of single-malt scotch over ice. A dash of water to help bring out the flavor.

Using a variety of aliases and forged identities, he had, like a rat in a pack, joined the fringes of serious crime. He maneuvered, he thought brilliantly, befriending certain criminal types, ingratiating himself with them, and at a certain point letting them know he was . . . well, head rat.

He was impossible to apprehend, because he wasn't greedy—at least not on the surface. He was financially secure from a year ago, when he'd spent a week of sex and pain with a crooked investment manager and his wife.

The killer knew enough to result in the man losing everything and going to prison. Probably his wife, keeper

of the secret books, would also do time. But the killer
had broken both of them, spiritually and physically, in
the investment manager's secluded cabin that was more
like a full-fledged house.

The wife, Glenda, in her forties, was not particularly
attractive, more of a greyhound than a cougar. She didn't
know it yet, but the divorce papers were about to be
served when, during a drug-enhanced night, the killer
taught the money manager, Hubby, how to induce and
manage someone else's pain.

Hubby was better at that than managing wealth. Under
his tutelage, Glenda learned how soundproof the cabin
was when she screamed and screamed and no one came
to her rescue.

Within a few hours she was eager to turn over to her
husband and the killer the secret set of books that she
kept, complete with numbers and names, and sometimes photographs.

This was just the sort of thing the killer sought. It
would have been silly, at this point, to set the wife free.
Besides, a plan was growing in his mind like a disease.

After a few days Wifey was trembling so that she
had to be spoon-fed so she wouldn't make such a mess.
Hubby the money man led her to a wall, made her lean
against it, and beat her with a beaded leather strap. By
now she automatically obeyed his instructions and
made no sound while she was being whipped. A gag
was no longer necessary.

When the husband's arm was almost too tired to lift,
the killer walked over, took the whip from his hand,
and laid the whip hard along the back of the wife's
thighs.

Wifey was sobbing now, her head bowed in submission.

"Take her to the basement and hose her off," the killer said.

Hubby looked confused. "Hose her . . . ?"

The killer grinned. "With water. If you want to beat her with the hose, maybe we can arrange that later."

He could barely stop smiling. These two were perfect.

When the killer went down to the basement, he saw that things were in order. Wifey's arms were tied over her head and she was hanging from a rafter with her toes barely touching the concrete. Quite a stretch. She tried to shift position now and then to relieve the pain when her stretched muscles cramped. Sheer agony. A hard rubber ball was jammed between her upper and lower teeth so her jaws were strained wide open. Her hair was soaked, pulled back, and fastened with a rubber band. She knew the rubber band was so they could see her face. Her expressions. That was great for photographs that could be sold and resold on the Internet. Her husband and their houseguest had taught her that.

The faint, rhythmic thrashing sound began, more vibration than noise. The killer was ready for it, knew that it would stop, knew how to stop it.

He stood with his hands pressed to his ears, his eyes clenched shut. Waiting.

Finally the thrashing noise reached a crescendo then subsided, and he was calm. The air that he breathed was like nectar.

The killer tested the strength of the ropes, felt the warm wetness of her body, then unnecessarily told Hubby the fund manager to stay where he was and went upstairs.

Ten minutes later the killer came back down the basement's wooden stairs with something obviously heavy beneath a blanket.

"What's that?" the husband asked. He hadn't so much as budged.

The killer smiled. "My equipment. Car battery. Cables. Alligator clips."

Terror paralyzed the wife. She emitted a lot of gagging and gurgling, and then lost consciousness.

The killer knew that unconsciousness was where they often went to escape. A country of painlessness and peace.

He had brought smelling salts.

35

Four people had been killed, seven injured, in the fall of the construction crane at the Taggart Building. Two of the dead were off-Broadway chorus line dancers, Betty Lincoln and Macy Adams. Their names and faces were known only to avid playgoers.

Not enough time had passed that Quinn and his detectives were done talking to the few witnesses who'd actually seen the crane come down, observed the panic, heard the screams. Then almost instantly the impact of the crane, followed by the landslide rumble and crashing of concrete, marble, and brick.

Quinn and Fedderman were doing the last of the interviews of witnesses, which didn't make for a long list. Usually they weren't technically witnesses, as it was the bomb-like crash of the crane that first drew their attention. It also scrambled their senses so that much of what they saw and said was wrong, forgotten, or irrelevant.

Now Quinn and Fedderman were in a modest apartment on the East Side, interviewing a giant of a man the others in SBL Properties called Little Louie. He had a bandage on the bridge of his nose and an arm in a sling. Quinn knew they were injuries from the crane accident. Next to Little Louie, on a faded but comfortable-looking sofa, sat Louie's wife, Madge.

Louie Farrato looked like what he was, a solid type who worked with his hands, simple but not stupid. He would have made a great Indiana Jones in the movies. Madge was a sloe-eyed beauty of the sort who would abide no nonsense.

Quinn glanced at the preliminary notes made within hours of the crane incident.

"Would you like some iced tea or lemonade?" Madge Farrato asked.

Quinn declined. Fedderman gave it some thought and settled for iced tea.

They both waited patiently, along with Little Louie, until Madge returned with a tray on which were four glasses of what looked like iced tea. "Just in case," she said with a smile that made her look like Sophia Loren. (Had Loren and Harrison Ford, who owned the Indiana Jones role, ever been in the same movie? Fedderman wondered.) "There's real sugar and some artificial on the tray." She set the tea on a glass-topped coffee table, and they all settled in as if they were going to watch a movie on television instead of talk about murder.

Quinn, who had changed his mind, sprinkled the contents of a pink artificial sweetener package in his tea and twirled the ice cubes with his forefinger. "We don't mean to irritate anyone by asking them to repeat what they've already probably said over and over. It's just that sometimes, after a traumatic event, people don't remember things until some time has passed."

Madge said, "Tell him, Louie."

Louie squirmed a bit, ill at ease. He had on buffed leather boots, a many-pocketed tan shirt, and faded Levi's, and sure enough looked as if he should be on an archeological dig.

He said, "Not long before the crane fell—say, about twenty minutes—I was working a jackhammer and I looked up and saw this guy in a yellow hard hat, carrying a clipboard and taking notes or something. I got a good look at him when I let up on the jackhammer and he became more than a blur. Still, he was some distance away. I got curious and walked over there."

"So you saw him close up," Quinn said, as if just to keep the conversational ball rolling. They might have a genuine close-up eyewitness here.

"Yeah," Louie said. "There wasn't anything really memorable about him. He was short. Built about average. Little, nimble type, but strong. Like a good flyweight boxer. Even had a cauliflower ear. That's what I remembered later, when I saw that drawing or something of him on TV."

"What did you say to him?"

"Asked him if I could help him. He kind of tugged his hard hat down like he didn't want it to blow off his head."

"What did he say?"

"Kept kind of doing his job, making notes, checking off stuff, like he was on a schedule. Said, 'Safety.' Like it was the one word that should explain it all. So I figured he was an inspector from one of the city agencies. We get 'em all the time, checking for workplace danger, long-term issues, lead-based paint, asbestos . . . that kinda thing."

"Did you talk about safety?" Fedderman asked.

"Naw. We didn't gab. We both had things to do."

"Then?"

"Then he left."

"Say good-bye?"

"Nope. I guess neither of us thought we had that kinda relationship."

"Did you see him get into a vehicle?"

"Nope, he just walked outta sight. I didn't think much of it at the time."

"When did you think of it?"

"A few hours ago. I was watching news on TV, and up pops this picture of somebody that looked familiar. Then, during the commercial, I remembered. The safety guy! Then I read about him on the crawl at the bottom of the screen. I still couldn't believe it, that I was just a few feet away from this guy, talked to him. So I read some more about him. The Gremlin. That just about scared the pastrami outta me."

Louie clamped his lips together, looking as if he was in conflict. Quinn waited for him to say more, not asking him, not wanting to be the first to speak. Fedderman maintained the same silence. Sometimes people who are the first to speak say the damnedest things.

It was Madge who spoke first. "Tell him, Louie."

"It's probably nothing."

Quinn said, "Everything's something."

"Tell him, Louie," Madge said again.

Louie looked pained, but he spoke. "The big noise when the crane fell was when it slammed into the ground. But there was a small noise before that. A smaller explosion up high."

"You sure? It could have been the crane hitting something on the way down."

"It came before the crane hit," Louie said. "Before it fell." He clamped his lips closed again. Then parted them. "I was in bomb disposal in Afghanistan. I know explosives. I can know some things by the sound of the explosion, the extent and kind of damage that's done. I'm pretty sure this was a shaped charge."

"Which is?"

"A bomb—and it can be a small bomb—shaped a certain way so that it directs most of the force of the explosion in one direction. They're used to take out tanks and other armored vehicles. I think one was used to separate the crane from the Taggart building."

Quinn and Fedderman looked at each other. They seemed to be thinking the same thoughts.

"Would it take an expert to build and plant such a bomb?"

Louie squeezed his lower lip between thumb and forefinger, then said, "An expert, yes. An artist, no."

Quinn thought, here was a man who loved his previous occupation perhaps too much. "Could you build one?" he asked, smiling.

"Probably, but I might blow myself up. My expertise was in disassembling bombs so they wouldn't detonate."

"He might have gotten killed," Madge said, patting Louie's arm.

Fedderman said, "My guess is he knew what he was doing, or he wouldn't be here."

"Could an amateur have made and set this shaped charge?" Quinn asked.

"A gifted amateur," Louie said. "Gifted and lucky. Like this Gremlin I keep hearing and reading about."

"I wouldn't jump to any conclusions," Quinn said. Fedderman shot him a glance. But Louie had jumped.

"I wasn't gonna say anything about it at first," he said. "It was Madge talked me into it."

"You're lucky to have Madge."

"I am that," Louie said, and gave Madge a hug.

When they were back out on the sidewalk, Fedderman said, "They've got a great marriage."

Quinn kept quiet. He knew the problems of a cop marriage. He wondered if his and Pearl's relationship would last, and if it had a better chance because they were both cops.

It took only a phone call for Quinn and Fedderman to ascertain that there hadn't been any kind of safety inspection on anything owned by SBL Properties the day of the crane collapse. And the company's hard hats were white and had a corporate logo on them.

"What now?" Fedderman asked, as they walked toward Quinn's old but pristine Lincoln.

"We get that high-tech artist who made the so-called sketch to get with Little Louie, and maybe Helen, and improve on it."

"The Gremlin isn't getting better looking."

"None of us is."

"With him, there should be a portrait in his attic, where the subject gets uglier with every rotten thing he does. Know what I mean?"

Quinn said, "You've been seeing too much of Harold."

36

Quinn phoned Renz and told him about the shaped-charge possibility. Renz thanked him, but told him the bomb squad had already been discussing the shaped-charge theory.

"Do they like it?" Quinn asked.

"They say it's unlikely, except for a guy who disarmed bombs in the Navy. He said somebody with a little knowledge and a shit pot fulla luck might make such a bomb."

"Why didn't we learn this sooner?" Quinn asked.

"We just figured it out ourselves. But it's only hypothetical. We're still trying to decide how seriously we take it. Look at it piece by piece, and it doesn't seem like much, so don't go getting all excited. And for God's sake, don't talk about this to Minnie Miner."

"Do I sound excited?" Quinn asked. "Or pissed off?"

"Do I sound gone?" Renz asked, and ended the connection.

* * *

Louie was still on sick leave, and still wearing the arm sling, when Helen and the NYPD sketch artist visited him in his and Madge's apartment. They'd stopped for breakfast on the way, but that didn't stop Madge from offering them coffee. Helen and the artist fell under the aromatic scent of freshly brewed coffee, though they managed to forgo the delicious but wildly caloric cinnamon-butter coffee cake.

The artist wasn't Warfield this time, but an affable kid named Ignacio Perez, on loan from the FBI, who asked everyone to call him simply "the artist." He set his laptop on the coffee table but off to the side. Then he ran some wires, turned on the fifty-two-inch screen on which Louie and Madge watched *Justified* and *The Good Wife*. He settled back on the sofa with a small mouse pad and a wireless mouse.

Up popped the digital likeness of the Gremlin, as it originally appeared on *Minnie Miner ASAP*.

"I wonder what he'd look like in a hard hat," Helen said. "Carrying a clipboard."

"I anticipated you," the artist said. "Except for the clipboard."

His fingers danced over the keys. He pressed some others, and there on the large screen was the Gremlin in a yellow hard hat that looked too big for him.

"My old friend," the artist said.

"See anything that doesn't look right?" Helen asked Louie, leaning toward the TV screen.

"No. That's just the way the hat fit him, like he was a little kid playing dress up. How's it look when you tug the hat down in front?"

The artist lowered the hard hat until the subject's eyes almost disappeared. "Something like that?"

"Yeah. That's more it. More hair sticking out."

Helen said, "Now make the ears somewhat visible beneath the hair."

"Like they'd stick out without the hair?" Louie said.

"Yeah, just like."

"Did you notice anything unusual about the ears?"

"Naw. Not on this guy. Except for the right ear."

"It sticks out more than the left?"

"Somewhat," Louie said. "But like I told you, he was built like a flyweight boxer. Had a cauliflower ear, it looked like to me."

The artist played electronically with the right ear. Made it slightly larger and more damaged by countless jabs and left hooks.

"That's good," Louie said. "But his hair should be a little longer, and slightly darker."

Again the artist made some adjustments while the others looked on.

"More chin, less nose," Louie said.

The artist complied.

"The ear that you can see all of, it is rather pointed, at least from a certain angle."

Helen squinted at it. "So close to the head. Not like the other ear."

"Other one probably came unstuck," the artist said.

"Unstuck?"

"Like with movie stars. A guy's or woman's ears stick out like open car doors, so they got this flesh-colored two-sided tape. Like carpet tape. An ear won't stay taped in for very long, but plenty long enough to shoot movie or TV scenes. And if it's still too much trouble, there's always an operation to make the ears flatter to the skull."

"So tell me who's had their ears operated on?" Madge said, from where she sat over in a corner where she could see the big screen.

The artist shook his head, smiling. "I couldn't reveal that."

"They've got their right to privacy," Madge said

"I don't know for sure about that, but they've got the right not to hire me if I shoot them or draw them with car-door ears."

"Shoot?" Madge asked.

"Photograph. Shoot pictures."

"Oh."

"Anyway, for photo shoots or short movies for TV scenes, there's always the two-sided tape. The stuff works pretty well. And if you don't like it, you can always do what this guy probably does . . . did—grow your hair long at the sides and comb it back over your ears."

The artist put together another screen image of the Gremlin, this time without the hard hat.

"Look like the same guy?" he asked Louie.

"Yeah. I wouldn't mistake him. Of course, some people do look different with and without caps or hats."

"But would you feel confident picking this guy out of a lineup?"

"Sure. Unless he's got a twin brother."

"Louie," Madge said, "don't make things more complicated than they are."

"So let's make some final adjustments," the artist said. "You never saw this guy's hairline, right?"

"Yeah, but he wasn't bald. He had sideburns, anyway."

The artist used the mouse to create sideburns on the screen image. He paused and looked at Louie.

"A little longer," Louie said. "There. Just right."

"We can put out images with different hairlines," Helen said.

"Good idea," the artist said. He created several renderings, finishing with one that left the killer bald except for a bush of hair around his ears.

"I wish we could have one of him smiling," Helen said.

The artist shook his head. "I'd have to see him smile to do that." He looked at Louie. "Did he smile when you were with him?"

"Not once. He was all business."

"Which you shouldn't be all the time," Madge said. "Remember you are not well."

They thanked Little Louie and left him with Madge. Not a bad situation, if you didn't count Louie's nightmares and broken bones.

As they were walking toward where their cars were parked, the artist said, "I'd like to draw that woman."

"You guys," Helen said, "for the kind of drawing you're talking about, you'd have to use a crayon so the other ten-year-olds would understand it."

"A crayon," the artist said, "would melt."

37

An hour later, Renz called Quinn on his desk phone. "No doubt about it," Renz said, when Quinn had picked up the bulky plastic receiver that fit hand and ear so well. "The crane falling was murder. There were traces of hydrofluoric acid found at the breaking points of the steel cables. It ate through the cables until enough strands popped that they finally broke apart under all that weight. That overloadcd the stress on the other cables, then a small bomb separated the crane from the building and down it came. The thing is, whoever was responsible had to have some basic knowledge of how that crane was put together. How the damned thing worked."

"Just like he knew about elevators," Quinn said. "Was this the same kind of acid used on the elevator cables?"

"Yeah. The base was hydroflouride, along with nitric acid. A devil's brew, according to the techs. If you want to tote it around, you'll need a special container. Most likely it was outta the same lab."

"Do the techs think our killer is a chemist?" Quinn asked.

"Not in any major way. But you don't have to be a chemist or engineering genius to know how to destroy something. Common sense goes a long way. To know how to build up is to know how to tear down."

"But we're not necessarily looking for a scientist or engineer."

"That's right," Renz said. "Matter of fact, most of the info you need, you can find on the Internet."

Quinn doubted if that would be reassuring to the public.

"The Internet and DNA," Renz said. "One helps find them, and the other helps prove them guilty. Life gets harder and harder for the bad guys."

"Can't get hard enough."

"That's what my ex-wife used to say."

"The crane cables are right out where anyone can see them," Quinn pointed out. "Or get to them, depending on the position of the crane."

"It gets better and better," Renz said bitterly. "Where do psychos like the Gremlin learn this crap?"

"Like the artist told us," Quinn said, "there's plenty of information on the Internet." The main air conditioner in Q&A wasn't quite keeping up with the heat, and his clothes were stuck to him. There was some not-quite-cold-enough diet cola in the little fridge by the coffeemaker, but he chose not to have gas.

"The Internet is a school for crime," Renz agreed.

"And the students get their advanced degrees in prison."

"It shouldn't be like that."

"Nobody's figured out a better way."

"I know one."

"I didn't hear that," Quinn said.

"The Gremlin. I really hate that little bastard!"

"We'll find him, Harley."

"Will we? They never found Jack the Ripper."

"They might have, if he'd ever been listed in the FBI database."

"Speaking of data . . ."

Quinn brought him up to date on the Little Louie and Madge interview.

"This is a mass murderer," Renz said, when Quinn was finished talking and reading aloud. As if Quinn needed reminding.

"We've got a reliable eyewitness that puts him at the scene of the crane collapse," Quinn said. "And we're working out a digital image that'll be as good as a photo, if it isn't already."

"We've got everything but the criminal."

"I wouldn't express it that way to the media," Quinn said.

"So can I tell the press predators what you just told me? When I step outta here, they're gonna be on me like a pack of mad dogs."

Quinn tried to imagine that but couldn't. Renz would surely have even larger mad dogs protecting him.

"I would tell the media only what I wanted them to know, Harley. At this point, we're using them instead of the other way around."

Renz seemed to like that observation. Quinn wasn't so sure it was true, but at least it gave the illusion of progress.

"We clear on everything?" Renz asked. "Or do you have any questions that won't be wasting my time?"

Quinn said, "I didn't know you had an ex-wife."

Renz hung up.

38

The next morning Quinn slept in and Pearl left the brownstone around seven o'clock to open the Q&A offices. The team of Sal and Harold were coming in early to prepare for an interview with the SBL Properties crane operator. He'd given his statement half a dozen times. Another wouldn't hurt.

So far there had been only the occasional small contradiction. The crane hadn't responded as usual to its controls. Quinn had heard that the operator was a red-headed guy named Perry, who looked about fourteen until a second look revealed he was about forty. He was still jumpy, and blamed himself for the crashing and carnage.

Of course, unless he was connected in some way to the acid that had melted some of the crane's cables, or to the shaped charge, he had no reason to feel guilt.

Quinn poured himself a cup of coffee and went out to the tiny secluded courtyard behind the brownstone. There was a small green metal table there, and three green metal chairs. They were rust-free and weather-proof as long as Quinn painted them every spring.

Randall, the bulldog that lived next door, began to bark up a storm, until he heard Quinn's voice and decided to be quiet.

One of these days, Quinn thought, Randall would be correct in his desperate prognosis of a catastrophe. Those were the odds, anyway. This kind of dog couldn't be wrong all the time.

After Quinn used a paper towel to wipe down the table and one of the chairs, he spread open the two newspapers Pearl had left for him, the *Times* and the *Post*. Despite them being already read by Pearl, and maybe by Jody, they were folded in reasonably neat fashion. He used another paper towel, folded in quarters, as a makeshift coaster for his coffee cup.

It was a beautiful, clear morning, with only a breath of breeze. Quinn fired up one of his Cuban cigars. He hadn't kept up on the Mickey Mouse ordinances he kept hearing about. Didn't know if the Cubans had become legal yet or not. Whether and where in the city he could smoke any kind of cigar didn't much concern him. People who robbed and killed and blew up other people concerned him. Not if or where someone somewhere else was lighting up some tobacco.

Scofflaw bastard.

He sipped, inhaled, read.

The press didn't seem as interested in the particulars of fires or crashing cranes or elevators as they were in the two dead, beautiful dancers who had both been elevated by the media to the chorus line in *Other People's Honey*. The producers of the play knew how to wring tears and publicity from their prospective audience. There were plenty of questions to be asked. Had the two dancers died at the same time? In the same way?

What were their last words? Did they suffer? Have husbands? children? (Neither was married or a mother.) What other plays or movies had they appeared in? What other celebrities did they know? Who were their favorites, not just in plays or in front of the cameras, but as real and dedicated human beings? Who was going to replace them in their current roles? Was the play now cursed?

Quinn sipped, smoked, and mulled over some of those questions, but not all.

In another part of town, Jordan Kray was avidly reading the same papers, plus the *Daily News*.

He was famous, all right. Not as his real name, but that didn't matter. He knew, in the heart and depths of his fear, that at some point his real name would be revealed. It would be engraved on his tombstone or plaque.

Not the brief stint he'd done in the military. That might never be known. Not for sure. He'd joined under another name, another age, another mission.

But he wouldn't lose his professional name. The Gremlin. The ghost in the machine. He liked the ring of it. It was memorable. When he thought about it, the throbbing in his brain, the relentless thrashing sound, would usually subside.

People would visit his grave. The public would finally recognize the voracious fire of genuine greatness. And how it could consume the bearer of the gift.

They would know real fame, real celebrity, when they saw it, heard it, feared it. Right how it was merely a speck on the horizon, a red carpet unrolled.

Right now.

39

Missouri, 1999

Jordan Kray thought he'd be given a simple instruction by the farmer, whose name was Luther Farr: Get out.

But Luther apparently decided there might be too much risk involved. Things didn't stop growing, or rotting, because the hired help was . . . precariously balanced. Jordan seemed all right physically. In fact, he was a good worker, and there was still a lot of work to be done around the farm.

Jordan understood that his days and nights at the farm were limited. There was no way the family or any of the other Freedom Farm workers would understand. He had dismembered the goat to investigate its bone structure, see the thickness of the bones and sinew that permitted such butting power in such a small animal. How could anyone not realize that nothing wrong had been done? The goat was one of those animals people relied upon. It was leather, it was insulation, it was meat.

It was also cuter than a cow, and possibly more intelligent. Closer to the human mind if not body of the cow or ox. Or even the horse. When you looked into goats' eyes, they often looked back at you with a certain calculation. A message: We're both smarter than the hens. We should be friends and partners.

But of course that wasn't true. Not the last part, anyway.

You should be food. You should be sacrificial. Like in Sunday school.

What he didn't know was that the goat was Jasmine's favorite pet. And Jasmine was the farmer's favorite daughter.

Jasmine was sixteen, but mature for her age. Jordan was fond of her, or at least saw her as a desirable object. She seemed to return his interest. In fact, he was sure she'd developed a crush on him.

That could be useful.

A few times, Luther Farr had caught his daughter smiling at Jordan in a way he didn't like. But all that had happened so far were some cautionary, scathing looks. Still, Luther was planting the seed of fear in Jordan. And Luther was on the edge of understanding that a boy like Jordan wasn't rich soil in which fear might thrive. Something quite different from fear had already taken root.

One evening, at Jordan's request, he and Jasmine met secretly in a copse of elm trees. They were well beyond the farmhouse and its clapboard addition. The addition was where the help slept. Including Jordan.

There were half a dozen youths living and working at the farm. Jordan wasn't the only one there who'd had minor brushes with the law. What did people expect, from someone usually alone and with practically no money? There was in the land a catalyst that not many people had to experience: Hunger. Usually it was hunger that drove Jordan to larceny. Hunger and cold sometimes teamed up to edge him toward more serious crimes.

(Though he didn't think of them as crimes. Not by their strictest definition. If it was about survival, it wasn't criminal.)

Jasmine, who had ripened that year with the crops, sat with her coltish legs crossed on a small blue blanket she'd brought with her. It was with great reluctance that she'd agreed to meet Jordan this evening. She was still heartbroken over the death of her pet goat, Sadie. Yet still she felt the magnetism of Jordan when he was near her. Like tonight.

"I just don't understand why you did that to Sadie," Jasmine said. Just thinking about it made her choke up so she could hardly breathe. But it was something she didn't understand. She truly wanted to understand.

Jordan moved closer to her. The toe of his shoe was on a corner of the blue blanket, as if it were a magic carpet and with one foot he could hold it down so she couldn't fly away. "I made sure she didn't feel any-thing," he lied. "I was humane. And you know your dad was going to sell the goat before winter. I saved her from a less humane death. Sometimes you have to be firm to be kind. Anybody grew up on a farm oughta know that."

"But still . . ."

"Also, I needed to see how Sadie differed."

"From what?"

"The other goats. I mean, inside. The bone and mus-cle, how it moved."

She stared at him with unblinking blue eyes. He could see she was not even beginning to understand.

"I don't see what the big deal is, if you think about it," he said. "I mean, we eat goats. Parts of them, anyway. They're even killed sometimes as part of religious ceremonies."

"Says who?"

"Says the Bible, Jasmine. You've heard of blood sacrifices?"

"Usually it's lambs that get sacrificed."

"Well, a goat is a kind of lamb."

"Not really."

"Read your Bible," Jordan said. "There are plenty of pictures of goats being sacrificed." He wasn't actually sure of that.

She had to admit that she'd seen such pictures, though she couldn't recollect when or where. Sunday school, probably, during those services she'd been forced to attend. And he was right, people did eat lambs and goats.

"But not Sadie," she said with brave certainty.

"It wouldn't matter to the goat," Jordan said. "Except in goat heaven, maybe."

Jasmine suspected he was putting her on, but that didn't make what he said untrue. Jordan liked to joke sometimes, and not take things serious that were serious. He was just like that, and when you came right down to it, she didn't mind all that much. He knew more of the world than she did, though he wasn't always as wise as he thought. He seemed kind of dangerous, even if he wasn't all that large a man. You didn't always see it, but it was there. She kind of liked that, too, in a way she didn't quite understand.

Jordan squatted down on the blanket's edge, producing a knife from somewhere. It wasn't a switchblade or any other kind of pocketknife; it had a broad, flat blade that came to a honed point. Like a bowie knife.

He smiled at her, and began tossing the knife in front of him so that it penetrated the blanket and stuck in the soil.

"That's the blanket I used for my dolls," she said. Not warning him or asking him to stop. Simply giving him a nugget of partial understanding. A glimpse of her early childhood.

He continued to flip the knife expertly, so it made one revolution in the air and then stuck with the same solid *chuk!* in the ground beneath the blanket. The rhythmic, brutal sound, over and over, was hypnotic. Like something killing her childhood.

Jordan gazed deep into Jasmine's eyes, holding her gaze so she couldn't turn away.

Through an understanding smile he said, "The Bible tells us there comes a time to put away childish things."

She knew that was true. She would have to face it someday. She fought back tears.

"I'll be here in the morning," Jordan said. "I'll earn my final pay, then come evening I'll be gone. If you're here, we'll leave together. A new life will be ours."

He wiped the knife blade clean with two swipes on the side of his thigh, then slid it into a leather scabbard. She saw that it had a yellowed bone handle as he sat down on the blanket and leaned toward her, kissing her, using his tongue, teaching her how to use hers.

Still kissing her, he bent her backward and placed her gently on the blanket. He began to unbutton her blouse, her shorts. Her clothes seemed to melt from her. She gazed off to the side, like billions of women before her, and for a second or two became as much observer as participant.

This wasn't supposed to happen. Not so soon. But now that it was happening, she didn't mind. Time kept rushing toward her, past her.

She lay back, her elbows supporting her at first, then all the way back, and spread her legs, welcoming him.

Afterward, Jasmine couldn't stop trembling. She knew what her father would think. Knew what he would tell her. It wouldn't be about Jesus and the blood of the sacrificed. It would be about commerce. The food chain.

Every living thing required a reason to exist.

A usefulness.

"Even people?" she would ask.

"Especially people."

"Why should that be?" she would ask.

She hadn't yet heard a convincing answer.

40

Jordan worked hard on the farm the next day, standing near Jasmine's father as the two of them shucked corn. Jasmine's father, Luther, was a gangly, powerful man. He wasn't intimidated, but he didn't like meeting Jordan's unconcerned gaze. Luther was smart in a direct, instinctive kind of way, and what he sensed in Jordan was a kind of darkness of the soul. An emptiness that in one way or another would have to be filled.

Luther had talked to his daughter earlier that day, and though she had told him nothing, he knew by looking at her that something had ended, and something had begun.

She could no more hide her feelings than could Luther. And Luther believed in God and demons and the reality of hell.

Side by side in the bright sunlight, the heat and humidity building, the two men shucking corn sometimes chanced to look at each other, and it was always Luther who turned away.

* * *

Jordan had a plan. Railroad dicks these days were mostly an invention of fiction. The expense of hiring so many of them just to keep freeloaders from traveling without tickets didn't make good economic sense.

The boxcars were going north again, most of them emptied of coal and produce, jingling and jangling along the rails with their sliding doors open wide. More than half the boxcars were empty, the train's engines so far ahead of them they were out of sight except where the rails curved.

After supper Jordan went out onto the porch, carrying a cold can of Budweiser. He was scheduled to meet Luther again in the morning and finish the bin of corn cobs. Both Luther and Jordan knew they probably wouldn't see each other again.

The screen door slammed and reverberated in the quiet sinking light. Luther came out, carrying a can of chilled Bud like Jordan's.

"Hot night," he said to Jordan.

"That time of year," Jordan said.

Luther glanced around. It was an obvious act. "Jasmine around?"

"Not that I know of."

"Seen her go upstairs after supper," Luther said. "Guess she's still up there." There was a high tension emanating from him, a crippling regret. The past was over. The future was going to change in a way that made Luther sick and afraid.

He'd known this day would come. When the cancer had gotten his wife, Jasmine's mother, Luther was left with Jasmine and her memories. He lived with his regrets. The silent truths that both knew were left unsaid.

Nothing could stop them from working their dreaded damage.

He couldn't leave the farm, and nothing would compel Jasmine to stay in a house haunted by her mother. A family had been destroyed by death. Luther knew what quiet horror would haunt his final days, and perhaps his eternity,

He hesitated, seemed about to say something more to Jordan, then lowered his head and turned away.

"See you come sunrise," he said.

Jordan didn't answer. Luther didn't look back.

The eleven o'clock *American Eagle* sounded its lonely trailing wail. Jordan thought it was like a wolf howl, carried on the wind.

He and Jasmine each carried a duffel bag just large enough for a change of clothes and some personal items. Jasmine had stood frozen in her bedroom before leaving, knowing it was the last time she'd see so many things, keepsakes, pictures, her mussed and longtime bed with its sheet dragging the floor.

Jordan had warned her: there was no way to move on without leaving the past behind.

Wasn't that the truth?

The *Eagle* wailed again. Jordan knew it would be audible back at the farmhouse, but not loud enough to wake anyone. Especially if they were used to it, as was Luther Farr.

The mournful sound of the train whistle signaled that

it would soon be part of the past, and the past would be fixed in time and place.

Carrying their bags slung over their shoulders, Jordan and Jasmine jogged so their course would cross that of the train tracks. But they wouldn't cross the rails. They would stop at them, then wait.

Seconds became minutes, then the *Eagle* came at them at an angle out of the east. It started small and then grew slowly, coming at them faster and faster. They watched in the moonlight as boxcar after boxcar, most of them empty and with opened doors on each side, clanged and clattered past.

As they'd agreed, approaching the train from the side at a forty-five-degree angle, Jordan hung back so he could run alongside. Then he quickly mounted a small side ladder near the front of a boxcar's open door. In the same smooth motion, he tossed his duffel bag in, then pulled himself up and around and into the boxcar.

He swiveled so he was on his hands and knees, looking ahead for Jasmine. For a moment a voice in his mind told him she wasn't coming with him. What was a promise from a girl so young? To a boy not much older?

He edged closer where he was kneeling at the open boxcar door, and there she was.

Jordan watched fascinated as she followed his instructions perfectly. First she hung on to the ladder of the moving car and with her free hand tossed her duffel bag up through the gaping side door. Then she gripped the small steel ladder built into the side of the car. Made her way along the side of the bouncing, clanging car, to the open door. As Jordan had taught her, she grabbed hold of the ladder with both hands and swung out and then inside the boxcar,

But only halfway.

Her heart took flight like a startled bird, then Jordan's strong hand closed around her wrist. He pulled, pulled, her shins sliding and banging painfully against the floor's edge.

Then she was in!

They lay together on the boxcar's rough plank floor, the train jouncing and squealing and very gradually building up speed. Fresh air streamed in through the open doors, along with the smell of the worked earth.

The train held its speed and the ride became smoother, the boxcar swaying in a gentle, rocking rhythm. The steel wheels began a steady ticking sound. The night breeze—or was it the moonlight?—played over them. Jordan and Jasmine were out in the endless fields and prairies, their dreams intact.

A man's voice from the dark shadows at the far end of the boxcar said, "I was glad to see you both made it."

41

New York, the present

Renz, seated behind his airport-size desk in his office, handed a photograph to Quinn. He had leaned so far over the desk, so he could reach Quinn's outstretched hand, that Renz's purple tie dragged and got defaced by what looked like eraser crumbs. Or were they pastry crumbs?

Whatever they were, Renz saw Quinn staring at them and deftly brushed them off and onto the floor behind the desk.

Quinn concentrated on the photo. It was in black and white, and grainy.

"It's a still from a security camera," Renz said. "From four nights ago, ten thirty-five p.m. Outside the Devlin Building over on Twelfth Street. The guys who run the coffee shop inside have been bitching about drug deals going down in the passageway. That's also where a big Dumpster sits, gets emptied every two weeks."

"So what makes them think this isn't a drug deal? Or some scroungers looking for a late meal?"

"Look closer at it."

Quinn moved slightly sideways so a better light would show on the photo.

"That was the best the tech guys could do," Renz said.

Quinn was looking at a slight figure, maybe a woman, turning and running away from what looked like a Dumpster. She was clutching something white in her (or his) hand, and looking back, as if to make sure no one was following. The camera angle was from approximately ten feet above the subject and at a sharp angle, so her face was barely visible. She was wearing a baseball cap, either blue or black, with the bill pulled down low so her features would be obscured. It did appear that the subject was glancing back.

Renz handed Quinn a magnifying glass. Quinn held the photo at the same angle to the sun and observed through the curved lens.

"That white object the character has in his or her hand looks like a foam takeout box from a restaurant," Quill said.

"Yeah, but look at the ear."

Quinn did. The subject's right ear seemed to protrude at a sharp angle from his head, and might very well be pointed. If it wasn't simply a shadow. Or an errant lock of hair.

Quinn said, "I don't know, Harley. Times are tough. This looks like somebody snapped a photo of a Dumpster-diver scouting around for dinner."

"Or it could be our Gremlin on the run. Taking meals whenever and however possible."

"With another killer with him? A copycat? Who'd want to be mixed up with a guy who slices and dices people?"

"Somebody who doesn't know what he's bumming around with. The worst of these sickos can seem the nicest and least dangerous. That's their cover, how they camouflage themselves."

"The public seen this photo?" Quinn asked.

"Yeah. The morning news," Renz said. "Thanks to *Minnie Miner ASAP.*"

"That would figure. Minnie can't stay away from murder cases. They make such compelling news."

"Well, you can't blame her for turning death into entertainment. That's her job. At least we know where she stands."

With a foot on your balls, Quinn thought, but didn't say.

The Gremlin put down his coffee cup in disgust. He was on the balcony of his apartment, where he often took breakfast. He didn't feel his best this morning, so it was coffee and orange juice only. No cream, no fat. He had to stay in shape. Small but mighty, he thought.

He laid the paper out flat and studied the photograph close up. Then he leaned back, satisfied. There was no way anyone could make a positive identification based on the grainy security camera still.

So what was going on? Or was it really only some good citizen who wanted his name in the papers and talked himself into thinking that the small person in the photograph was the Gremlin? And that the Gremlin was Jordan.

The more the Gremlin thought about it, the less likely anything representing a threat, or a plan, had been in evidence. He had simply parked half a block down from the restaurant and then carried his three large black bags from his car's trunk to the passageway. Quickly he'd lifted the lid of the Dumpster and tossed inside the black plastic bags, listening to them land softly on trash that had built up for the past two weeks and now had a familiar, sickening stench when the lid was raised. That was good, because when the Dumpster was lifted and emptied in the truck, what was on top would be on the bottom, and least likely to be found.

42

The shadow in the corner of the boxcar moved, then stood up and became a tall, potbellied man with a dark beard and gray-streaked hair grown down to his shoulders.

"You two hopped rides on trains before?" he asked.

"First time," Jasmine said. She sounded almost cheerful, as if they were talking about learning to ride a bicycle.

The man smiled. A couple of teeth were missing, giving him a jovial, carved-pumpkin expression. "I'm Kirby," he said. He was holding what looked like a gin or vodka bottle. He started to take a drink, then realized the bottle was empty. He skillfully dropped it on the leather toe of his shoe so it wouldn't break on the boxcar floor and leave grass shards. It rolled whole and harmless away. The whole process looked as if he'd done it countless times before.

Jordan hadn't moved since noticing the man. "Jordan," he said, by way of introduction.

There was a slight dip in the rails, causing the car to

lurch and sway. Everyone flexed their knees and rode it out.

Looking dubious, Kirby said, "You two sure this is new to you?"

"We're sure," Jasmine said.

Kirby stretched as if to show off his height and muscles in contrast to Jordan's slightness. He looked anything but fit, yet he still held the undeniable advantage in size and strength over Jordan.

"What we gotta do right off," Kirby said, "is get these boxcar doors partway shut so we won't draw any attention. Y'unerstan'?"

"Sure," Jasmine said. "We wanna look like the other boxcars, but not so much that we won't have enough hiding space to stay outta sight."

Kirby smiled at her, looking like a happy pumpkin with selectively missing teeth. Then he aimed his smile at Jordan. "This is a smart and sexy little gal you got here."

Jordan didn't know what to say to that. Simply muttered, "Thanks."

Jasmine looked at him, as if for the first time a balance had shifted. He seemed scared, and that scared her.

She wasn't the only one scared. Jordan wished he had a weapon. A stout club. Even a gun. The only thing he had that could do damage was his folding knife in his jeans pocket, with its four-inch blade. He knew it would take too long to fish the knife out of his tight jeans and open it with both hands.

He was standing near one of the wide-open doors, his feet spread wide so he could maintain his balance in the swaying boxcar. Outside, only a few feet from him, green scenery glided past.

"You kids'll get used to it," Kirby said.

"Used to what?" Jordan asked. He saw that Kirby was now standing closer to Jasmine.

"Bein' on the road. It's hard till you know the ropes, then you catch on."

"To what?" Jordan asked.

"To where you can grab some sleep, find a meal. An' stay outta harm's way. Y'unerstan'?"

"Sure."

"An' you gotta know who your friends are."

Kirby moved suddenly, causing Jordan to jerk his body and step protectively toward Jasmine.

But Kirby was merely moving to one of the wide-open boxcar doors.

He pushed sideways on the heavy steel door to close it, but it didn't move.

"Sometimes they don't close so easy," he said. "This one slides rough. Gimme a hand, Jordan."

Jordan made his way over, and the two of them leaned hard into the door. It didn't budge.

"Sum'bitch is like it's welded," Kirby said.

Suddenly the door slid easily halfway closed and then jammed. Jordan had fallen to his knees. As he stood up, he saw that Kirby was watching Jasmine. He couldn't keep his eyes from her.

"Only open it partways," he said to Jordan. "Leave it about two feet from bein' closed, then we'll do that to the other door. That way we'll have some cross ventilation and light in here, and we'll still be outta sight unless somebody pokes his head in and looks around close."

Jordan recalled how invisible Kirby had been in the

shadows when he and Jasmine first got into the boxcar. Kirby had been nice enough so far, but Jordan knew enough not to eat the whole apple.

His right knee was plenty sore where he'd bumped it on the floor. He crawled over to where Jasmine sat near an open door, then sat down beside her with his back against the boxcar's plywood side. Along with Jasmine, he stared out at the trees and fields. At the distance. He'd never been this far from home.

Kirby was sitting across from them, near where the other door was open but only a few feet.

"How far you two goin'?" Kirby asked. Here and there straw and white packing tablets lay on the boxcar's plank floor. He had a strand of straw stuck in the corner of his mouth like a toothpick. It rotated in a wide arc as he moved his tongue around.

"All the way east," Jordan said.

Kirby stared across the boxcar at Jasmine.

"This train's gonna stop at Jeff City," he said. "Then it'll go on to St. Louis, where it'll switch out."

"Switch out?"

"Uncouple and sit empty till it gets hooked to another engine. We just need to avoid the railroad dicks."

"We'll figure out how to make our way," Jordan said.

Jasmine smiled at him, reaching over and squeezing his wrist.

Kirby sneezed, spat out his straw, and struggled to his feet in the swaying boxcar. He reached into a back pocket as if to draw out a handkerchief.

Instead he was gripping something in a small gray cloth bag the size of a sock.

"What's that?" Jasmine asked.

Kirby smiled, then said, "Candy."

Only it wasn't candy; it was gravel. And it formed a hard lump in the toe of the sock that made it an efficient sap.

43

Kirby swung the sap hard at Jordan's head but hit his shoulder instead, said, "Sum'bitch!" and swung again. This time he missed entirely and almost fell as the boxcar jerked.

Then the girl, who appeared to be so frail, was on him like a tiger and much stronger than she looked.

"Ow! Friggin' country bitches," he yelled as her sharp fingernails dug hard into the sides of his neck.

He pushed her away and she fell back. Got halfway up then stumbled and fell again.

The pulsing and swaying boxcar was Kirby's friend now. He could dispense with these two easily.

He turned toward the boy, but he was no longer there. That puzzled Kirby. He thought he'd hit Jordan hard enough to break a collarbone. The kid should be incapacitated.

So what'd he do? Jump outta the boxcar? Was the feisty little bastard lying in the darkness? Was he off the train and running and hiding in the night?

Jordan charged out of the blackness at the other end

of the boxcar and hit Kirby at the knees; Kirby went down hard, and Jordan crawled up his back and twined an arm around Kirby's right arm and was twisting it, causing Kirby to yelp. He tried to push himself up with his left arm so he could stand, but Jordan punched the arm out from beneath him and Kirby went face-first against the hard floor.

Kirby yelped again. Damned farm kids spend their lives at hard labor, gettin' strong before they get smart. Twice as strong as they look. Kirby spat blood and figured he'd be lucky if his nose wasn't broken.

This is wrong! I don't deserve this! I need to be left alone!

But he knew he was too late. He couldn't surrender to himself. And nobody else was listening.

Here came the girl again. What the hell was she doin' now? Wrestling with both of them. Almost like she was attacking Jordan.

But that notion was dispelled when her teeth sank into Kirby's bare heel, and he was angry with himself now for using the sock as a sap and then missing his target. Friggin' Jordan kid should be the one down with his head split open.

What was the bitch doin' with Jordan now? Tryin' to take his pants down? What the hell? Was fighting for her life getting her hot?

Despite his bruises and bite marks, Kirby was feeling more confident. Jordan might be on top, but he was weakening. Jasmine kept clawing at him like she was trying to work down his Levi's.

What she would do then, only God knew.

Then he realized what Jasmine was attempting to do. Sum'bitch!

* * *

Jasmine felt another fingernail bend back and tear as she clawed at the rough denim of Jordan's jeans. She grabbed the edge of a side pocket, gripped and pulled, and the fingernail felt as if it had torn completely loose.

She felt the wetness of blood.

It made her fight all the harder.

Jordan was squirming around now, understanding and trying to help her. He couldn't help much. One of Kirby's arms was pinned beneath him, the other bent back and pinned by Jordan, but he was a powerful man and still plenty dangerous.

"You kids stop this right now!" he yelled. As if they'd attacked him and started the hostilities.

Jasmine got three fingers into Jordan's side pocket and felt the smooth handle of the folding knife he always carried. She was elated. If she could just work the knife all the way out of the pocket, she could use one hand to open it with her teeth, then this struggle would end and that would be the end of Kirby.

How she hated him at that moment. He'd attempted to steal their future for whatever he could loot from their cold dead bodies.

Their future!

Her blood served as a lubricant. She worked, worked with her mangled fingers and felt the handle of the knife clear the edge of the pocket.

It was halfway out.

"You kids stop this now!"

"We ain't kids," Jordan said.

"And we ain't gonna stop," Jasmine added.

"I'm warnin' you!" Kirby yelled. "You're gonna be in a lotta trouble!"

"For doin' to you what you were gonna do to us?" Jasmine said. And the knife was free.

Jasmine gripped the knife as best she could in her uninjured hand. Like most folding knives it had a groove along the back of the blade where you could hook your fingernails into it and pull the blade open.

"A lotta trouble!" Kirby chose for his last words.

Jasmine didn't have the fingernails for this task. She gripped the knife carefully by its handle, holding her torn nails so they were under the least possible pressure.

Kirby knew death was on its way and bucked powerfully.

Jasmine was straddling him now, staring at a pulsing blue artery in his neck. She fixed her eyes on it, knowing the knife would go directly to its target. Drew her knife hand back and gripped it hard.

Too hard.

The blood from her torn nails had made the smooth knife handle even smoother, and too slippery to hold.

Jasmine felt it slide out from between her fingers like a watermelon seed. She made a futile grab for the knife, praying even that she could catch it by the blade.

But Kirby had worked his pinned arm free and grabbed at the knife while it was suspended in midair. He couldn't get a grip on it but he knocked it away. It went skittering across the boxcar floor, out of everyone's reach.

Kirby used his free arm to punch Jordan in the side of his head, then shoved him away along with Jasmine.

He started to crawl toward the knife. Jordan was only half conscious, and Jasmine was winded

"I'll show you little pissants somethin' now!" Kirby wheezed.

Jasmine was terrified that he was right. He was closest to the knife, and could move faster and was stronger than either of them. She and Jordan were as good as dead.

Until her hand closed on a sock full of gravel.

She started crawling faster toward Kirby, not toward the knife itself. That puzzled him for a few seconds.

A few seconds were enough.

The first blow with the makeshift sap dazed Kirby.

Then Jasmine mounted him like a horse and hit him again and again and again . . .

The train was on the flat now, and in vast darkness. It speeded along, making time, toward the bright mystery of its wavering light far ahead. The train wouldn't go anywhere but straight for miles, and the source of the light was unseen, a wavering unsteady glow up ahead and off to the sides.

Jordan and Jasmine were still breathing hard, in concert with the rhythms of the train rattling through the fields.

Jasmine said, "Let's get rid of him."

Jordan, leaning with his back against the swaying boxcar wall, looked over at Kirby stretched out motionless on the floor. It was too dark to see for sure, but there seemed to be a lot of blood around Kirby's head. Kirby's mouth was open. His eyes looked to be only half closed. His expression was that of a man slyly planning, except for the fact that he was so still. The dead didn't plan.

Jasmine got up, her body swaying with the boxcar so she could maintain her balance. Jordan used the boxcar wall as a support helping him to get to his feet. Fighting off dizziness, he almost fell.

They made their way to where Kirby lay.

"He gone?" Jasmine asked.

"Far as we're concerned," Jordan said. "Time for Mister Kirby to get off the train."

Together, they gripped Kirby by his shirt and leather belt and inched him toward the open steel door. He'd left a large bloodstain, glistening black in the darkness.

Jasmine sat down on the floor and shoved Kirby along with both feet. Jordan, with a wide stance, stood over Kirby and used Kirby's belt to lift him slightly and shove him toward the black rectangle of the door.

They pushed together, using all their might. Kirby's arm jammed in the door, as if he didn't want to leave.

Then the arm came loose, and he was out in the black night, as if plucked from the train by someone or something that had been waiting for him all along. Jordan leaned out the door and looked toward the back of the train. There was Kirby, his momentum still tumbling him along near the steel wheels. Then he bounced into invisibility and the night had him.

"Dead or alive," Jordan said, "nobody's gonna find him for a while. And if he's dead, or even just unconscious, it'll take a while to figure he fell off a train."

Jasmine knew the rails would be all the clue the police would need to tell them where the body had come from, but she didn't mention it to Jordan. He was still shaken up and not thinking straight.

He leaned back against the swaying boxcar wall and closed his eyes.

The train rattled on through the night.

44

New York, the present

It was a surprisingly cool morning. Quinn and Pearl were walking along Broadway toward Zabar's to have breakfast and then buy some pastry for the rest of the Q&A personnel.

It had rained slightly during the night, but now the sky was cloudless. The colorful lines of traffic-stalled cars were punctuated by the occasional yellow cab. Sunlight glancing off concrete, steel, and glass made everything look recently washed, which in a way was the case. Here and there, glitters of dew still clung to weeds or grass that had inched their way up between edges and cracks in the pavement.

Pearl's cell phone chimed and she walked slower and fished it out of her purse. She was afraid the caller was her mother, whom she deliberately and shamelessly saw too little of. But when she squinted down at the phone she saw the caller was her daughter, Jody.

Pearl and Quinn slowed to a near stop. A passerby

bounced off Quinn, glared at him, and then looked closer and sweetened up.

"What's up?" Pearl asked her daughter. It was a question she never asked without some trepidation.

"I went out to see Gramma at Assisted Living. She says she misses you, told me to let you know you should give her a call at the nursing home."

"Nursing home" was what Pearl's mother called Sunset Assisted Living in New Jersey, where she had a well-furnished one-bedroom apartment. The kind of place that would have cost a million and a half dollars in Manhattan.

"That all?" It was a short message to be coming from Pearl's mother.

"No," Jody said. "She wants us to buy her something here in the city."

"You know about real estate prices in Manhattan. She's better off—"

"No, no, Mom. She doesn't want a better apartment—at least not now. She needs one of those folding contraptions with metal claws on the end of a long pole. For picking up objects she can't reach."

"What kind of objects?" Pearl asked.

"I suspect desserts, snacks, wrapped candies. She uses a walker now and doesn't like it."

"So she wants to use her walker and a grabber on a pole?"

"No, no. Just the pole contraption, like a lot of the other patients have here."

"Tenants."

"And maybe a new wheelchair."

"Good God! Are they going to joust?"

"She's your mother and my grandmother. Don't make a joke of it."

"Okay. Sure."

"The longest pole they make, she said."

"Sure. But with her walker she's standing up."

"It's getting to things," Jody said. "Her walker isn't fast enough. Some of the other women are always ahead of her. She gets the last or the smallest or what's broken."

"She has tennis balls on her walker," Pearl said. "If she puts oil on them she'll have the fastest walker. Oil on the tennis wheels, and those walkers will blow your hat off."

Jody giggled.

"What's that I hear?" Pearl asked. "You're an attorney. You're supposed to be serious."

"Oil your tennis balls," Jody said, through her giggling. Pearl started to giggle. She couldn't help herself. More giggling. Quinn looked at her as if she were insane. But then, that could happen, talking to Jody.

"For God's sake," Quinn said. "You're a cop."

Pearl looked over at Quinn and opened her mouth to explain.

That was when they heard the three loud explosions.

Quinn put his hand on Pearl's shoulder, while she told Jody she had to go.

"Business?" Jody asked.

"Business."

"Be careful, Mom."

"I'm a cop."

Quinn and Pearl ran toward the source of the explosions.

45

When they got to the end of the block, a crowd was beginning to build. Three police cars had arrived, two of which were parked to block traffic and turn it around to detour. A potbellied, uniformed cop was wandering around, waving his arms and shouting for pedestrians to get back. Two others were knee-deep in debris, trying to find people and dig them out. Several civilians had ignored the uniforms and entered the field of wreckage. A ten-story building housing a dry cleaners and apartments had collapsed on a five-story office building. Broken bricks, bent iron rebar, twisted steel, chunks of concrete and marble, stretched before them for blocks. A cloud of dirt and drywall rolled over the scene, the breeze snatching it away from where Quinn and Pearl stood. They could hear a man screaming nearby, beneath the debris.

Sirens yowled, horns blared, voices screamed and pleaded for help. Quinn heard a child's voice somewhere in the grit that was airborne and distorting the source and direction of sound. It was also blocking his nose and leaving a horrible taste on his tongue.

He was close to the child who had screamed and, along with others, began to dig through and throw debris.

Five feet away, Pearl was working to free a woman who was trapped beneath what looked like a large fallen beam.

Quinn and the others concentrated on the child, who was almost completely buried.

Five minutes later several others joined their efforts. Quinn was surprised to see that one of the rescuers was Pearl. Her expression told him that the woman she'd been trying to save had died. Pearl found space next to Quinn and began gripping whatever wreckage she could reach and tossing it away. She was gasping for breath and he could hear her sobbing.

Someone yelled, a joyous whoop, and across the jagged and blackened pile of rubble two men were carefully removing the child they'd been working to free. No more than three or four years old, the child appeared to be in shock, but definitely alive and still protesting with healthy lungs.

More noise, more calls for help, more people trapped in the rubble. Quinn and Pearl continued to work near where a woman stood sobbing and pleading for help to free her husband, who was trapped beneath bricks and shattered glass. When the woman wasn't screaming, he could be heard from where he was virtually buried.

A particularly large chunk of concrete was eased aside by several bloody hands, and the man who'd been screaming but now was quiet was carefully removed from beneath the debris. He was white with shock, and his right leg was missing. The sobbing woman who'd directed searchers to him rushed toward him but was restrained by several men and a teenage girl.

Quinn took off his belt and fashioned a tourniquet to stanch the injured man's bleeding.

Movement and noise around him, more voices. Quinn was nudged aside, not all that gently. The belt was removed and replaced by something else. Something more effective. Then hands wearing huge gloves worked their way beneath the injured man and lifted him. More huge gloves, helping to locate and remove the injured, the people in shock. Playing out hoses. Wearing black T-shirts with white lettering—FDNY.

The Fire Department had arrived.

Sirens of every kind of emergency vehicle were still yowling. Uniforms at both ends of the blocked street were letting them pass in and out with alacrity. No one wanted to come in here unless compelled by compassion or occupation.

A woman obviously in shock, wearing a tattered pants suit, stumbled over to Pearl and collapsed. Pearl held her, helped her to walk, urged her to keep breathing, and led her toward where at least three ambulances were parked, their light strips putting on a colorful but muted display in the thick dust.

Exhausted, Quinn trudged on. He'd taken only a dozen steps when a hand like a claw closed on his arm and squeezed hard.

"Take him, please!" a woman's voice pleaded alongside Quinn.

He turned and saw a woman holding an infant less than a year old. She was obviously about to pass out and drop the child.

She thrust the infant at Quinn. Said, "My other daughter's in there."

He could think of nothing to say, nothing to do but accept the child. The woman turned around and made her way back toward the center of hell. Quinn thought for a few seconds that he'd go after her, help her. But there was the child in his arms.

He gripped the silent, staring boy and walked toward the ambulances. As he strode in shuffling, zombie-like strides, he felt a glimmer of hope that the damage was less than it might be. There seemed to be some control of it now, since more police and the fire department had arrived.

When he reached the ambulances he turned the boy over to white-uniformed paramedics. As the back of the nearest ambulance opened, he saw the woman Pearl had been helping, sitting with others in the ambulance who were sobbing or simply sitting and staring.

He glanced around, walking along the line of parked ambulances, looking for Pearl. Finally he saw her sitting on the back of one of the vehicles with an open back door. It struck Quinn that she was staring with the same dazed expression as the woman who'd just handed him her baby.

When she saw Quinn she smiled, and he felt immensely better. He walked to her and stood next to her.

"The woman find her other daughter?" he asked.

"I think so. Yes." She seemed to have no idea what he was talking about. He realized she thought he meant the first infant they'd help rescue.

"I meant the second baby," he said.

"There was a second one?"

He smiled again.

Two in one day, she thought. Not such a tough guy. She drew a deep breath and stood up. "Wanna go back for more?"

"Like you do," he said.

They walked back toward the fallen buildings. The volunteers, cops, and firefighters were swarming over the debris now, searching for survivors or more of the dead. At least half a dozen dogs and their handlers were roaming the wreckage.

"Let's pace ourselves this time," Quinn said, seeing that there were signs of order and progress. "It's almost twilight."

Pearl was so tired she simply grunted her agreement.

Quinn knew that even if he tried he couldn't stop her. Not anymore than she could stop him.

"The Gremlin, you think?" she asked.

"Probably. The little bastard might very well be part of the crowd, standing at the edges, watching and enjoying. And learning."

"Infuriating," Pearl said.

Quinn was silent for a few seconds, then stopped and stood still.

Pearl looked up at him.

Quinn said, "I smell gas."

46

Quinn and Pearl stood still, working the calculus of
death. If the buildings had been brought down
with bombs, there might still be a few of them around,
timed to kill rescuers as well as trapped victims.

Quinn clutched Pearl's arm and turned her around.
They passed a few rescuers going the other direction,
toward the collapsed building.

One of them was a cop, covered with grit and what
looked like dried blood.

Quinn blocked him, standing squarely in front of
him and clutching both his shoulders. "Gas!" He shook
the man. "We've gotta turn these people around!"

He simply stared at Quinn.

Seeing that the man was in deep shock, Quinn tried
to turn him around, but he pulled away and resumed his
shuffling walk toward the two buildings that had been
reduced to ruins. Half pulling Pearl with him, Quinn
started walking faster toward the NYPD sawhorses and
yellow tape, and the seemingly impossible geometry of
dozens of hastily parked vehicles.

"Gas!" Quinn shouted again, waving his free arm. "The gas lines are broken! We gotta get outta here!"

A few people heard him, then stood still and listened to see what he was yelling about.

When they finally figured it out, they began walking away from the collapsed buildings.

The smell of the gas was stronger now. And constant. More and more people left the scene of the bombing. Some began to jog. Any second another, even worse, explosion might occur.

Almost everyone, rubber-necker or rescuer, was moving away. Several NYPD cops were yelling as Quinn had, and waving their arms, trying to hurry people along. This wasn't simply someone who'd left the stove on without the pilot light. Cars within the crazy mosaic of parked vehicles tried to cut in on each other, fighting for distance. Metal screeched. Fenders crunched. A uniform was trying without success to recover some order in what had become a panic. He was knocked down by what looked like a football player dressed like a banker, then got up and ran after the man. One engine after another was starting up. People shouted. Starters ground. Horns honked.

"Every time an engine starts, there's a spark," Quinn told Pearl.

"Thanks for that information," she said.

The word spread quickly, and the word was *gas*. Everyone outside a vehicle was running now, picking up speed. Within seconds traffic jammed up and cars were being abandoned. Pearl stopped fighting Quinn and ran alongside him.

The screaming began.

Close behind them, the morning burst into flames.

Blocks away and upwind, the Gremlin sat at a rooftop restaurant window table and watched what was happening. He had a throwaway cell phone and was describing the scene to Minnie Miner, who sounded genuinely aghast.

The Gremlin knew he'd been on the phone long enough for GPS to pose a threat. He said good-bye to Minnie.

She said, "No, please! Tell me why you did this! Why in God's name did you do this? Please!"

He turned off the phone, then under cover of the tablecloth, used his butter knife to pry it apart. The cheap plastic case snapped open easily. With powerful hands, he broke the pieces into smaller pieces. He put the broken phone in his sport-coat pocket. When he got a chance he would fold a newspaper around the phone and drop it into a trash receptacle. Why not today's paper? He'd used the tablecloth so his fingerprints weren't on flat surfaces of the broken phone. All the dishes and flatware he'd used had already been picked up and transported from his table to the kitchen. He wasn't leaving any accidental clues.

Diners without window seats were drifting across the restaurant now to stand at the wide windows and gawk at the dark smoke rising from the city. He hoped Minnie's minions would get a lot of good video out of this. Maybe they'd use that asinine artist's rendering of him to show along with the video. It was an unflattering likeness, but that was the one thing he liked about it. It didn't resemble him at all.

He cautioned himself. Overconfidence could lead to minor missteps while he was focusing on avoiding major mistakes.

Though everything had gone as planned, he still had the broken cell phone in his pocket. For all the talking or listening it could do, it might as well have been a stupid drawing of a cell phone. But it could become evidence. It might be a good idea to buy yesterday's newspaper and turn the phone to trash as soon as possible. There were probably thousands of discarded copies of the *Times* on streets and in trash receptacles around the city, waiting to be picked up. In a few days they would be unfindable in a landfill.

And in a few days he should be able to view up close the wreckage his bombs had created.

There should be enough of the buildings left standing that they would provide almost an X-ray view. People's homes, people's lives, how people lived, how they died, all would be naked for observation and calculation. The guts of the bombed buildings, their lines of water, gas, electricity, would be visible. Secrets would be exposed.

How things worked.

This was very much like reverse engineering. Everything was a learning experience.

He decided to skip a second espresso and let someone else watch the city deal with its wounds.

That was what someone who cared might do.

*   *   *

Later he stopped at a park. There seemed to be no one else around, so he stood for a while and tossed the pieces of the shattered cell phone one by one into a lake, pretending he was feeding the ducks. Though there were no ducks.

Next time, he told himself, bring some bread crumbs.

Or some ducks, if any of them are dumb enough to eat plastic.

He laughed at his own humor.

There was, if one looked in the right places, some amusement in life.

47

Quinn looked up from what he was reading at his desk and saw Renz stomping into the offices of Q&A with a folded morning *Times* tucked under his arm. He drew the paper out as if removing a sword from its scabbard and slammed it down on Quinn's desk.

"See a fly?" Quinn asked.

"I see a goddamned hurricane!" Renz said. "It looks like a gigantic Minnie Miner."

Quinn leaned back in his swivel chair. "She hasn't blown up any buildings."

"She's about to blow up One Police Plaza—with me in it."

"You're making a strategic mistake, Harley."

"Which is?"

"Instead if concentrating on apprehending the Gremlin, you're concentrating on covering your ass."

Renz propped his fists on his hips and walked in a tight circle. "I oughta fire you."

"You don't really want to. Besides, I have a contract."

"Then fulfill it."

"Okay." Quinn adjusted his tie knot and shrugged into his suit coat. Best to look like a detective, if that was your game. "Let's go," he said.

"Where?"

"To look at some collapsed buildings."

"They're still digging out the dead and wounded over there," Renz said.

"Maybe somebody will dig out a clue."

"Already we've got twenty-seven dead and sixty injured. What a hellish mess."

"Like a war zone," Quinn said.

"I'm thinking more of the political side."

Quinn held his silence. Renz apparently didn't know that when you had dead and wounded, there was only one side.

As soon as they stepped outside, the heat hit them. They took Quinn's old Lincoln, with the air conditioner on high, and Quinn drove toward the disaster area.

For a while it seemed they were in normal New York traffic. Then, three blocks away, they began to see police barricades and detours and No Parking signs. They parked the car and went ahead on foot.

The two uniforms handling traffic and trespass problems recognized both the commissioner and Quinn, letting Quinn duck under one of the NYPD sawhorses and holding the yellow crime scene tape up so the corpulent Renz could get under it.

When they reached the corner they looked at the blocks of damage. The desolation caused by the original bombs was more than bad enough, but the gas explosions spread fire and more gas explosions, and damage that encompassed what seemed like the entire neighborhood.

Three bulldozers were roaring and snorting, working among the debris with cautious, elephantine delicacy, and Quinn could hear another close by. Workers with picks and shovels were making their way toward rescue or removal of dead bodies. That only twenty-seven had died was, in Quinn's mind, a surprisingly small number, considering the field of destruction they found themselves in. Certainly that number would grow.

"I know it's early on," he said to Renz, "but has anybody come forward as a witness?"

"Only to be on TV or in the papers. Your people learn anything that might be helpful?"

"Might. Yeah. But it's a meager might."

Renz said, "Maybe security cameras caught something."

"If they didn't cook in this weather," Quinn said. "I've got Sal and Harold looking into that."

"So you haven't just been sitting on your ass."

"Nope. Did I mention, I've got a contract?"

"Now I'd like for you to have a clue."

After a depressing twenty minutes, during which everyone other than Renz moved wreckage to reveal more wreckage, one of the uniforms came over and told Quinn and Renz that the Gremlin had phoned in to the Minnie Miner show and claimed credit for the destruction of the buildings, as well as for the deaths. The call was, of course, brief and impossible to trace, but the voice tracks appeared to be the same. The Gremlin's, in both instances.

Quinn said, "Seems like a clue, Harley."

Renz, flushed and puffed up from the heat and pervasive smell, called for his limo to pick him up.

Now that he'd delivered his message, Renz had little use for Quinn. He didn't so much as glance in Quinn's direction as the gleaming black town car with NYPD plates glided away.

Only to reappear on the opposite side of the bomb blast area and fire damage. Maybe Renz had thought of something helpful. A clue.

Quinn watched Renz from half a block's distance. Renz was out of his car and talking to a woman with a microphone. Another woman was frantically leaping around the limo with a small camera, finding good angles for shots of Renz.

Renz was helping her as much as possible. He removed his suit coat and rolled up his white shirt-sleeves. He found a high spot in the debris so the photos would have a flattering upward angle. For some shots, he propped his fists on his hips and raised his chin. A portly Mussolini.

Quinn watched and waited for a while, but he never saw Renz actually touch anything.

That was Renz's talent.

48

That evening, in his office, Renz was less circumspect in talking to Quinn. He knew there were no hidden video cameras or recorders here. And like a beast in his lair, he was most comfortable in familiar surroundings.

The conversation was so amiable that Renz gave Quinn one of his best cigars and fired up an identical one for himself. He confided to Quinn that the cigars were illegal and from some South or Central American country that Quinn had heard of only in a Woody Allen movie. Now they were partners in crime.

Quinn sat in a comfortable leather armchair, holding the cigar and a glass ashtray. The armchair faced Renz's desk, behind which sat Renz. If the desk had been any bigger, Quinn thought, he might need to shout to be heard.

"Now that we're off the record we can talk," Renz said.

Quinn didn't remember anything about being on or off the record, but he let it slide.

Renz tilted back his head as if about to administer eye drops. He made a perfect O with his lips and blew an imperfect smoke ring.

"Are we really getting any traction in finding this Gremlin bastard?" he asked. "Something or somebody we can toss to the media wolves?"

Quinn blew a perfect smoke ring. "Tell them we're making progress."

"They won't believe me."

"They won't believe you no matter what you say, so why waste the truth on them?"

Renz chewed on his cigar but didn't take smoke into his mouth. "This Gremlin guy would be easier for us to get a line on if he was a professional. But real experts in those fields always peg him as a talented amateur. New to his work, maybe, but he knew or learned enough about killing that he manages to make the hit and then get away unseen." Renz produced a white handkerchief as big as a surrender flag and wiped his forehead and neck with it. Watching him made Quinn realize the office had gotten much warmer. It might have been the cigars, or the futility.

"For instance, he knew how to neutralize all those elevator safety brakes in the Blenheim Building," Renz went on. "All those floors." He tapped ashes from his cigar into an ashtray on his desk and made a face suggesting he was nauseated. "God! All that bone sticking through flesh. And the fires! The arson guy said it took some knowledge and some jerry-rigging to bring off what this guy has done. Imagine the planning, learning what those buildings are made of, when and how they were constructed—their materials and vulnerabilities. He must have made studies before he made plans."

"You would think so," Quinn said.

"He knew where the flammable wooden support beams and joists were," Renz said. "How the fire would dance its way through the place. Which walls were load-bearing. Everything that'd cause the fire to feed on itself and turn buildings into ovens."

"Fire seems to fascinate people who like gadgets."

"Does it follow that people who like gadgets like to kill?"

Quinn thought about that. "People who like gadgets want to know about how the insides of things work. They can only gain that deeper understanding through careful observation and examination. Which is why our gremlin has a compulsion to disassemble things so he can study them. Even women."

"So he thinks that by abduction and torture he can learn about women?" Renz looked skeptical.

"Only some things," Quinn said. "Other things he'll learn in other ways. We have to learn those things, too, if we're going to find him."

"It sounds reasonable when you say it," Renz told Quinn. He snubbed out his cigar.

Quinn took that as a signal from Renz that their tête-à-tête was finished.

Quinn didn't think so. Still seated, he said, "There is something you might toss to the circling news vultures, Harley. Tell them we're studying closed-circuit security camera stills and videos of people at the Taggart Building fire. The people in the street, observing the flames. Images from before, during, and after the explosions and fire. We think we might be able to do a facial match with the killer and the artist's rendering. Mix in a picture of Kray as a youth, and we may come up with some positive identification."

Renz looked surprised. "Are we doing all that?"

"As soon as you supply the cameras and cassettes."

"Nobody uses cassettes anymore," Renz said.

Quinn ignored him and stood up. He knew Renz had the political clout to get whatever he needed to get something done in a rush. The man had his connections. That was how it worked. The favor would also subtract from Renz's stock of favors owed. Some might sniff weakness, but who knew if there really were such images that hadn't been destroyed?

Renz stood up and said, "You are really a prick, Quinn."

As Quinn was leaving, he paused at the door and said, "Nice cigar, Harley. But it's only that."

When Quinn arrived at Q&A, he found Jerry Lido there, along with Pearl and Fedderman.

Sal and Harold were still occupied interviewing witnesses to the bombing and burning. Sal had called earlier and talked to Pearl. She'd told him two witnesses had surfaced and reported glimpsing a child of about twelve running and dancing through the flames. Neither witness had gotten a good look at the quick, lithe figure.

Pearl gave Sal and Harold names and addresses and sicced them on the witnesses.

"Could have been a small adult," said one of the witnesses, a hard-looking but glamorous woman named Philipa.

"Or a large child," Harold said.

They were in her living room, in a modest but cozy ground-floor apartment that looked out at ankle level at passersby on the sidewalk. It was on the upwind side of the field of wreckage left by the explosions and fire. Half the buildings on the block looked untouched, in contrast to the others.

Harold wondered about Philipa's ethnicity. She had a certain earthy magnetism that intrigued him. When she caught Harold staring at her breasts, she gave him a look that startled him with its clarity of meaning. She knew what he was thinking she was thinking, but he was wrong.

Exactly.

"I was just curious about your ethnicity," he said, laying it all out there. "Where you're from."

"Philipistan," she said. "And before you ask, yes, I am named after my country."

"Like Odessa," Harold said.

Sal glared at him. "Or Miss Australia."

Philipa's husband entered the room then, and that was that.

"I wasn't here during the event," he said. Meaning he had nothing to add, and neither did his wife. Interview over.

Harold thought "event" was an odd thing to call a bombing and conflagration. And to Harold, the man didn't look at all Philipistanese. More Irish.

"Thanks for your cooperation," Sal told the husband, feigning dead seriousness. He gave the wife one of his cards. "If you remember anything else, please call."

As Philipa accepted the card, she glanced at him,

then up and to the side. Something in her eyes sent the ancient wordless message: I know you know I know . . .

"Where exactly is—" Harold began, as Sal pushed him out the door to the hall.

Back in the unmarked, with its engine and air conditioner running, Sal riffled through the many interviews. What he and his fellow detectives were doing didn't seem productive, but he knew how some small item or phrase, or even silence, could unexpectedly yield up a fact or physical piece of evidence. He squeezed the bridge of his nose between thumb and forefinger. Some people thought doing that could help to make a headache go away. Sal wasn't one of those people. His headache had a name: Harold.

They drove for a while, Sal behind the wheel. He knew that sooner or later something would click. The trick was to recognize it when it happened. The legwork of the investigation was only beginning. When a little time had passed, the same witnesses could be interviewed again. Differences or contradictions in the results could be useful.

Sal continued to drive what he thought was the perimeter of the recent catastrophe. Harold sat and fiddled with his iPhone.

Fifteen minutes passed before Harold spoke: "It's nowhere on Google."

"What's that, Harold?"

"Philipistan. As far as Google's concerned, it doesn't exist."

After a while, Harold muttered, "Those countries come and go. Sometimes they even overlap."

* * *

Back at Q&A, Quinn sat slouched in his desk chair and listened while Sal and Harold read their reports in noticeably weary voices. Quinn didn't mind, not only because he wasn't doing the drone work on the Gremlin chase, but because he believed that sometimes what's not noticed in one sense is noticed in another. Listening to reports differed a shade from reading them to oneself. Quinn had once persuaded Pearl to touch her tongue to a sheet of paper to see if it tasted the same as the rest of the paper in a tablet. The papers had tasted the same, but Quinn pretended that one was more acidic than the other, which convinced a suspect to roll over and implicate his codefendant in a series of burglaries.

I know that you know I know . . .

49

The Happy Brat sandwich shop was close enough to the ballpark that, when the ball club was in town, there was no shortage of customers. Fran and Willie had opened the place after the previous owner had put it up for sale and retired to Kissimmee, Florida. They had themselves retired two years ago, almost died of boredom, and saw it as their fate to at least make an offer when the diner went on the market. Their offer was rock bottom, but the owner knew them and liked them. And sold them the Happy Brat.

Willie was a big man, and strong, but he was in his seventies now. His hair was thinning and gray, his back bent, but his arms were still powerful. There was a hitch in his gait. He knew he'd soon have to have a hip replacement. Fran was wiry and stronger than she looked, but she, like Willie, was surprised to discover that retirement had been wearing. They needed help, full-time and part. A fellow retiree, Henry Lodge, who was a longtime friend of Willie's, bought a percentage of the diner and sometimes spent weekdays there with them. There were days when business dragged.

When the Cardinals ball club was in town, it was another story. The Happy Brat couldn't afford much, but hired a series of short-order cooks and countermen to handle the additional business. Henry helped, especially on those busy days when the Chicago Cubs were in town for day games. Baseball fans loved bratwurst on a bun with sauerkraut and mustard. And what could go better with that than beer, which Fran and Willie sold on draught and ice cold?

All went well beneath the neon bratwurst on a bun sign until, during a long home stand, a need for a dish-washer and sometimes short-order cook became too obvious to ignore.

This home stand, the Cardinals stayed in town almost three weeks. Fran was beginning to look haggard and tired all the time. Willie and Henry took to sniping at each other.

"Enjoy the backbreaking work while you can," Willie was fond of saying. "There'll be plenty of slow days in our future."

But this was the present, profitable even if it was a test for nerves. The economy was such that it would be easy to hire temporary help, maybe for the rest of the baseball season.

Hiring seemed the solution to their problem.

Fran put a help-wanted sign in the lower right corner of the window, and within an hour the kid turned up. He was small, said he actually wanted to become a jockey. But things other than horses were slow at the track across the river in Illinois, so he was looking for a job he could do for a while.

Fran, who was at the register, listened carefully to the boy, and motioned for him and Willie to come to her end of the counter where she could take part in the job interview.

Up close the boy looked to be in his teens. Willie, with his aging linebacker's body, dwarfed him. The kid wasn't the cleanest, but he probably hadn't planned on seeing a help-wanted sign. The hand-printed sign also said "part-time," down at the bottom, but that was okay, if a person was getting desperate.

"What's your name?" Fran asked.

"Pablo Diaz."

She looked at him for what seemed a long time. Then: "You don't look Mexican."

"On my father's side," he said, as if that explained any questions about his ethnicity.

Fran was the practical one, but there was something about this boy that made her feel maternal. A basic goodness that was more than youthful idealism. On the minus side, there was something he was holding back.

Fran decided to put it aside, for now. "If he's not afraid of hard work, I say we hire him."

"Can we do that on our own?" Willie asked. "Remember, there's three of us that own this place."

"Henry might make it two out of three, if it comes to a vote. But I don't think he would. Ain't no reason not to hire this lad."

"What about the girl?" Willie asked.

When no one answered, Fran said, "She tells me her name's May, and she and the boy are married."

"We hiring her, too?" Willie asked.

"Not likely. She don't look strong enough to lift a pea."

"They'll fool you, though, those country girls."

"You think any of that's true?"

"I dunno. Do you?"

"Like I'm married to Robert Redford," Fran said.

50

New York, the present

Despite the effectiveness of Lido's software, the composite image of the alleged Gremlin struck a note with no one. Possibly when finally they ran the Gremlin to ground, there would be no real resemblance.

"This guy," Harley Renz said, "is at least as lucky as he is tricky."

He and Quinn were seated on a bench in one of Manhattan's pocket parks. Though it was near a busy street, the park had a lot of greenery. It seemed more private than it was. A man in a gray suit and a woman with a ponytail sat on another bench, side by side and facing away from Quinn and Renz. The woman appeared now and then to toss bread crumbs to the pigeons. Three of the birds seemed to take turns in pecking at the gift of bread. Others stood nearby and solemnly observed. Quinn knew what they were thinking, like all the earth's creatures: It might be a trap.

"Nobody's called in with any information or identi-fication of our artist's rendering of the Gremlin," Renz said. "Probably if anybody gets a good look at him, they still won't have paid enough attention to recognize him from that composite."

"It hasn't worked so far," Quinn admitted. He was wondering why Renz had suggested this meeting.

He didn't have to wait long to find out.

"We've got another victim," Renz said. "Woman over on West Seventy-seventh Street. Dora Palm."

Quinn felt the stab of anger and sadness that he always felt when informed of a victim, especially a victim given a name. Somehow the name made the murder even more grotesque, the victim more real and alive—a person with a past and present. Until a short time ago, a fu-ture. "Any doubt it was the Gremlin?"

"None. The ME even says he can tell it was the same blade. Says the killer used a sharp knife here and there, but a jigsaw for hard to reach parts or heavy-duty cut-ting."

"When did it happen?"

"Last night around ten o'clock. After a steak dinner with a good Merlot. At least she got that."

"We all get that," Quinn said, "sometimes not know-ing when it's coming. Maybe it's better that way."

"Or not."

"Crime Scene techs find anything useful?"

"Not yet. But they're still looking. Why I called you about this one was to warn you to be careful."

"Careful of what?"

"What you say. Who you say it to. Extra careful. This is a somewhat complicated case."

Quinn leaned back on the bench, watching the woman with the ponytail feeding the pigeons. "Tell me what I need to know, Harley."

"You like dogs?"

"Depends on what kind."

"Greyhounds."

"A couple of them have run fast enough to win me money—but not much."

"We're talking about a racing dog," Renz said. "Here's to You."

"Huh?"

"That's the dog's name."

"This a racing dog?"

"Doesn't matter," Renz said. "It's a dog."

"How old?"

"About eight years."

Quinn understood now what Renz was trying to say. "Here's to You was probably a rescue dog, saved from an abbreviated life by some animal lovers' organization that arranged homes for dogs that found themselves without owners. Here's to You was probably adopted by Dora Palm when it retired from racing. Along with its new owner, it had been killed by the Gremlin."

"You might say the killer autopsied the dog," Renz said.

Quinn thought that over. "The bastard wanted to see why it could run so fast."

"You know, that might be possible," Renz said. "It was a greyhound, poor thing."

Quinn knew Renz was making a joke by stating the obvious about his concern for an aging racing dog that had come to a bad end. That was contemptible but not unexpected.

Renz was aware that Quinn was a dog lover. A simple all-around pet lover. While Quinn felt genuine concern about Here's to You, Renz felt none. What scared him was that Quinn might say or do something the public or some organization like PETA might build into an issue. Renz knew that if it helped to nail the Gremlin, however the dog was used would be okay with him. He would not be thinking of the dog.

Quinn would be.

That was a weakness.

Renz glanced at his watch and stood up, buttoning his voluminous suit coat. "Uniforms are still at the victim's apartment. They and the ME know you're on your way." Renz tried to impress Quinn with an unblinking stare, but Quinn stared back mildly, unimpressed.

Beyond Renz, the pigeons had finally gotten out the word. Over a dozen now hopped and pecked around the bench where the ponytailed, beneficent woman sat casting out bread.

"I'll swing by and pick up Pearl," Quinn said.

Renz grinned. "Make sure she behaves."

"Like always," Quinn said, and walked toward where his black Lincoln sat gleaming in the blazing sun.

51

Once in the hushed quiet of the Lincoln, Quinn called Pearl on his cell and told her he'd be by the office to pick her up for the drive to Dora Palm's address. Pearl said she was having lunch with her daughter, Jody, and would take the subway there as soon as possible.

Quinn told her he'd meet her at the victim's address but to take her time, the person they wanted to see wasn't going anywhere. "Better, too," he said, "if you don't bring Jody."

"She wouldn't be interested anyway," Pearl said, sotto voce. "She's all involved in an animal rights case. Can lizards be classified as pets that—"

"Never mind," Quinn cut in. "I don't want to hear it."

"The lizards just might have a case. Of course, the roaches wouldn't—"

"Still don't want to hear it," Quinn said, using his thumb to break the connection and turn off his phone.

He hadn't told Pearl that the medical examiner assigned to the case was her antagonist, Dr. Julius Nift.

She was, after all, eating lunch.

* * *

Dora Palm's apartment was in a midtown brick and stone structure that had once been an office building. Like many midtown buildings these days, its face was made temporarily anonymous by scaffolding.

Quinn saw a uniformed cop within the maze of scaffolding about the same time the cop saw him. When he flashed his ID, the cop motioned him over.

After parking the car, Quinn went on foot and zigged and zagged through the scaffolding, along a temporary plank walkway.

The cop motioned again, this time to indicate the building entrance. Quinn thought he might know the cop, but he wasn't sure. The guy had one of those average-this, average-that faces. They might simply have glimpsed each other along the way. Be a cop long enough and faces were indelible once seen, stored somewhere along with identifying marks and bloody crime scenes and the indignities of death. A cop's mind . . .

"This way, Captain," the cop said. That was when Quinn recognized him. Vincent Royston, from Homicide South. It had been a couple of years.

"How you doing, Vince?"

Royston's face lit up. He was pleased to be recognized by Quinn, whom he saw as someone reasonably famous. At least in cop circles.

It was a rhetorical question, but Royston said he was doing the best he could.

"Aren't we all?" Quinn said.

But sometimes he wondered.

"Third floor," Royston said, realizing he wasn't going to be engaged in a lengthy conversation. "Left off the elevator."

Quinn went through a narrow, unmarked doorway he would never have guessed was an entrance. He found himself in a fairly large foyer that had been created when several other spaces were taken down. It was the kind of place that ordinarily would have a doorman, if it weren't for all the remodeling. Eight or ten people were coming and going through the maze of iron pipes supporting the scaffolding in the lobby. Almost everyone wore work clothes, and some had on hard hats. A sign was nailed crookedly to a vertical support beam reading EXCUSE OUR DUST.

The elevator looked purely functional on the outside, but when Quinn stepped inside and the door closed, everything looked finished, mostly in oak and brushed metal. Quinn's mind went back to the elevator in the Blenheim Building, to what must have gone on among the passengers during the five or six seconds it took to reach the basement once they realized what must be happening. His mind recoiled.

The elevator stopped smoothly and the door opened on the third-floor hall. Quinn stepped out, turned left, and saw that on this floor everything looked as finished and usable as in the elevator. Oak wainscoting and brushed metal was the theme here, too. It appeared that interior rehabbing had begun in the upper floors and was working its way down. Probably a money thing, Quinn thought. Rents collected on the high-priced upper-floor apartments would help to finance the lobby's modern curved marble registration area, and what might someday become a fashionable bar and restaurant.

A stalwart uniformed cop stood next to an open apartment door about fifty feet down the hall from the elevator. Quinn was sure he hadn't seen the man before, who looked capable but about twenty pounds overweight. Gained recently, Quinn suspected, noting the cop's youth, and the taut material stretched over a stomach paunch.

When Quinn flashed his ID the uniform stepped aside so he could enter.

Quinn was directed to the apartment's one bedroom. Techs and the dance of the white gloves were everywhere except the bedroom. They'd finished in there, interpreting the bloodstains and gathering possibly minute evidence to be examined later. Trying to recreate what was.

Nift, the atrocious little medical examiner, was kneeling beside this victim in the way Quinn had often seen him, more intensely curious than somber. His lips were moving slightly and silently. It was almost as if he and the corpse were getting to know each other on the most intimate terms, which in a way was half true.

As he saw Quinn, Nift said hello, removing from the torso of the dead woman what looked like an indicator to probe for liver temperature, a valuable part of the calculus that would provide time of death.

The victim, Dora Palm, was on the floor, lying in an awkward position that needed a second look to be sure she was real. The observer would see that her arms, legs, and head were about a quarter of an inch from where they should have been attached.

"Skillfully done, isn't it?" Nift said.

"Strange skill, though. And why in this cramped little room did he put her on the floor instead of the bed?"

Nift looked thoughtful. "Could be he wanted her in the lowest position possible. A measure of her importance compared to his. Gremlin the conqueror, his conquest lying on the floor like a detached and broken doll."

"Or it could be that it's difficult to pose a dead woman on a soft mattress, especially with her limbs and head severed."

"I could think of more interesting poses," Nift said, looking beyond Quinn.

"I'm sure you could," said a woman's voice.

Pearl had walked in. Nift looked instantly interested. Pearl had on a light tan raincoat over a gray pants suit and a white blouse open at the neck. The neckline was low enough to show the swell of her more than ample breasts. Why would she unfasten that top button on her blouse, knowing Nift might be here?

Or had the blouse come unbuttoned and she hadn't noticed?

The things women did that made men think. But then, he was the one doing that kind of thinking.

"Hello to all three of you," Nift said.

Quinn considered saying something to Nift, then decided Pearl could speak for herself. She had once punched out an over-amorous police captain when she was in the NYPD. Promotion was difficult for her after that, if not impossible.

Nift began packing his instruments in a container that would keep them separate from the sterile ones. He straightened up slowly, as if his back hurt. Pearl hoped it did.

It occurred to Quinn that Nift was getting up in years to be acting like a nasty lothario who might have a strain of necrophilia in his horror-house mind.

"Unless you have some reason for her not to," Nift said, "it's okay now for Dora Palm to leave for our rendezvous in the morgue. I'll phone you later and give you facts and figures, among them a more accurate time of death." He glanced around to make sure he wasn't forgetting anything.

"By the way," he said, "there's a uniformed officer downstairs, a big cop named Vincent something. He can give you the name of the guy who found the body. Lives in Brooklyn and works for the company that's doing the work now on rehabbing this area."

"I'll talk to him," Quinn said.

"His name's Stan Gorshin. You'll recognize him. He's the only hard hat out there in a suit."

Quinn said, "Did he have on the hard hat before all the unscheduled demolition?"

Nift thought for longer than a minute. "Yeah. I think so. But I can't be certain."

"Seems nothing in life is certain."

"Or in death," Nift said.

There Quinn disagreed with him.

52

St. Louis, Missouri, 1999

Fran came in early the morning of a doubleheader that was going to be played because of an earlier rainout. Downtown St. Louis was still snoozing, as were most of the suburbs. But Fran knew that within a few hours, parking space would become a rare commodity, and expensive when you parked anywhere near the stadium.

She'd left the car near the double-wide where she and Willie lived and taken the Metro downtown.

By the time she was walking the short distance from the Metro-link stop to Busch Stadium, the slight drizzle had ceased, as the weather wonders on every TV channel had predicted, and the low gray sky had become blue. Probably, Fran thought, the temperature would reach ninety-five degrees, as predicted, and the sun would be blasting away most of the day. Baseball fans approaching and leaving the stadium would want bratwurst, which would make them want beer or soda, which would make them want bratwurst. A vicious, profitable circle.

Fran picked up her pace and smiled. It was going to be a good day; she could feel it. She could take the register, spelled now and then by Willie or Henry. The new kid, Pablo, could work the kitchen. The Happy Brat was the kind of restaurant where no table service was expected. Alcoholic beverages could be ordered at the counter and would be brought tableside, but customers served everything else to themselves. To eat here or to get food to go. It always impressed Fran to see how many people liked to eat and drink while they walked.

Multitaskers, Fran thought. That was okay with her, as long as they paid and didn't make a mess of the public sidewalks.

As she rounded the last corner before reaching the Happy Brat, she saw that the lights were on inside, from the fluorescent ceiling fixtures. They cast a ghastly glow, adding age and angst to everyone inside. But it was summer and it wasn't dark outside now. The night had been chased away, but recently. The diner shouldn't yet be open. The notion that something might be wrong stirred in Fran, but she dispelled it. Henry had closed the diner last night, and had most likely simply forgotten to switch off the fluorescent overhead fixtures.

She was pleased that the red neon open sign in the window was off.

Fran realized her heart was banging away and told herself to slow down. Nobody was burglarizing the diner. Maybe Pablo had overslept again and Henry was getting a jump on things in the kitchen. It wouldn't be the first time. She could smell the scent of the bratwurst rotating over the open oven, the special sauce crusting on the meat.

At least she thought she could smell it. She did have a powerful imagination when it came to food.

She saw now that someone, probably Henry, wearing a white shirt, dark pants, and a dark apron, was working in the kitchen, visible through the window and beyond the serving counter pass-through. Henry, all right. Or maybe the kid. Certainly not Willie. He was still home in bed, breaking the sound barrier with his snoring.

Or was he? He might have beaten her to the diner, if he'd left the double-wide right after she had.

The red neon bratwurst sign was still off, and most of the light in the diner was coming from the fixture in the kitchen, directly above the sink.

When Fran opened the door, the figure at the sink had his back to her, wearing the white and black outfit with the apron. He either heard or sensed something.

As Fran stepped inside, he turned.

The kid. Pablo.

When Pablo turned and saw her, his expression didn't change for a few seconds. Then he forced a smile.

"Where's Henry?" she asked.

"Still asleep."

"What about May?"

He looked confused.

"Your wife," Fran reminded him.

"Yeah. She's still asleep. I couldn't sleep, so I decided to get some brats ready to go. You know, for early customers."

"I don't know," Fran said reasonably.

Pablo turned away from the sink to face her squarely.

She saw the knife in his right hand. What looked like blood was on the blade.

"We need some buns," he said. "We've got plenty of brats, but we need buns." He placed the knife on the sink, wiped his hands on a towel, and removed his apron. "I'll go see if I can find some."

Fran decided there was no sense in arguing. Let the kid get out, get some fresh air in his search for buns.

She stepped around him, looked at what was on the cutting board, and recoiled. Her eyes were huge and horrified. "My God! What are you doing?"

"Nothing, really!" he said, backing away. Pablo had picked the knife back up. Time seemed to have solidified. He was the only thing in the diner moving.

Henry opened the door and came inside. His shirt was untucked and his hair was still wet and slicked back from showering. He glanced around. "What've we got going on here?" he asked.

"Good question," Fran said.

Pablo noticed the others were staring at the knife, and he tossed it backhanded so it fell clattering behind the burners on the stove.

"What are you cutting there?" Henry asked calmly. He stepped toward Pablo, then to the side, and stared at the cutting board. "That what I think it is?"

Pablo couldn't prevent a frightened smile that quickly disappeared as he regained control.

"It's a rat!" Fran said in a horrified voice. "My God, he's carving up a rat!"

"I got it here, in the kitchen," Pablo said, as if that explained everything.

"This is a diner!" Fran said. "A restaurant!"

"That's how the rat saw it." He actually sounded sincere.

Henry glanced again at the carving board on the sink. "What were you gonna do with that?" he asked in a calm voice.

"I was just . . . looking at it. Studying it."

"Studying a rat?"

"They do that at Harvard," Pablo said.

Henry shook his head. "This ain't Harvard. You ain't Jonas Salk."

"Jonas who?"

"Salk. He found a way to fight polio."

"Who was polio?" Again he seemed serious.

"Don't play dumb," Fran said. "Like we're supposed to believe you just happened to find that rat in here."

"You can believe what you want," Pablo said.

"Okay. You're a medical doctor doing cancer research."

"You got it first try. Now, I'm gonna leave here. Anybody tries to stop me, I'll have to tell them about that rat. How I found him in the corner by the stove."

"Maybe you're not so dumb," Henry said.

Fran walked behind the counter and scooped a handful of bills from the cash register. She placed the money on the counter where Pablo could reach it.

"Take that," she said. "All of it. And then leave us the hell alone."

Pablo kept his eyes on her as he picked up the money and stuffed it into a side pocket of his jeans.

"Now go someplace else where they'll believe you and your so-called wife are Mexicans."

"Gracias, señora," he said, patting his bulging pocket.

He backed out of the diner, almost falling as he spun in his worn-down boots and ran away.

Fran walked to the door, held it open, and watched as Pablo—or whatever his name was—joined his wife, May, or whatever her name was.

They cut across a level stretch of bare earth that would, within about four hours, become a parking lot. Then they both turned to look back. May waved at Fran, looking as if she might be smiling. Then they disappeared into downtown St. Louis, where Cardinals fans, and Cubs fans from Chicago, would soon be roaming the city streets, looking for new places to eat lunch, or find that bar or restaurant they'd been to during their last trip to St. Louis. Some of them would recall the delicious bratwurst served at a neat little diner not far from the stadium, in an area soon to be developed by the city.

"Better wake up Willie and give him the bad news," Fran said.

Henry said, "I best get rid of that rat, first."

When he went to the sink and got a better look at the rat, he was surprised by how neatly it had been carved and partially skinned by Pablo. The incisions were neat and precise, as if the kid had studied medicine and at one point wanted to be a surgeon. When Pablo worked at the grill, he always wore a do-rag, knotted at the corners so it made a sort of skullcap. Henry had assumed it was to keep his hair out of his eyes and out of the food. But he'd glimpsed the kid's ear once, when he had the do-rag off and was splashing cold faucet water on his face to cool down in the heat. He remembered the kid's right ear. It looked something like Dr. Spock's ears in *Star Trek*.

It took only a few seconds for Henry to figure out what he should do about the events of the morning—which was nothing. No way was he going to let anyone find out about the rat on the cutting board in the Happy Brat. Henry would tell no one. He might have been born yesterday, but it wasn't at night.

He lifted what was left of the rat by its tail and dropped it into a plastic bag, then put everything else on the board down the garbage disposal.

"I'll go drop this in the trash, then go wake up Willie," he said to Fran. "You think we should tell him about the rat, and what the kid said?"

Fran said, "I don't see why we should. It would just give him something else to worry about."

"That's for sure," Henry said.

53

Quinn felt a helplessness about Dora Palm's death that he hadn't felt after the other murders. It wasn't that the severing of body parts and removal of internal organs was that much more vicious and sadistic than the other murders. It was more of a wearing-down process. Quinn knew his patience was getting thin.

In a case like this, where the investigation seemed to go nowhere, there came a time when the strain reached its breaking point. The killer was aware that he could stretch his good luck only so far, then something he overlooked, or some little something that was supported only by a mass of lies and an alternative reality, would finally give. He would be tripped up, and he knew that moment would someday come, had been getting closer all the time.

Quinn knew that some part of the killer's mind yearned for luck that would see him through, and at the same time he wanted something out of his control that would end the suspense. In glory and gunfire, it would end. And no one would ever forget what the Gremlin had done.

No one would ever forget the Gremlin.

The public would eventually forget what Quinn had done. Who remembers who arrested Son of Sam? Or Ted Bundy? The age of tech didn't help as often as it upset balances. Computer mice were clicked. Buttons were pushed. Digital blood was spilled. It all confirmed that death and murder could be reduced to a game. And even if the players were acutely aware that their luck, good or bad, couldn't run forever, who was afraid of a game?

Quinn felt about that the same way he knew his quarry felt.

As if a noose were around his neck, and tightening.

This game was going to end soon, along with someone's death. It must end that way. Both men understood that. Someone's trust would be misplaced, or an informant would whisper in the wrong ear. Or someone's will would break. Someone would have to die.

To help make sure he wouldn't be the one, the NYPD photography director carefully selected enlarged backgrounds and photos.

The photographs of what was left of Dora Palm looked as if they'd been taken by someone with more than mediocre skill with a camera. Still, they would accomplish their purpose, which was to encourage Minnie Miner to cooperate with the law. Minnie was glad to give Quinn a few minutes to describe any progress on the Gremlin case, and to answer a few questions. Quinn gave her the questions.

Minnie, who had been in Renz's office when Quinn arrived, gave Quinn a baleful stare and asked him if Renz had known about the use of her program, *Minnie Miner ASAP,* to help lay a trap for the Gremlin.

"Maybe," Quinn said with an enigmatic smile.

But it was smile enough for Minnie, which is how Quinn came to find himself on her early call-in TV show the next morning.

This was one interview, Quinn knew, that would have to go right.

Not like the few, dream-filled hours' sleep he had last night worrying about it.

54

After the round of applause for Quinn, Minnie let the callers talk about the Gremlin investigation. Quinn sat in one of the big easy chairs angled toward the audience, and Minnie sat in the other.

She made a big deal out of using Quinn's clout so they didn't have to reveal the questioners' names. For safety's sake.

"This man looks friendly," Quinn said, about the composite rendering of the Gremlin on the big screen centered on the wall behind the easy chairs. Quinn wished he had a laser pointer. "He isn't. He's thirty-five years old. He was released from detention in Louisiana recently because some DNA in sperm found near a young girl's dead body had been contaminated and so couldn't be matched to his, as the prosecuting attorney had pointed out over and over to a grand jury. It was also confirmed that, while the grand jury had thought him guilty, they had their reasonable doubts about whether he should be indicted and tried in criminal court. Not only would the judicial process be futile, it might be unfair to the defendant."

"We could use fewer of those cases of mistaken identity," Minnie said. She raised a hand palm-out. "I don't mean we should railroad people, just that we get tough with the real criminals. The violent ones."

There was a great deal of applause from the studio audience.

"We're trying," Quinn said. He continued to lie about the sprung prisoner in Louisiana, who didn't exist except as a ploy created by Quinn. "The Louisiana defendant was released, though the jury made it clear they thought he did the crime. They were also sure that with the compromised DNA evidence, he would probably not be found guilty. In the court of public opinion, he would become a victim.

"A range of other expert witnesses were called," Quinn said. "But they couldn't prove beyond some people's idea of a reasonable doubt that the defendant was in any way implicated in what could have been an extremely unfriendly separation, like so many others wherein both parties became losers.

"The prosecutor didn't know it, but he was a pawn in a small game inside a large game.

"Here's the thing," Quinn said, leaning forward in his chair. "This woman had been raped and killed, and now the law can prove it. And if it weren't for contaminated DNA, there wouldn't have been a chance in hell of the suspect escaping punishment. All of you know, or think you know, that he's beaten the justice system. All of us also know that sometimes the justice system isn't enough, and that's because we subscribe to the idea that it's better to let a guilty man go free than to imprison, or even execute, an innocent man." Quinn looked directly at the camera. "This refusal to bring an indictment will be appealed."

Knowing all the time that an actual appeals court would never act on this matter. It couldn't, without an actual potential defendant.

"We did good," Renz said to Quinn later, in Renz's office.

Quinn's gaze slid over the wall festooned with framed photos of Renz receiving medals, winning awards, posing with celebrities.

"We only did half a job," Quinn said.

"Now don't go getting all wishy-washy, Quinn. We put a dagger through the heart of whoever it was who's trying to ruin my political career. You might be able to make it look like we solved your case."

"We solved nothing," Quinn said. "Not for sure, anyway."

Renz shrugged his meaty shoulders. "I'm suspicious of that word, sure. What the hell's for sure in this life or the next?"

"I'm sure I'm the lead investigator on this case," Quinn said.

"In a way."

"In a way that might have got my brains shot out."

"Prepare to be shocked, Quinn: I don't care a rat's ass about who gets shot or who's guilty."

"Speaking generally, what about the hypothetical guy in a jail cell who's innocent?"

"He's just that—hypothetical, not real."

"You're all politics and games," Quinn said.

Renz shrugged. "You forgot heart."

"No," Quinn said, "I didn't."

Renz was now occupied in making sure his expensive pen was working well so his signature would be unbroken and impressive. He was way, way beyond inkblots.

Quinn felt anger rise in him, along with a kind of pressure. He absently reached into a shirt pocket and pulled out a cellophane-wrapped cigar that he'd been given earlier as a kind of harmless bribe involving Krispy Kreme doughnuts.

Harmless bribe?

Renz raised a pudgy hand. "You can't smoke cigars in here."

"I have before, just like you."

"We've got rules, regulations."

"Laws," Quinn added. He lit his cigar, drew smoke into his mouth, and exhaled. All with a stare fixed on Renz.

"Look at yourself," Renz said. "You're no different from me. It's just that you won't admit to yourself that you're like the rest of the world. You are definitely not the type who wouldn't jaywalk even if there wasn't a car for miles. Just look at you."

"We're dealing with rape, torture, murder." Quinn said. "Not jaywalking."

Renz smiled, his jowls spilling bulbously over his white shirt collar.

Then he leaned sideways and opened a desk drawer. He withdrew a yellow envelope with its flap fastened by a clasp. "And then there's this." He laid the envelope on the desk where Quinn could reach it.

Quinn worked the clasp and opened the envelope. Its contents were photographs. A dozen eight-by-tens in black and white.

"These are copies, found hidden in Dora Palm's kitchen."

Quinn looked closer at the photos. They seemed to be of the same scattering of pieces, large and small. "What the hell is this?" he asked Renz.

"They were found by the crime-scene people when they did their deep search. And don't give fingerprints a thought."

"Wiped?"

"No, but the killer was wearing latex gloves."

Quinn looked more closely at the photos. Whatever had been found torn to pieces in the dead woman's kitchen didn't look very familiar. "So what was it, a blender?"

"Some kind of coffeemaker that uses compression, so it forces the grounds through a filter." He pointed. "There's the handle. The way it's shaped, that glass part, is what makes it look like a filter."

"Our gadget guy again," a voice said.

It belonged to Nift, the Napoleonic little ME.

"My secretary let you in?" Renz asked.

Nift smiled his oddly reptilian smile and stuck out his pigeon chest. "I charmed her."

Neither Quinn nor Renz knew how Nift had sneaked or lied his way into the office. But they were sure he'd entered of his own accord. Otherwise Renz's receptionist/aide would have called and alerted Renz that someone was on their way, in case Renz or a guest wanted to maintain privacy and leave by the rear exit.

The rear exit was a way out of the building, supposedly secret, that almost everyone knew about. If the news was hot enough, media types would have someone posted to see if anyone of any consequence was sneaking out. Those with something to hide usually fabricated stories authenticated by friends or lovers. Or by the police, who didn't like to be one-upped in the media.

If they didn't remember that secrets known by more than one person were no longer secrets, people who should have heeded the old adage would often get tripped up. The relationships between the criminal world and cop world involved people knowing secrets about people with secrets.

People forgot that, even though it was no secret.

PART THREE

And now I see with eye serene
The very pulse of the machine

—WILLIAM WORDSWORTH,
   "She Was a Phantom of Delight"

55

New York, the present

Quinn lay in bed listening to Pearl's deep and regular breathing. They had enjoyed sex last night; he couldn't imagine not enjoying it with Pearl.

She sighed and rolled onto her side. One of her ample breasts spilled halfway out of her unsnapped nightgown. The city, an hour before the dawn, lay beyond the brownstone's bedroom window. Its sounds, made fainter and less definable by distance, seemed to ebb and flow with Pearl's breathing.

Quinn's own breathing did not seem as regular, almost as if he didn't belong in this room, this city, with this woman. As if he didn't deserve them. Some kind of celestial accident must have occurred, and, improbable as it seemed, here they were.

That was how lucky he felt some mornings.

Pearl let out a long breath and rolled further onto her side, almost resting on her stomach. Her head was turned toward him, and she sensed his attention, opened her eyes, and smiled.

He propped himself up on one elbow and rested his chin in his hand, still looking at her even though she seemed to have fallen back asleep.

He felt rising in him again a thought that was becoming stronger and more powerful.

He wanted a family.

A certain family.

Pearl, Jody, and himself.

They were already much like a family. They lived together and had become that close, that dependent on each other for the various things that kept a family together.

It wasn't that family life was foreign to him. He'd had something like it with his former wife, May, and their daughter, Lauri. He still, in a less forceful way, loved them both—especially Lauri. But he knew he had never loved as he loved Pearl.

He reached over and ran a knuckle gently across her cheek, waking her halfway. Still only partly awake, she turned toward him.

Quinn whispered to her, "We should be married."

A long several seconds passed before she answered. "Is there a law?"

"Probably none we haven't broken," he said.

"Then we can't fail," Pearl said.

He drew her to him. Kissed her.

"There is one thing," she said.

"Like in all marriages," he said.

"I think we should wait until this case is over."

"Kind of a distraction," he said.

"A distraction," she said, "would be Renz watching us walk down the aisle while a murderer is still walking his streets."

Quinn said, "There you have a point."

56

New York, the present

Anyone watching the woman walk along First Avenue would have guessed her age at about seventy. Her walk was slow and indecisive, as if she had no destination. Which was probably true. Her back was slightly bowed, and her hair was dull and frizzled, too long in back and sticking out in clumps on the sides. Her complexion was pale and there were sores on the sides of her neck. From the way she thrust out her jaw and held her lips, it was obvious that she needed cosmetic dental work. She must have been in her thirties.

She kept her chin up as she walked, slowly looking to the right then the left, like a turtle gazing from a shell that was a tattered green coat. The coat, which she had stolen from a used clothing store, was already too warm, but it would keep the rain at bay at least for a while, until it became soaked through.

She was approaching the doorway of a closed beauty salon. A few months ago she'd been shooed away from that same doorway by the woman who ran the place and was the main beautician. Most likely because the woman had been too much of a smart-ass with her customers, the shop was now permanently closed, its windows soaped. The blank white show windows lined the entrance. They did a slight zigzag to a door that was now locked and featured a red-lettered CLOSED sign.

The woman moved back and out of sight in the doorway until she was out of the drizzle that would eventually soak her only coat. A low, fierce wind swished in, whirling a mini-tornado of trash out on the sidewalk. A loosely crumpled sheet of newspaper broke away from the other litter, skipped into the doorway, and wrapped itself around the woman's leg.

She bent over, peeled away the paper, and tossed it aside.

The breeze picked it up, and the airborne newspaper page swirled around and again found the woman's leg. She bent slowly, as if her back hurt, snatched the paper away from her ankle, and was about to crumple it into a tight ball when she noticed something and stopped.

She smoothed out the crumpled newspaper and read it.

On the front page was news about the so-called Gremlin, who was by now, if you believed all accounts, responsible for over a dozen victims. The captions beneath renderings of the Gremlin were pretty much like others. No one seemed to have gotten a clear look at him. The woman mostly used newspapers to line her clothes so she wouldn't become chilled in the early morning hours. She didn't read much, and sometimes wondered if she'd lost the knack.

Here was good reason to find out, and maybe sharpen her skills.

She studied the crinkled newspaper and laboriously read the tawdry, horrible accounts of the victim's death, as theorized by the police.

But there was something else that caught her attention. For some reason the killer had taken the time and risk of disassembling the latest victim's expensive and complex coffeemaker.

When the old young woman turned the newspaper page over, she saw the composite rendered image, as imagined by the police and media. She still couldn't be positive, but the more she stared at the composite, the more she thought she knew him. Or had known him.

Something about his eyes.

Her memory suddenly gave up the man's identity like a prize. My God! He was a childhood friend! More than a friend.

Years ago she had helped him throw a man out of a boxcar that was coupled to a moving train.

She and Jordan Kray had saved each other's lives.

Their childhoods were far away from them now. Though the sketch in the newspaper wasn't all that accurate, the artist had captured something of his subject. There was no doubt that it was Jordan. It was difficult to imagine him as a serial killer, though not so surprising to learn he was probably the prime suspect in a series of murders.

She recalled how Jordan liked to take things apart and put them back together—if he could. Things that were simply objects, and things that were alive.

A curious boy, Jasmine Farr thought. Her seamed face broke into a smile.

In those days they had both been curious.

Maybe they both still were.

The newspaper had been a door-opener. Jasmine had fallen low and fallen again and again, and she had contacts, if not friends, in low places.

It hadn't taken her long to learn who in New York she could contact if she knew the identity, and even the whereabouts, of the Gremlin. Maybe the Gremlin was back in St. Louis. That was where they'd departed the train, and near where they had left, sprawled alongside the dark tracks, the body of a railroad dick.

Surely the man had died. Jasmine could still remember how the knife had felt when she slid it into his side, the surprised and frightened cry that he couldn't suppress. Had she really heard the knife's sharp blade scrape a rib? That was how it was in her memory.

Whatever the reality, Jasmine and Jordan had known that after the man died, the sooner they got out of St. Louis, the safer they'd be.

The wisdom of that had been confirmed by the next day's *St. Louis Post-Dispatch* newspaper. Railroad detective Ellson Ponder had been stabbed to death and was found alongside a train car. Police theorized that Ponder had discovered his killer or killers hiding in what was thought to be was an empty boxcar. A struggle ensued. Ponder had tried to fight off his attackers, but he was beaten, stabbed, and apparently had then been left to die. Ponder had lived with his wife, Charlotte, and their ten-year-old son, Ivan, in the St. Louis suburbs.

While Jordan and Jasmine had known they'd be safer somewhere other than St. Louis, they'd also known the police had most likely tracked them as far as St. Louis. From the police's point of view, the two of them might still be in the city, made to lie low so they couldn't run. They were pinncd down.

At least for a while.

Two people running from murder could attract a lot of attention in ways they couldn't guess at.

It was just a matter of time.

57

New York, the present

It was easier to find Jordan than she'd thought it would be. Jasmine knew where people who didn't want to be found might be located. The invisibles who took form only when worlds overlapped.

Past and present worlds overlapped here, as Jasmine and Jordan stood on opposite sides of Canal Street. While he was unaware of her presence, she studied him.

He seemed even smaller than she remembered. His light jacket was wrinkled, as were his brown slacks. There was no shine on his shoes, and he was wearing a shabby fedora that looked too large for his head. Jasmine noted his dark hair was tufted beneath his hat brim, and that he needed a shave. The stubble on his chin and along his jawline was also dark.

He raised both hands and held his palms pressed to his ears, as if a loud noise that no one else could hear was torturing him.

The traffic signal changed to walk and he dropped his arms, stepped down off the curb, and came toward her.

As they passed each other, their eyes met only briefly, but it was enough to make her breath catch in her throat.

He looked older (of course he did). And he was slightly bent forward as he walked. He was the shorter of the two, even with the fedora.

After five steps she turned around and followed him. That was when she noticed that something didn't ring true about him. It took her a while to figure it out. His forward bend was more a matter of posture than of age and hard luck. His clothes were those of a home-less person, but they didn't match his attitude.

She said something not usually heard in New York City: "You finish shuckin' that corn?"

Jordan took a few more steps, slowed, and turned around.

He looked at her, and a smile slowly formed. She wasn't surprised to find that she couldn't look away from him. She had already felt the attraction.

He said, "Jasmine?"

"'Fraid so." She was trembling. Could he see that? Could he not?

He reached forward and touched her shoulder, as if assuring himself that she was real. She laid her hand on top of his.

They realized, at the same time, that the past had bound them, and now they shared the future.

"Come with me," he said through a smile. "We'll have some coffee."

She looked at him, then bowed her head and sur-veyed herself. "Will they let us in? I mean, we can't go someplace where I usually check the Dumpster for leftovers."

The traffic signal had changed again. Now a horde of cars was moving toward them. He held her elbow and escorted her up on the curb and safety. She felt like a parody of royalty. "I don't know about this, Jordan." Saying his name felt good.

"Don't worry about how we're dressed. I have money. I wear these clothes to walk around the city without drawing a lot of attention. It works if I stay in the right neighborhoods."

"Clever," she said. "You always were clever."

They were walking now, him leading her slightly, toward the coffee shop.

"Had breakfast?" he asked.

She shook her head no, and was astonished when he drew a fat roll of bills from his jacket pocket. The top bill was a twenty.

"This'll fix that," he said.

"Are you always in disguise?" she asked.

"Not all the time. But I've found it's the best way to take advantage of the city's gift of anonymity."

"I can vouch for the invisibility," Jasmine said. "Sometimes I think I could walk right in and rob a bank and nobody'd notice."

"That would be a crime."

They exchanged a secret smile.

Both were aware they were exploring the bond between them. It was powerful. Binding in a way that neither of them quite understood. After all, this was the man who had claimed her virginity. The man with whom she had murdered.

Jasmine found herself wondering, Is murder an aphrodisiac?

She remembered the Gremlin, and decided it wasn't time yet to bring up that subject.

"I always wondered," he said, "why you left me in St. Louis with no explanation."

"I was young, afraid, and I was going to go home. But then I didn't."

After they'd gotten doughnuts and coffee, he said, "I've been thinking about going where I can be even more unnoticeable."

Jasmine added cream to her coffee and sipped. She had been beautiful, in her way, and still was, even though time and events had worked their way with her. Hers was an indestructible kind of beauty. The crow's feet, the mottled complexion, the crazy hairdo that was all curls. It was as if wear could change her, but she was impervious to time.

"What city would we go to?" she asked.

"Where we'd be least likely to go. St. Louis."

58

St. Louis, the present

Now here they were, back near the banks of the Mississippi and its muddy secrets. Jordan had a friend in St. Louis, name of Christopher, who would lend them a vacant apartment he often subleased while he was away on business trips in Mexico. There would be no paperwork. The rent money had to be fast and up front, and beyond the attention of the IRS.

Jordan didn't ask Christopher what kind of business he tended to in Mexico. And Christopher didn't ask Jordan why he wanted to keep a low profile in St. Louis. Jasmine didn't ask where the money came from. Or how.

If pressed hard enough, she would have to guess it involved gunrunning. Or perhaps people smuggling. There were a fair number of illegals in and around the city, and trafficking in them was said to be wildly profitable. She deliberately didn't think too much about it.

Everyone profited by not knowing too much.

Jasmine and Jordan had finally stopped running, in

body and spirit, the first time since they'd originally arrived in St. Louis.

The landlord Christopher, from whom they'd subleased the condo unit, was short but hefty in a muscular way, built like an offensive lineman. He had a nervous air about him. Jordan and Jasmine were sure he was wanted by the police. That would explain why he was so eager to leave St. Louis.

Four days after Jordan introduced Christopher to Jasmine, Christopher left for Mexico.

He didn't say where in Mexico.

"Can we trust him?" Jasmine asked. After living on the streets in New York, the St. Louis apartment, which was actually barely adequate, seemed luxurious to her. And it was their sanctuary.

"We won't stay here any longer than we have to," Jordan said.

"How long are we going to have to be on the run?"

"For the foreseeable future."

Jasmine lowered her head, said, "God!"

Jordan looked at her and smiled. "We can survive anywhere, and for as long as it takes."

As long as what takes? Jasmine wondered.

Jordan paced to the window of the small living room and looked out toward the neighborhood beyond Grand Avenue. So many cities took on another identity at night. Outlined and punctuated by lights.

He felt the throbbing, heard the thrashing noise, growing louder, and massaged his temples with his fingertips.

Jordan actually didn't mind staying here for a while. Now and then he would buy a Southwest Airlines ticket and fly to New York to check the condo he had on the Upper West Side. He wasn't prepared to share that information yet with Jasmine. He was reasonably sure she was loyal and dependable, but that person might be the old Jasmine. People changed. To know that, you had only to look at the haggard and worn Jasmine and compare her with her younger self.

He smiled thinly. Did we all finally have to live in the clothes that we disdained, with the faces we deserved?

They might have left St. Louis for the larger, more anonymous city of New York. But they felt safe there, and a Midwest apartment was a hell of a lot better than the New York streets. That was where he would be, along with Jasmine, because he didn't like the thought of her knowing about the New York apartment.

Stay, do nothing noticeable, and keep a low profile. Let time wash some more of the past away. That was Jordan's plan. He couldn't figure out Jasmine's plan, but was sure she had one. The longer she lived in St. Louis, the safer she seemed to feel, and that scared Jordan. She would follow his lead for a while, but not forever. How could he totally trust her?

Totally.

Life for Jordan and Jasmine flowed easily enough for a while in St. Louis. They really did feel separate from the rest of humanity. Detached and reasonably safe in their isolation.

They seldom went out, but each morning Jasmine

would walk to a corner bakery and get two toasted bagels and two coffees to go. No one paid any attention to her. She was simply another creature of the city, scraping to get by like others in a lower-middle-class neighborhood in a lousy economy.

So, too, seemed Jordan, but in two neighborhoods half a continent from each other. He didn't have to explain to Jasmine that he had another apartment in another city, or where he got his money. She didn't know he was moderately wealthy, and didn't need to know. She only now and then brought up the past, as she had this morning when they were seated at the small kitchen table having their breakfast. She had learned early that they both ate lightly for breakfast, and shared a liking for bagels and orange juice with coffee.

She also knew that this man she was living with killed. And he knew that she knew. That she also had killed.

They pretended otherwise.

The reason why was, to Jordan, irrelevant, though not all that hard to understand. If these kinds of very private arrangements didn't take place, a functioning modern society wouldn't be possible.

One thing Jordan couldn't get Jasmine to do was to stop collecting news items from Web sites and newspapers. What bothered Jordan was that the items she seemed to be saving were mostly about the Gremlin.

Days passed, Jasmine shed some of her street-person habits and mannerisms, and regained some of her belief in herself. She looked people in the eye now, and carried herself differently, with a straighter back and a bolder stride.

While Jordan had come to trust and admire her

more and more, he still didn't trust Jasmine enough to reveal how he'd nurtured a sub-rosa stock portfolio, though he was aware that she knew he was the Gremlin. He always established an escape hatch in life. He could, if need be, disappear quickly and without a trace. From time to time, he did.

Once Jasmine had found a playbill from a Broadway theater in his suit coat pocket. Another time, a receipt from a New York restaurant.

All right, Jasmine thought. We can still lead our private lives. Better that right now, Jordan was leading some of his in New York and not in St. Louis.

What Jordan did that sometimes irked Jasmine was to bring home gifts that she considered to be mostly junk. It was never a surprise to get up early, or in the middle of the night, to find some gadget, either whole or dissected for analysis, laid out on the kitchen table.

The man simply loved gadgets, and delighted in disassembling them so he could better understand them. It was a sort of obsessive-compulsive behavior, Jasmine knew, and not the only obsession he had. That was okay with Jasmine. She understood and could accept addictions.

At times, these gadgets, or renderings of them, would appear in the media along with explanations or further description. Everyone seemed to know who was responsible. What was obviously the work of the Gremlin dominated the news and the online speculation at the fringes of news. Jasmine was saving just about everything in print. Sometimes photographs or video. Crime in the time of tech.

Jasmine clipped most of the horrific news items describing how a riverboat had sunk with six of its passengers. It was thought at first that the boat had struck some flotsam. Later it was learned that the stern near the paddle wheels had been damaged by a small, homemade underwater mine.

Jordan knew that at a certain point, he would destroy this potentially incriminating information.

As for Jasmine, as much as she trusted Jordan, which was more than she could trust anyone else, it was getting to be not enough.

59

New York, the present

The Mary Contrary line of clothing was taking off. If sales figures continued to climb at their present rate, it would make Lola Bend independently wealthy.

That word, *independently,* was important to her. It was one of the reasons she used her maiden name in the world of fashion. It also meant that at times there were people who referred to her style of clothing as the Lola Bend line. She tried to stamp this usage out with the determination and grim enthusiasm of a gardener stamping out weeds.

It was this new line that was selling like crazy. Anything with Mary Contrary on it seemed to be flying off the shelves and transforming itself to profit.

Lola was getting rich.

She herself was rather plump to be wearing Mary Contrary, especially the new luxury line, Effin' Right! It hadn't sold well at first. A long, raked hemline and a pinch at the waist had done the trick. Now it was selling so well that Lola took a giant step she would have only dreamed of six months ago.

Lola and her husband, Roland, had discussed buying a Manhattan condo so she could be close to her work—what he called "her venture." Lola had bought the expensive unit with a down payment of fifty percent. Had agreed to, anyway. Not only that, it was fully furnished. Lola wasn't crazy about the antique French provincial in the largest bedroom, but the hell with that. She could change things over time, eventually make the condo hers. That, in fact, would be the most enjoyable part of this transaction.

She had an appointment now to meet with the real estate broker and make arrangements so the only thing left to do was for Roland to sign on the dotted line. She knew Roland well enough to be sure he would do that.

She hoped.

After a long lunch, Lola took a short cab ride across town, back to the Whitworth Arms. A uniformed doorman opened the cab's door for her. Lola gave the driver a backhanded wave rather than accept change for the twenty-dollar bill she gave him, thanked the doorman, and entered the lobby.

It was as sumptuous as she remembered it. Acres of red-grained marble, rich brown leather furniture, and two elevators. A chandelier straight out of *Phantom of the Opera* graced a vaulted ceiling.

The doorman had followed her in and gone behind a marble counter. Lola stopped gawking and walked over to him.

"I'm here to meet Charles Langley in 303," she said.

The name, which had been on the business card Lola had taken from the coffee shop bulletin board, seemed familiar to the doorman. "Third floor." He motioned toward the elevators.

Lola thanked him and could feel him watching her as she walked toward the elevators. She gave a little hip switch but didn't glance back, thinking, Soon you'll be working for me, pal. As long as the condo board okays Roland and me as unit owners. Lola didn't have the slightest doubt about their approval. She thought about the latest sales figures on the Effin' Right! Line. This was one of those times when it was okay to be rich. Plenty of designers would love trading places with her.

The elevator made not a sound and seemed to take about three seconds to rise three floors. The door slid open silently.

Her footfalls in her high-heeled shoes were as hushed as the rest of the building. Was she dreaming? Floating?

The doorman must have called up to Langley, because the real estate agent was standing waiting for her with the door to 303 open. He was a small man in a well-tailored gray suit. His hair was long and combed down in back, puffed up in spikes on top. Despite his diminutive stature, the hairdo didn't make him look feminine.

He beamed. "Lola!" Like an old friend greeting her after a long absence.

She smiled back at him. "Were you afraid I wasn't coming?"

"I never for a second doubted it. Such a bargain this is!"

She felt somewhat ashamed because she didn't actually know if the condo was a bargain. It must be cheap, if its address was scribbled on a business card pinned to a coffee shop bulletin board, with no price, no photograph. And it was being sold by an independent broker.

But it was precisely, give or take a few blocks, where Lola wanted to live, so she took down the card and called the number.

The sales agent, a man named Charles Langley, picked up after five rings. Lola had heard that they did that, letting the dream dangle enticingly. Still, she felt great relief when he identified himself. She still had her choices. It created the illusion of being in charge.

Langley had the knack of speaking in a way that made interruption almost impossible. He knew she would love the condo, and she would understand the factors that made it such a bargain. The couple who owned it were locked in a nasty divorce and wanted to return to England, where they'd lived previously. The husband could retain his employment in London only if he could report there by a certain date. Time was growing short, and any buyer had to accept that and use it as an advantage. Right now, the owners wanted to get rid of the place, furniture and all, and had priced it so they could stop thinking about it and walk away without looking back on it or anything else American.

"But they will take American dollars," Lola said.

"Or anything that converts." Langley smiled again, a kind of devilish, inclusive grin. "If you want to look around again, that's okay. I have some paperwork for you to sign—nothing final, but it will lock up this place for you."

Lola pretended to think hard. "We could still back out of the deal?"

"Sure. But you won't want to." He glanced around. "Heck, you could probably sell this place for a big profit even if you didn't want to live in it. Or lease it." He shrugged. "You can't lose."

"I could probably figure a way," Lola said. "But I'll sign. I just want to see the expression on my husband's face."

"Me, too," Langley said, and laughed.

He reached down and got a large brown leather briefcase from where she hadn't seen it alongside a chair. He opened the briefcase and paused. "Oh, before you do sign, there's something you should see in the main bedroom."

He strode toward the hall and she fell in behind him. As they passed the open door to the kitchen, she noticed something silver and black on the countertop. It looked familiar but she couldn't quite place it. Some kind of gadget.

Then they were past it.

When they reached the bedroom door, Langley stepped aside so she could enter first.

"If you'll concentrate and look up near that light fixture . . ." he said, pointing.

60

Eddie Amos, the doorman at the Whitworth Arms, was conflicted. He'd accepted five hundred dollars to let this friend of the real estate agent, Langley, into the unoccupied condo so he could make a deal. If the friend did land a temporary tenant and make a deal, Eddie had another payment, of a thousand dollars, coming. He knew that if he revealed that arrangement he would lose his job, not to mention the thousand-dollar cut. After all, he wasn't in real estate, he was a doorman.

What got to Eddie the most was that Lola Bend turned out to be a hotshot designer, on the verge of becoming very, very rich.

Now she was very dead.

And now there was the package. It was small, wrapped in brown paper, with Eddie's name printed on it in black felt-tip ink. He'd come in from hailing a cab for one of the tenants and found the small, square package on the marble desk where the building's log was kept, with a record of every visitor coming and going at the Whitworth.

So far, Eddie hadn't opened the package, knowing that if he did so before talking to the police, he'd be a coconspirator in a murder. If they didn't already think of him that way.

But then there was the key to the condo. How reliable was Eddie's story that the condo's real owners were in England? The police would wonder soon how the killer got into the condo unit without a key. Or with a key. How many people knew that Eddie had a master key that fit all the units?

That was something else Eddie needed to think on. Sooner or later the police were going to find out about the master key anyway, so would his best move be to hand the key to them and explain what it was? Eddie knew they'd find the key anyway, so why not play it like a card first?

He slid the package down into the shadows of the marble pedestal where the black leather logbook lay. Unless someone for some reason reached way in there and felt around, the package would be safe. It also took the pressure off Eddie. He could think more clearly and calmly about his position. He could always tell the police he'd known nothing about the package, if they happened to find it. Or, if he decided to come clean, he could tell them about Langley and then pretend that he'd just found the package.

Almost certainly, Langley had left the package.

Eddie wasn't sure about all the details yet, but he knew what he had to do.

When finally the police were finished talking to him they would cut him loose.

Loose but not free.

61

The corpse of Lola Bend yielded information but no surprises. She lay on the bed, where apparently she had been dragged after being left to bleed out in the bathtub. The tub itself, and the bathroom, were fairly clean, considering. The killer had dissected the victim, mostly drained of blood, on the bed. She had the now familiar puppetlike look, her torso, head, and limbs laid out in their anatomically correct positions.

"It almost looks like there was a medical seminar here," Nift the ME said. He broke into song, providing his own lyrics: "Oh, this bone's connected to that bone . . ."

If the bastard broke into a dance, Pearl was going to slug him.

Out of deference to the CSU techs, who should show up any minute, no one had touched anything,

"Got a time of death?" Quinn asked Nift.

Nift rubbed his chin. "About ten thirty, but I can be more precise when we talk later." He looked down at the victim. "Some of the injuries are ante mortem." He smacked his lips. "He tortured her, probably for a long time, before letting her die. Maybe hours."

"So what's the mess on the sink counter?" Renz asked. Quinn followed him into the kitchen. Pearl and Fedderman stayed in the bedroom with Nift and what was left of Lola Bend. Neither of them trusted Nift to be alone with the dead body. Not that it made any difference. He'd shortly be alone with Lola Bend in the morgue, and doing intimate things to her, if the rumors about Nift and his dead women were by all accounts accurate.

Pearl waited so she'd be among the last to leave the apartment. She could swear that Nift had leaned down and whispered something to the corpse. It sounded like, "We'll never have Paris . . ."

"Place looks brand new but lived in," Quinn said.

"It's fully equipped and furnished, according to the brochure," Pearl said. "If you're wealthy enough to afford it, you shouldn't have to go to the trouble of picking out wallpaper."

Fedderman said, "The rich they are a funny race."

Quinn, Renz, and the others were standing in the kitchen, staring at the various Bakelite and metal parts scattered on the countertop.

"Looks like he disassembled a Monsieur Café," Pearl said, "and couldn't put it back together."

"Sounds like our man," Fedderman said.

Quinn said, "I can see why he couldn't get it back together. It looks like it's manufactured so no one can. But what is it?"

Pearl picked up some of the parts and sniffed at them.

"It's a very expensive gourmet coffee brewer," she said. "It presses the beans."

"Why?" Quinn asked.

Pearl shrugged. "Flavor." She knew Quinn's favorite cup of coffee was hot, with cream, and in near proximity to pastry.

"Presses the beans," Fedderman said slowly and thoughtfully, mulling it over. "Maybe we should test what's left of that coffee brewer to see if anything other than coffee was pressed in it."

62

Eddie the doorman waited until the time was right. He'd made a study of the building's security cameras and knew how to move among them keeping to the blind spots. He stood just so, for only a few seconds, but with his back to the camera that was slowly sweeping across the lobby where the marble podium with the visitor log sat. He stood at the podium and appeared to be checking the logbook. Then, when seconds counted and the slowly rotating camera was turned away, he removed the small, wrapped package he'd stowed in the shadowed space beneath the writing surface.

With smooth, casual motion, he kept the package between himself and the podium as he slid the little rectangular, wrapped box into a side pocket of his uniform jacket.

Squared away again behind the podium, he pretended to scan the logbook idly, sure that within a few seconds he would again be on camera.

An hour later Robert, one of the building's two other doormen, came on duty and relieved Eddie.

Robert was in his mid-thirties, classically handsome

and as well groomed as a film star. He made his rather plain uniform, exactly like Eddie's, look like a spit-and-polish general's outfit, complete with epaulets. Though he'd never served anything anywhere, other than restaurant food for a brief stretch, his bearing was military. It was a shame he'd missed the British Empire.

He gave Eddie an appropriate little half salute. "So whadda we got, some excitement here today?" He didn't talk like a general.

"Woman dead up on the third floor," Eddie said.

Robert held the street door open for a guy in a wrinkled suit who sure looked like a cop. "The fox that plays her television too loud?" he asked, when the cop was out of earshot.

"No. This one hadn't closed the deal yet. Too bad. She was kind of a looker. And the sort who flaunted it."

"You seem to know a lot about her, considering she hadn't even moved in here."

Eddie shrugged. "I see them come, I see them go. She looked good from either direction."

"So what happened?" Robert asked. "She have a heart attack brought on by sexual arousal?"

"Somebody killed her. What I hear, he played with her for quite a while, then he finally killed her."

"Holy Christ! They know who shot her?"

"She wasn't shot. The Gremlin got her."

Robert didn't seem surprised. "You, uh, see what was left of her?"

"Yeah. I don't want to look again."

"Not much bothers me. I seen some shit in Afghanistan. You mind hanging around a few minutes while I take a look?"

"Treat yourself," Eddie said again. "Just don't ask me to join you."

"Back in a jiff," the general said, and stormed away toward the elevators.

Eddie waited until Robert returned from upstairs. Robert's face was ashen, and he looked like he might have to vomit. Eddie thought about asking him when he'd served in Afghanistan, then thought better of it.

Eddie gave a quasi-military salute as he left the building, and wasn't surprised when Robert saluted back.

Eddie followed company rules and didn't wear his red jacket with its decorative brass nameplate when he was away from work. They didn't want him looking like a commoner dressed up for some kind of TV commercial. He carried the neatly folded jacket over his right arm, careful to keep the wrapped package where it couldn't be seen and wouldn't fall out.

The subway surprised him and wasn't crowded. He sat near one of the doors, the jacket folded in his lap, his hand resting on it so he could feel the tiny package inside.

63

Eddie's wife, Kellie, watched Eddie hang up his red uniform jacket and brush it off. He was always careful to hang it neatly in the closet when he was finished with work for the day.

After brushing the jacket, he used a sticky roller to go over it and lift off any dust or hair or dandruff that might have collected during his shift. Satisfied, he started to walk into the living room, when he remembered the package. He got it from his jacket pocket, sighed, and went into the living room.

Kellie went into the kitchen. "Want a beer?" she called.

Eddie called back that he did and carried the package to the secretary desk, where unpaid bills were stacked in chronological order. He sat down at the desk and dropped the writing surface.

Kellie came in from the kitchen, carrying two bottles of Heineken. She placed one of the bottles on the desk, on a square cork coaster advertising Guinness stout. Held the other bottle by its neck.

"A cop left here a little while ago," she said.

Eddie wasn't surprised. "Figures," he said. "Some woman in an upper floor got herself badly hurt today."

"Killed, is what the cop said. He was a big guy, tough-looking in a nice way, if you know what I mean."

Eddie didn't.

He looked seriously at her, but calmly. Letting her know that, just in case, he, the alpha male, had everything under control. "Accidental?"

"From what I heard, it's murder," Kellie said. "I guess that's why they'll want to talk to us, you working there and all. He left his card."

"Thoughtful of him," Eddie said.

Seated at the desk, he quickly began filing those news articles he wouldn't want Kellie or a few other people seeing. When Kellie finally understood what was going on, she was certain to be all for it. It was time for a fresh adventure. Even if she didn't yet realize it, she was about to have a brush with good fortune.

When Eddie was done with his filing, he went to his wallet and removed the half dozen or so business cards he'd collected during the day. After placing them in a drawer with others, he cleared the desktop and slowly began unwrapping the package. Kellie stood up from the chair she'd been sitting in and wandered over to look over his shoulder.

The package contained a small music box that looked like an antique. On its porcelain top was the painted figure of a beautiful woman in a white gown, seated on the lap of a prosperous-looking Edwardian gentleman with a long beard.

There was a small key taped to the bottom of the music box. Eddie found the edge of the cellophane tape and turned it back with his thumbnail. He sat with the key in one hand, the miniature music box in the other.

His wife Kellie hadn't moved. She remained staring curiously at the music box. It looked genuinely old. And harmless enough. And valuable in an *Antiques Roadshow* sort of way.

"That filigree around the edges looks like real gold," she said.

"Maybe it is," Eddie said.

"Wind it," she said. "See if it still works."

Eddie didn't need much encouragement. He was the curious sort.

Kellie watched as he inserted the tarnished key in its slot in the side of the box, then gave it a few tentative turns. The box ticked and whirred, and then began playing some song she didn't recognize. The kind of simple, chime-like notes shared by most of the music boxes ever made. It was faint. Couldn't be heard unless you held it close to your ear. Even then, Eddie couldn't place the tune.

Tired of standing, Kellie took a sip of Heineken and went over and sat down on the sofa.

Eddie looked over at her and shook his head. She watched silently as he held the music box even closer to his ear, so he could try to identify the haunting and familiar tune.

It remained faint and unidentifiable.

The tune was nothing she'd associate with what happened next. The small block of Semtex concealed in the music box, and ignited by a watch battery, sent its spark to the detonator. Eddie was holding the box close to his ear so he could hear the tune when it exploded.

It wasn't a large or loud enough explosion to destroy everything in the room. Still, it was more than efficient, and narrowly targeted. Half of Eddie's head was blown away, and landed halfway across the room, in Kellie's lap.

She stood up immediately, brushing the thing onto the floor. There was no sound other than a high-pitched, constant scream, and she seemed to be moving in slow motion as she made her way to the secretary where Eddie was slumped dead and bloody. At least the ruined side of his face was turned away. Thank God for that.

She moved her right hand carefully around Eddie, not looking at him, and opened one of the secretary desk's small drawers.

With a trembling hand she delicately reached into the drawer and withdrew Quinn's card that he'd pressed into her hand before leaving.

She wondered if the screaming in her head would ever stop.

64

They were in the Q&A office—Quinn, Pearl, Fed-derman, Lido, Helen, Sal, and Harold—engaging in what had come to be known to them as a confab of the fab. Nobody knew where the terminology had come from, but everyone assumed it had started with Harold. No one regarded such a description as totally self-effacing humor. It smacked of the truth.

"He's going to kill again," Helen the profiler said. "And soon."

Quinn said, "We need to use our resources."

"You mean Jerry and his tech genius?" Helen asked.

Jerry Lido looked at her, wondering if she was being sarcastic. He decided he didn't give a shit.

"That might be part of it," Quinn said. "We need to get that refined photo of the Gremlin out to every site on the Internet where it'll be Facebooked, tweeted, and retweeted."

"And LinkedIn," Harold added.

Lido, slouched on a chair near the coffee brewer, said, "Sounds as if you don't need me."

"Just sounds that way," Quinn said. "When I hear the word *blog* I think *Hound of the Baskervilles*. And I don't know a sound bite from a mosquito bite."

"So what resource are we talking about?" Helen asked. She knew about Quinn and his resources. They scared her, though she realized that sometimes she loved the thrill they provided. "Is this resource of yours legal?"

Quinn gave her the kind of smile that should itself be declared illegal. Said, "More or less."

Great! "I am in the NYPD."

"So are we all, temporarily." He regarded her as if she might be growing another head. "You want out, Helen?"

"Depends on what this resource is and what you want to do with it."

"The news media," he said. "Specifically, Minnie Miner."

"Marvelous!" Sal growled. "Why her?"

"She's got moxie," Pearl said.

"The Marvelous Minnie Miner Media Moxie plan," Harold said.

Sal glared at him with disgust.

"Putting planning in progress," Harold said, still in the grip of alliteration.

"There's someone else involved," Quinn said. "Somebody we've trusted before."

"How did those times turn out?" Fedderman asked.

Quinn said, "She seems always to wind up in hospitals."

Helen looked at him sharply. "Likes sex, heals fast?"

"Well . . . yes."

"Nancy Weaver?"

"Jackpot."

"Every time she heals up and gets out of the hospital, she goes back to the Vice Squad," Helen said. "She belongs in the Vice Squad. Maybe on the other side."

"She enjoys getting the snot beat out of her," Fedderman said.

No one disagreed. When it came to Weaver, they simply didn't know what to think.

Helen looked around. Said to Quinn, "Everybody you're involving in this is the sort of person who would skydive without a parachute."

"That's how I got here," Nancy Weaver said.

No one had heard the street door open, but there she was, in four-inch heels and a businesslike pants suit that was a size too small for her and looked completely unbusinesslike.

She displayed no injuries.

Helen, in the complete silence, watched Weaver move all her parts as she crossed the room and sat down in one of the desk chairs. Her pose and posture were calculatingly prim. The effect looked nasty.

Helen crossed her arms and glanced around. All the maniacs were present.

All of us.

Except for the police commissioner.

Quinn smiled at her, reading her thoughts while she was reading his. "Renz doesn't want to know."

Helen knew he was right. Not that anything would prevent Renz from throwing them all under the train if it was to his advantage. As long as he held that strategic position he was fine with whatever they did.

"Okay," Quinn said. "I'll clue in Minnie Miner later."

"What if she doesn't want to play?" Helen asked. Knowing how foolish the question was even as she spoke.

"She'll play," Quinn said. "Here's the plan."

He felt the familiar thrill as he realized that at that moment no one in the room wanted to be anywhere else. Feel anything else.

Be anyone else.

Two hours later, after her show, Quinn made his pitch to Minnie Miner. As he spoke, he saw in her face what he'd seen in the faces of the others. In their eyes and in the slight forward lean of their bodies.

An acknowledgment and a readiness.

Wolves and gray wolves.

She said, "I'm in."

When Quinn got home he found a message on his answering machine.

It was Renz, informing him that the pieces of the broken coffeemaker were clean of fingerprints.

What they'd both expected.

The coffee-bean press was only a coffee-bean press.

65

They were by the river, just north of downtown St. Louis, in the commercial part of the city. The doors of the empty shipping container opened out and were cracked just enough to let a breeze in. Jordan wished it had been luck instead of a breeze.

Things had gone wrong for Jordan and Jasmine. Jordan had been turned down for half a dozen jobs. Most places simply weren't hiring, or at least told him that. The last place he'd applied, unloading cargo from one of the many barges that moved up and down the river, had resulted in a fight with the man who would have been Jordan's boss.

He was a large man whose face was like a map of madness. Yet he succumbed early and turned away from Jordan after a brief exchange of punches. There was something about the boy's eyes. The man had seen eyes like that in a winded fox that had been cornered by half a dozen hounds and knew it was going to die. It had fought even harder, and almost survived. It wasn't going to give up—ever. That in itself could be a force.

"You're the only man I know," Jasmine told Jordan, "who can lose a job and a tooth in the same day."

"Least it's a molar," he said, flashing his handsome smile.

"But you can't chew your steak," Jasmine said.

Jordan spat off to the side. "I don't anticipate that's gonna be a problem."

"We can go to that diner up on South Broadway." For the first time, she noticed that the knuckles on his right hand were reddened and cut. The hand was slightly swollen.

"We get done eating," he said, "and we're gonna experience an issue."

"Issue?"

"They're gonna be unreasonable at the diner and want money from us after we eat. You know how they are. They'll see it as some kinda trade."

"They'll just have to learn to share," Jasmine said.

"Share?"

She smiled. "Somebody say something about sharing?"

Jordan felt something shift in the core of him. Where his heart maybe should be. The thought amused him.

Jordan remembered telling Jasmine that if two people knew a secret, it was no longer a secret. That had seemed wise then. It seemed wise now.

Even if they trusted each other totally now, and felt they would share that trust forever, they both knew a day might come—would surely come—when things would change. If they delayed long enough, the secret that was murder would become again a real secret.

Jordan knew it, and was sure that when the time came, he would act in his own best interest.

Jasmine also knew this, and had contemplated killing Jordan first. Then she'd become resigned.

She decided that if Jordan didn't want her enough to let her live, she wanted to die.

Love? she wondered.

Actually, she thought, there was no titanic struggle raging in her breast. It was really kind of obvious and simple. She and Jordan were like two shipwrecked people in the middle of an ocean, starving in a lifeboat. Neither spoke what each knew the other was thinking. Eventually, one could only survive by eating the other.

66

Jordan had this persistent notion that the police were gaining on him. He had plenty of net worth, and stolen credit and debit cards that were too hot to use. He knew the police could quickly trace that kind of plastic, so he stayed with the rapidly diminishing cash that he kept hidden in a money belt.

Only now the ready cash had about run out, and the dangerous cards beckoned more and more to him. There seemed to be only one thing to do—or rather several things. They all had to result in the acquisition of money.

Jordan noticed what seemed to be a young college guy walking toward him. He changed course slightly and approached the boy, making note of his expensive-looking sweater tied by the arms around his neck. Mr. Preppy. A closer look took in deliberately worn-out jeans, and expensive-looking leather boots that had built-up heels that made the kid appear taller.

They were pretty much alone, in a place not far from where the Eads Bridge crossed into Illinois. Across the Mississippi the grim outline of East St. Louis was sharp against the cloudless sky. Down here on the levee the sun seemed to burn with an extra brightness, casting sharper shadows. River traffic seemed not to move until you looked away and then back at it and realized the scene changed slightly. It made Jordan wish, in some part of him, that he was a French impressionist painter, wise to the ways of light and shadow.

A man and woman walked close together and stopped now and then to kiss. They were the only other people in sight. Jordan waited until they disappeared into what looked like some kind of parking structure.

A car emerged five minutes later. It was a dented convertible with the top up, and was in no way a rental. The woman was driving and was alone. She was in a hurry and didn't look anywhere except straight ahead. She didn't apply the brakes as she pulled out onto the road.

Almost immediately, the preppy-looking guy reappeared and walked along the levee, seemingly enjoying the lingering morning and the nearby rush of muddy water.

Jordan approached Mr. Preppy, keeping his hands in his pockets so he'd seem more casual than dangerous. Noting that the boy appeared scared, he smiled with false assurance and said, "You look like a fella who'd give a desperate man a small loan."

Now the kid did look afraid. His eyes darted around, seeking company or some sort of help.

But there was no one.

He tried a smile and a head shake. "Sorry, I don't have a cent on me." He stepped to the side and walked around Jordan.

Jordan moved to block him and took his hands out of his pockets.

At first he thought the kid was going to turn and run. Jordan didn't want that. In fact, he decided that if the boy did break and run, he, Jordan, would run the opposite direction.

Instead of running, the boy sighed and said, "All I've got on me is ten dollars." He pulled his brown leather wallet out of a hip pocket and flipped it open, showing Jordan that it was empty except for a single ten-dollar bill. Jordan held out a hand and was given the bill. It seemed so easy, he thought he should do more of this. "Give me the entire wallet," he said. "I'll give it back. I just want to make sure there are no secret pockets."

Decision time. The kid looked as if he might bolt, but instead complied.

Thumbing through the wallet, Jordan found no more money.

He discovered nothing more of value. The usual junk. A driver's license revealed that the kid was Samuel Pace, and he was nineteen years old. The clothes . . . the cheap wallet . . . Sam didn't figure to be the scion of a wealthy family.

On the other hand, the trendy clothes suggested the family probably wasn't poor.

A plastic charge card didn't interest Jordan; he knew that once reported stolen it would be a trap. There was another card in the wallet. Two cards, actually, in a little envelope that had the name of a hotel and a room

number on it. Inside the envelope were two key cards
for the nearby Adam Park hotel, room 333. There was a
photo in the wallet, too, pressed in plastic—an attractive young blond girl seated in a wooden swing and
smiling. "This your girlfriend?" Jordan asked. Pocket-
ing one of the hotel key cards. Probably the kid would
think he misplaced it, or that he was given only one key
card when he checked in.

"She is my girlfriend."

"She here with you?"

"No. Yes. Coming in tomorrow."

An obvious lie.

"I bet her name is Cherry," Jordan said.

Samuel Pace looked slightly confused, not knowing
if Jordan had just insulted his girlfriend. "Her name is
Eleanor," he said.

A tugboat chugged upriver, its air horn blasting a
low, mournful note. Samuel Pace glanced at it with brief
hope in his eyes. No one was on the boat's deck. No
one to look back at him.

Jordan said, "What size shoe do you wear?

Samuel blinked at him. "'Bout an eleven."

Jordan shook his head in disappointment. The boots
were too large for his feet, even if he stuffed something
in the toes.

"I ain't got any money in my boots," Samuel said,
getting the wrong idea.

Jordan smiled. "I'm gonna believe you." He knew
that he could, or Samuel wouldn't have brought up the
subject.

He handed the wallet back to the boy, keeping only
the ten-dollar bill and the photograph, which he slid
into his shirt pocket. He didn't count the hotel key card

as loot; plucking it out of its tiny envelope when the kid's head was turned had been almost automatic. It was one of Jordan's cardinal rules, not passing up a chance to use somebody else's charge or key card.

"I know where you live," Jordan said. "And I can find out about Eleanor. Neither of you know where I live."

He took a careful up-and-down look at Samuel. He was skinny, but also tall. Probably close to six feet. Nothing he was wearing would fit Jordan. Everything would drape on him, making him look even smaller than he was. Lost in his clothes, as his mother used to tell him. His late mother. His father hadn't minded his diminutive stature. It made Jordan easier to control.

"You seem not to believe I think of that ten dollars as a loan," Jordan said.

Samuel stared at him, still afraid, but curious.

"You be here this time tomorrow and I'll pay you back, with interest," Jordan lied. "You believe me?"

"If you want me to."

Jordan smiled. "I'm not sure I know exactly what that means, but yeah, I want you to. I told you it was a loan. I don't lie."

Samuel was in no position to contradict Jordan. He simply stood with a stupid half grin on his face.

Jordan stuck out his right hand. "I'll bring the photograph, too. The one of Eleanor."

Samuel thanked him because he couldn't think to say or do anything else.

"See you tomorrow," Jordan said. He shook Samuel's sweaty, trembling hand with its slender fingers.

As an afterthought he added, "I know a famous glamour photographer who'd love to shoot Eleanor. Maybe I'll bring her, too. He might wanna shoot both of you."

Thinking, always leave them confused.

Jordan had noted on the Missouri driver's license that Samuel's address was here in the city, though he was staying at a hotel. He was most likely here for an assignation with Eleanor. One that he didn't want anyone else to know about.

Or tell anyone else about.

Samuel was smart to be so suspicious, Jordan thought.

He walked off in the direction of Jasmine.

Later that day

Lying in the cool air-conditioning with his eyes closed, Jordan thought about his master plan. The plan that would play out as tragedy so vast it would be pondered and admired for generations.

The witnessing of what the famous architect and engineer Ethan Ellis had done to a ten-year-old boy ensured Ellis's cooperation and his silence. He had understood immediately what Jordan wanted.

And why, like Jordan, he had long ago made his choice of evils, and it had enveloped him like a shroud.

PART FOUR

A righteous man regardeth the life of
 his beast;
but the tender mercies of the wicked
 are cruel.

—PROVERBS 12:10

67

New York, the present

Minnie Miner was not so much amenable as eager to be part of the plan. Quinn decided Helen the profiler would be best for the opening gambit, the softening up. Helen was skilled at turning unease into fear, fear into horror, horror into mindless panic.

"My vote for someone to explain these gruesome murders goes to a woman who knows all about the people who might perpetrate them," Minnie said with all sincerity to camera 2's red light. "I give you police profiler, psychologist, and author Helen Iman."

Helen, all six feet plus of her, strolled out onto the set. Despite Helen's towering height advantage, Minnie matched her presence with pure energy. Fireball meets lackadaisical.

Applause was enthusiastic. Minnie made a welcoming motion with her right arm, and Helen sat down in one of the wing chairs angled at forty-five degrees so they both faced the low coffee table. She was wearing a red dress with a low neckline, and a high hemline that showed off her almost impossibly long legs.

Minnie sat in the other chair, on the very edge of the seat cushion, and smiled while the audience applauded. She waited, waited . . .

When the applause began to flag, she heaped more praise on Helen: "This woman has a sixth sense when it comes to getting inside the heads of the bad guys." Minnie laughed. "And she knows a lot more than anyone else I know about weaponry, villains, law enforcement, and serial killers." She turned her attention away from the audience and faced Helen. "And one interesting thing I've heard you say in the past, Helen, is that such killers are like ticking time bombs. At a certain point they very much want to get caught and stopped. That happens when their murders make it begin to seem like they're the ones dying a little at a time with each death they cause, each life they stop. Killing does that to the murderer, male or female."

Helen looked beyond Minnie and spoke to the studio audience.

"Have you ever eaten something you thought was delicious, knowing it wasn't good for you?"

She pretended to count members of the audience, observing the various heads nodding yes, yes, they knew the satisfaction of stuffing food into their mouths to the point of gluttony. And Helen knew it. They had that in common, being human beings. But Minnie wasn't any kind of criminal. So how could she know the cost of disregarding the lengthening shadows? The ticking bomb? Her background surely precluded that.

"Helen?"

Minnie was looking at her expectantly.

"Sorry," Helen said. "We push the food away. We've had enough. We can eat no more. Finally, it is time to stop."

The audience applauded at the pause, without a cue. They liked this woman. Minnie decided to let it roll.

"Usually one person can understand another only up to a certain point," Helen said. "Going beyond that point is what I do. That is what I've done. It's my job, and it's my calling.

"The Gremlin," she continued, "is not a good person. Not in any way heroic or iconic. He has a curious mind. That we know. And he is sick. He might be clever. He might be deadly. He might be three moves ahead of his pursuers. But he is also sick. He can't stop his increasing use of the knife. He can't stop torturing before killing. He can't help reverse engineering every interesting device he comes upon. He can't help this; he can't resist that; he can't reverse this; he can't change that. He is not the skilled genius who always must know more. He is simply a simple man with a simple problem. The solution is also simple. He wants to be caught now. Finally. Even more than he wants to kill. He wants to be locked up for life or die by needle. But not just that. He wants to chose the time and place of his death. He wants to be an observer as well as a participant. He needs to stop. On the other hand, he needs to continue.

"He needs to know how death works."

68

"I heard most of the conversation," Pearl said, when Quinn and Weaver had broken their connection. They'd recorded most of the Helen/Minnie conversation on their cell phones.

Quinn laid his phone on a bookcase. Most of the best mystery writers' books were there. Tricky folks, those. Had they influenced him? He hadn't mentioned to Pearl that she would be the primary target in Quinn's plan. The bait. She was the one in the killer's sights, whatever the condition of Weaver. Had been his ultimate target almost from the time of his arrival in the city.

It was Helen's opinion that Pearl was the most important piece on the killer's imaginary game board, the queen that had to fall.

That Weaver ostensibly was the ideal bait also made her the ideal diversion.

Pearl was what the killer had to claim to complete the mad symmetry of his purpose in life. And in death.

"You don't have to do it," Quinn repeated to Pearl.

She smiled. "I want to do it. I want to stop this bastard just as much as you do."

"Why?"

"You know why. The reasons that sound corny if you say them out loud."

"The lady in the harbor?"

"I don't want to get all metaphysical before I brush my teeth," Pearl said.

Quinn poured a cup of coffee, then sat down at the kitchen table. He sipped as he stared out the window at a ledge of the building next door. A small pigeon kept landing there, which seemed to drive the other pigeons nuts, because they would flap around and coo and fly at the intruder. As Quinn watched the avian combat, it occurred to him that he had never before seen a tiny, half-grown pigeon. He wondered if for some reason there weren't any, or if he simply hadn't been looking. Were they the victims of hawks? He knew there were hawks in Manhattan. Their presence had been called to his attention, and he had seen them.

Quinn wondered what else in life he simply hadn't noticed. He had so far seen a certain kind of life a great deal, but there was more, much more.

There had to be.

Quinn drove to Faith Recovery and parked the Lincoln on the street.

The amazing imaginary woman who'd been in a car accident and lost her memory was on his mind, haunting his thoughts. He almost believed it himself, that he and she were going to enter a maniac's mind and de-

stroy him. All or most of the plan had been hatched by
Helen the profiler, in partnership with a former cop
who'd learned psychology on the streets.

Their plan—their trap—should work, and perhaps it
might even evolve into something that surely would
work.

Quinn and Helen hadn't simply been burning up
calories when they jogged twice daily around the block.
Helen moderated her pace, and with Quinn had memo-
rized their surroundings, the layout of Faith Recovery
Center's reception area, the location of the elevators,
the entrances and exits, including the ones only for staff,
the fire escapes, numeric sequences of the rooms, radiology, cardiac, and operating areas.

The place was a large enough facility to have a park-
like area behind it, as well as a small gift shop and cafe-
teria.

Quinn glanced at his watch and saw that it was almost
seven p.m. Time to go to the room adjoining Weaver's,
through an open, wide door designed to admit gurneys
and wheelchairs.

Weaver was good at her job. She actually appeared
injured and drugged. She was convincing as a woman
who'd died and come back. The power of suggestion.

Can you do that? Ethan Ellis wondered, putting
down the *Times*. Actually return from the dead?

Not long ago he would never have asked himself
that question. But maybe he should have. Now the bit-
ter pill he could never swallow was the truth. There
were no second chances. And even if there were, he

knew in his heart he wouldn't have taken the smarter and more honorable road.

He knew he had to pull himself together. His wife, Cynthia, and his son, Jeremy, would wonder where he was.

Ethan was in the lobby of the recently rebuilt AA AAL building, financed by oil money and the tax-payers. He was the creative genius who'd figured out the best way to add marble and stone and glass and at the same time make the building almost twice as tall as its original thirty stories. Already the building was sixty percent rented. Now he was to accept his second Golden Architectural Award.

It was a night for celebration.

But damping high spirits was the subtle but persistent rhythmic *whack, whack, whack* that pounded through his head.

Then came the images of what Manhattan could become.

The pain.

Ellis bowed his head and sobbed.

69

Minnie Miner's voice thrummed with excitement when she called Quinn the next morning on his cell.

"It's working, Quinn! I made sure the Helen Iman interview was the hottest thing online, and that got us a lot of the print media. Not to mention even more video. CNN and Fox News are still running it on their loops. On Twitter it's—"

"Sounds good so far," Quinn interrupted. "Odds are that one place or another, the Gremlin will see it, hear it, or read it."

"According to Helen, he's bound to come in contact with it because he'll be looking for it hard. He's hooked on his own infamy. He can't stay away from watching and reading about himself, no matter how hard he tries. This is what the sicko has been working for. It's what they all want. To become legends. Their life is a story, and what's a story without a slam-bang ending?"

"Helen isn't always right."

"Yes, she is," Minnie said. "She's my hero."

"Mine, too. If this continues to work."

"Nobody said it would be easy."

"That oughta tell us something," Quinn said.

He turned off his cell phone alarm and went into the bathroom to take his shower.

Quinn was toweling off, and was going to wake up Pearl, when the landline phone rang. This ring was louder than the cell phone's alarm, and should have been loud enough to wake Pearl. He imagined her fluffing her pillow and gradually rising from sleep. He managed a gruff "'Lo . . ." as he picked up the phone.

"Quinn. It's Nancy Weaver. How come you aren't in your office?"

"I just got awakened by a phone call at my home. In my bed." *A small lie to help make his point.*

"No need to be pissed off," Weaver said. "I'm the bearer of good news. I think. Homicide called about fifteen minutes ago. There's this couple in St. Louis, Fran and Willie Clarkson, that owns and operates a brat stand."

"A what?"

"Brat stand. People in St. Louis like their bratwurst. You know, they look like hot dogs."

"The people in St. Louis?"

"I'm barely awake, Nancy. Get to the point."

At the mention of Nancy's name, Pearl sat straight up in bed. "Dammit, Quinn!"

Weaver said, "The male half of this couple, Willie Clarkson, called about something that happened in their bratwurst stand about thirteen or fourteen years ago. They saw the stories about the Gremlin and his ear and thought they'd better call." Quinn waited silently, staring at Pearl while she stared back, and listening to Weaver tell about the young couple, Pablo and May Diaz, and the episode with the knife. And the eviscerated rat.

"All this might have nothing to do with anything," Quinn said.

"I wish I could e-mail you a photo of the rat."

"Never mind that," Quinn said.

"The Clarksons cleaned up the place at the time anyway. There was nobody there to tell them otherwise, and Fran said the rat was creeping her out. There were no investigations at the time, either. But word got around. Somebody crossed out the *B* in their stand's outside menu."

"Cruel," Quinn said. "To you, me, the Clarksons, and the rat."

"Minnie Miner is spreading the word about my 'accident,'" Weaver said. Her voice was eager, without a tremor of fear. He could imagine the diamond glint in her sly eyes. Weaver was born for action. The huntress was on the scent.

"I want to go through it again," Quinn said.

"I don't want to recite it again, Quinn."

"Good. I want you to listen. The news-starved media will grab this story as if it's a hamburger. You'll be reported as being on the critical list after the auto accident. The doctors will have put you in an induced coma. They'll express amazement that you're still alive after your heart stopped beating for over five minutes. You simply came awake after you were pronounced dead and had no vital signs. There seems no reason that, when aroused from your coma, you won't return to normal."

"Gee, I feel better already."

"You'll stay in your hospital bed at Faith, supposedly making the first meager beginnings of a complete recovery. You'll be touted as a medical miracle."

"And the killer will be obsessed with finding out how I . . . work." She said this with little emotion.

"What he won't know is that you'll be watched every minute, and we can be in your room within seconds. Just in case, you'll be wearing a Kevlar bulletproof jacket beneath your hospital gown."

"I want my nine-millimeter," Weaver said, still with her calm, flat voice.

"You'll have it, but you probably won't need it."

"Such a plan we have," Weaver said.

"You should be safe. Helen is certain of one thing. The woman the killer will want more than anyone in that hospital room, and whose death will be a personal tragedy and defeat for me, is Pearl. He's chosen the time and place. Everything else will be a diversion."

"And he'll assume I'm Pearl."

"Yes. Pretending to be someone else."

"Who is also pretending to be Pearl."

"Uh-huh. He won't be sure, though. He can't be."

"Won't he notice the bulky flak jacket under my gown?" Weaver asked.

"He shouldn't, what with all the distracting plastic tubes and medical paraphernalia around you."

"At the least, he'll hesitate."

"Right. His target is the real Pearl, pretending to be someone else. He'll surely expect something like that.

Much like a marble under one of three walnut shells a huckster keeps moving around."

"What prevents the Gremlin, and not you, from being the last to incorporate a switch?"

"I know him," Quinn said. "He likes back-and-forth trickery, but not if it gets too complex "

"This is too complex?"

"I honestly don't know. Three women are involved, and one of them isn't real."

"Thank God!" Weaver said, "that not everything happening around here is real."

"Don't be too thankful," Quinn said. "Remember that the woman in Pearl's bed, beneath the black wig, all the Kevlar, and Pearl's bandages, will be you. Pretending to be Pearl pretending to be a woman who already died once."

"Pretending to be pretending," Weaver said. "Because Helen has convinced you that the Gremlin wants Pearl even more than he wants the woman who cheated death."

"She didn't exactly cheat death," Quinn said. "She only visited."

He worked the miniature keyboard on his iPhone.

"Who are you calling now?" Weaver asked.

"LaGuardia," he said. "Flight to St. Louis. Old habits die hard."

70

St. Louis, the present

Jordan knocked on the door to Samuel's riverfront hotel room.

Light shifted in the peephole. An unintelligible voice sounded from the other side of the door. Jordan moved over so Samuel could see him.

He knocked louder, so it could almost be said he was about to make a scene.

The door opened, and there was Samuel, wearing nothing but a pair of jeans. He looked worried and scared as he shut the door behind Jordan. Then he made a show about looking at his watch. Rather the white mark on his wrist where the watch would be after he got it from the nightstand in the bedroom and slipped it on.

"We were supposed to meet farther down on the riverfront, at ten o'clock. It's only nine fifteen."

"I thought this would be more private," Jordan said.

Standing there in worn loafers, sockless and shirtless, with his hair looking like it had been in a blender, Samuel made a face that was probably meant to scare Jordan, or at least gain the offensive. Some offensive. "I don't like you changing the rules as we go along," he said.

"Not to worry," Jordan said.

"Did you bring the money I lent you?"

"Of course I did."

There was another soft knock on the door.

Jordan ambled over and opened it. Behind him, Samuel Pace took a few steps and then stopped, trying to get a handle on what was happening here.

"Who's that?" he asked in a tight voice, as if someone had him by the neck but hadn't yet squeezed in earnest.

"The photographer," Jordan said. "Remember? You said you might bring your lady, Eleanor, so she could pose for some shots."

He opened the door and stepped aside. Jasmine slipped in quickly. She had a digital camera slung around her neck on a broad black strap. Jordan thought she looked old beyond her years.

She got right into the flow, looking around. "Where's Eleanor?"

A slight noise came from the direction of the bedroom. Three heads turned that way.

Tall, blond, and very young, Eleanor opened the bedroom door and stepped into the sun-drenched main room. Her long hair was tousled but in a wild way that was strangely attractive. She wore a sheet like a toga, and looked like something out of a Shakespeare madness play.

She smiled and said, "I'm Eleanor. I hear you want to photograph me."

As she talked, her gaze traveled from Samuel to Jasmine to Jordan. Her look lingered, and she appeared to want to say something about Jordan's jockey-like size, and then changed her mind.

Still she seemed amused. That didn't set well with Jordan. Neither did Eleanor's seemingly unshakeable confidence. He wanted control of this again. He said, "You're from money, right, Eleanor?"

"Money?"

"Your family."

Her smile became wider, displaying perfect white teeth. "It shows?"

"Very much so. And I'm thinking you booked the hotel and paid the way for Samuel to be here with you."

Eleanor glanced Samuel's way and flashed a reassuring smile. Surely somewhere, sometime, she had been a cheerleader.

"That's none of your business," Samuel said. Feisty, but he could no longer disguise his growing fear. There was an off-key note here that he was beginning to hear but Eleanor hadn't yet discerned.

She moved slightly toward Jordan, who smiled and said, "You ever hear of the Gremlin?"

"No. What is it?"

Jordan seemed surprised and miffed. He stared at her, noting with disgust that she was the taller of the two. "Don't you watch the news?"

"No. I don't have time for that crap. It's all lies, anyway." She stood more erectly and spread her legs so the sheet was stretched taut between her thighs and emphasized her figure. "The Gremlin . . . Didn't that used to be a car or something? Or wait a second—that building in Russia?"

"Your first guess was right," Jordan said.

"Anybody'd buy a car called a Gremlin would have to think it was guaranteed to give them trouble. They should have stayed with Jaguar or Rolls."

"You think your money can buy you out of any kind of trouble, don't you?" Jordan said.

Eleanor sneered. "Matter of fact, I do. My family has attorneys that will drain you like a sun-dried tomato. Not like your pro bono public defenders, you miserable little pissant."

Uh-oh! The discord was out in the open where everyone might hear and see it.

Samuel said, "Eleanor . . . please!" He could feel his heart hammering.

Jordan had had enough of this. Had really had enough.

He went into the bedroom and returned with a pillow. In his right hand was a small .25 caliber Ruger handgun. He wrapped the pillow around the gun, pointed it at Eleanor, and said, "By God, girl, you've got spirit." It was a line he remembered from an old movie. Or close enough, anyway.

She stiffened her spine and stared down her nose at him. "You better believe I've got spirit. Enough that—"

He squeezed the trigger.

The shot from such a small gun was muffled by the pillow and didn't make much noise, but feathers from the pillow flew.

Eleanor looked startled, then plucked one of the pillow feathers from the air, stared down at it where it was held loosely in her hand, and said, "This is real goose down. This is a good hotel."

She closed her eyes and fell.

Jordan looked over and saw Samuel standing rooted to the spot. He saw that the front and one leg of Samuel's pants were stained where he had relieved himself. Walking close, careful where he stepped so he wouldn't get a shoe wet, Jordan used the gun and pillow again, placing the bullet perfectly between Samuel's eyebrows.

It was a hell of a shot, considering the pillow tended to spoil your aim.

Jasmine was standing stunned, her mouth hanging open. Then she looked around as if coming out of a trance, saw all the goose down in the air, and began a crazy, cackling laughter, catching and releasing the feathers, repeating, "My God, it's snowing! It's snowing!"

She fixed her wild stare on Jordan. "I know what you're going to do, you bastard! It's monstrous!"

How could she know? Guessing? She must be guessing.

"Isn't it?" Jordan said.

"*Monstrous!*" she repeated.

He shot her twice just behind her left ear and she dropped straight down to her knees and sat with her legs folded back and her feet pointing in opposite directions. It was probably the way she had sat as a little girl.

Jordan glanced around, waiting for his breathing to level out. The strange thrashing, beating sound rose up around him. Like the earth was vibrating. He fought it back. Everything was under control. If he kept to his plan, things would turn out all right. He kept telling himself that. Repeating it. Believing it more each time.

Calm. That was what he could do better than anyone. Stay calm.

God, his breathing was loud!

He'd known he had to kill Jasmine. He'd had no choice. If two people held a secret it was no longer a secret. And if ever a secret called for solitary possession, it was the one he held so close. When he chose to loose it into the world, there would be storms that had nothing to do with weather, tectonic shifts that had nothing to do with earthquakes.

He slid the gun into his pocket and went into the bathroom, where he brushed and picked the snow-like goose down from his hair and clothes. Then he used a washcloth to wipe his fingerprints from the few places he'd touched.

He put on rubber gloves and went to the living room to get the backpack he'd brought with him. All the implements he'd need were in there, along with a tourist guide to New York

No one seemed to give Jordan a second look as he left the hotel and strode out into the sunshine, wearing Foster Grant sunglasses and carrying his backpack slung by a strap over his right shoulder. He had no remorse. Just as he'd had no recourse.

He'd done fine. He was sure of it. Believed it more with every step away from the carnage. Planned well enough, and executed with speed and conviction, there had been no doubt of the outcome. And when the unexpected had occurred, he'd done what was necessary.

He was safe now, and no doubt about it. Certainly safer than before. That was undeniable. Hell, it was mathematical.

Two people plus one secret equaled no secret.

Even if one of them, like Ethan Ellis, was bound tightly in the web of his past.

71

New York, the present

Pearl supposedly lay in the bed of the woman who'd only visited death. Supposedly because Quinn had invented that woman. The various plastic tubing and wires attached to her were mostly affixed by tape. The electrodes dotting her body sent no signals. At least, none that meant anything.

Nancy Weaver was in similar condition in the adjoining room. Leading to that room were folding doors that could be cast aside to allow full access and create one large room. The Gremlin would be stopped before he could pull a trigger. Probably he would be tackled and cuffed even before he could remove a gun from his belt or his ankle holster.

Probably, Quinn thought, the Gremlin would try to use a weapon with a silencer.

That was the polite thing to do, considering there was staff along with genuine patients in the recovery center. It was one of those medical facilities pretending to be hospitals yet at the same time managing a kind of

homeyness that belied the truths of illness and death.
There was a small library, a game room, a conversation
room, and a dining room for those on the meals plan.
There wasn't much conversation about the occasional
empty chair.

A lot of life, Quinn decided, was the art of pretending. That way lay a lesser madness, but a madness none-
theless.

Alone in her half of the adjoining rooms, Pearl glanced
around, fixing objects in her mind—the various equipment rolled near the bed or mounted on the wall by the
headboard, monitoring, softly beeping. The partitioned-
off part of the double room where the other bed was
concealed. There was a visitors' easy chair. Another,
smaller wooden chair, and a steel rack on wheels. Pearl
glanced toward her wristwatch lying on the metal tray
table next to her bed. There were also a green plastic
pitcher and a matching cup on the tray. Pearl felt like
taking a drink, then decided against it. She might dis-
turb some of the tubing and wires that were only
loosely fastened to her.

The idea was to trick the Gremlin into snatching
Pearl; he would suspect Quinn of replacing the once
dead, now living woman—only to find to his surprise
and delight that he had instead what he really wanted
the most. Given the not completely unexpected opportunity, he would take Pearl.

Helen had assured Quinn that the killer couldn't resist at least trying for the remarkable if fictitious life-
after-death patient, but even more he couldn't resist
choosing Pearl as his next victim.

Moving her head slightly on the hard pillow so she
could see her watch's face, Pearl noted that it was al-

most ten o'clock. It was Quinn's bet that the killer would pay his visit sometime during the night, when the center was on a looser schedule and there weren't so many doctors and patients in the halls.

Pearl knew that Bill Casey, a uniformed cop who was an old friend of Quinn's, would be getting up from his chair out in the hall by the door to her room. He would walk down to the elevators but veer into one of the small, semiprivate waiting areas—called conversation nooks—where there was coffee along with some vending machines.

Pearl was right. Carrying a half-eaten candy bar, Casey strolled to the conversation nook. He glanced around and moved a small sofa slightly, so if he sat on it he'd have a clear view down the hall. From there he could see the doors to Pearl's and the adjoining room. Fedderman was in the opposite direction on the same floor, seated in an area similar to Casey's. Harold was down in the lobby, watching the building entrance and elevators. Sal was wearing a white robe and might have been mistaken for a patient, idly walking around as if he couldn't sleep.

Quinn saw Casey drift past, peeling the wrapper off a candy bar, and guessed he would have a gruff bedside manner. Soon enough, that shouldn't matter.

They were all in touch with each other via two-ways that would work in hospitals, rehab centers, and other places with radiology and imaging equipment.

Quinn said, "Me," and entered Pearl's room from the adjacent one.

"Me, too," Pearl said.

He walked over and kissed her gently on the forehead, as if she were a real patient.

"Everything a go?" she asked.

He smiled. "We just need another player."

"Weaver all set next door?"

"She's always set," Quinn said.

"She's gotten the crap kicked out of her more than once when it could have been me instead."

"She's an adrenaline addict."

"So are we, Quinn."

He didn't argue with her.

"So is he," she added.

Quinn knew who she meant.

He bent over and kissed her cool forehead again. "Get some sleep," he said, then went into the adjacent room.

The idea was that, faced with a choice between the two women, the one the Gremlin really wanted would seem all the more genuine. If Helen was right, and unless everything she'd learned about human behavior was wrong, the killer would pass on the supposedly back-from-the-dead woman and go for Pearl.

He'd be pressed for time, and would have to make his choice quickly if he were to take a hostage and escape from the building before his presence was known and staff and police would close in.

That was when things would start happening fast.

Pearl thought, Let the games begin.

She closed her eyes, but not all the way.

72

St. Louis, the present

It was mid-afternoon when Marta Jones, a maid at the Adam Park hotel in St. Louis, opened the door to room 333 and saw a white feather drift out. She knew immediately that it was from a pillow, and it might signify that the room was a mess. It always surprised Marta how destructive some of the guests were, especially if there was liquor involved. The Adam Park wasn't cheap, and Marta thought it was people with more money than they needed who caused most of the trouble and made most of the mess.

She hoped this wouldn't be too bad as she rolled her linen cart back a few inches so she could make the turn, then pushed it past the opened door and backed into the room.

My God! The place looked as if there'd been a snowstorm inside. More goose down. So much white and red.

Red?

The snow was spotted with red here and there, and

smeared with red. As if it were real snow and someone had taken swipes at it with a paint rag.

Then Marta saw a young blond woman lying on the floor, with blood on her shoulder and chest and one side of her face. There was something awkward and not quite right about the way she was lying in the goose down. She was on her back, legs and arms akimbo. Almost as if trying to make a snow angel. Marta was momentarily paralyzed. Arms and legs didn't bend quite that way. She moved two steps closer.

Stopped and stood still again. Peered without moving forward. She didn't want to get closer to the blond woman, yet she wanted to see her better. She leaned forward and focused.

And saw that there was some space between the bloody neck and the head. She realized with a lurch of her stomach that the woman had been beheaded. And her limbs had been detached and lain or propped so they were close to where they'd be if only they weren't severed. One arm was slightly longer than the other. It was a man's arm, with an expensive-looking gold expansion-band wristwatch. Marta looked closer and saw that the watch was a Timex.

And there was the rest of the dead man, lying near the sofa, his limbs severed and carefully propped or laid near where they'd been removed. Marta didn't know him but thought she recognized him. He'd made a pest of himself with some of the hotel guests.

Marta had been numb, but now she was slightly dizzy. And more than slightly nauseated. Fearing she might vomit, she hurried into the bathroom.

From the bathtub a pair of infinitely sad blue eyes

stared up at her. Dead eyes. The nude dead woman in the white porcelain tub was almost as white as the tub itself. Water had been run on her until most of her blood and other body fluids had been washed down the drain.

Her body was taut and shapely and looked young, but her face looked prematurely old.

In a way, it had been old.

Marta bumped her hip painfully on her linen cart as she ran from room 333, down from the steps leading from the catwalk, then the shallow wooden steps leading toward the levee.

She screamed as she ran, waved her arms, pointed back toward the hotel. One of her shoes flew off and she felt cool mud squish between her toes. At first people thought she might simply be enjoying herself, joking, a vacationing refugee from some boring job, suddenly set free and screaming with relief.

But it didn't sound like relief.

"*Mortandad! Policia!*"

Someone said, "I think she wants the police."

The federal park ranger for that stretch of waterfront had been observing this from the beginning. His name was John Randall, but most of the river people who knew him called him Rocket.

Rocket saw now that the woman had a maid's uniform on, and she was definitely headed for the river. She was limping now, dragging one leg. Soon she'd be close enough to the brown rushing water that he wouldn't be able to catch up and save her, if she was one of those who needed saving. A swimmer didn't have to get very far out in the river before the deceptively powerful current would take charge. Some people who went in here had been found dead as far south as New Orleans.

The decision was made for Rocket when he suddenly recognized the woman. Marta! One of the maids at the Adam Park.

Marta seemed unhinged, and definitely was headed for the river. He didn't know if that was on purpose or if she simply didn't realize how soon she'd be getting wet. The way she was waving her arms and yelling, it was obvious that she wasn't going to slow down.

He began to run. He was a big man, a year out of Florida State, where he'd gone on a football scholarship as a wide receiver. It was no mystery why he was called Rocket.

He almost caught up with Marta, calling her name, reaching out for her and barely missing.

She seemed to run harder.

He tackled her, but as gently as possible, and they both were down on the edge of the water. What felt like gravel was only a few inches beneath them. Rocket thought it might have cut up his right knee.

The water lapped coldly at Marta, and she stopped struggling and began to tremble. Rocket held her close, saying over and over that she should take it easy, take it easy.

Marta calmed down somewhat and stared up at him. It gave him a jolt, how horrified she looked.

"*Policia!*" she said.

"Yeah," he said, smiling at her to keep her calm. "Show me. If we need to, we'll call the locals." He held his grin. "What happened, Marta? you see a mouse?"

"*Policia! . . .*"

73

St. Louis, the present

St. Louis, Quinn decided, was a hotter place to live than New York. Most of the people in and around the Adam Park hotel had on casual clothes, jeans, shorts, pullover shirts, moccasins, sandals, or jogging shoes. Cross the street, stroll down to the river bank, and you were near the Mississippi. The wide, lazy river that held its secrets.

Even before it soared over the riverfront, the famously beautiful and utterly useless Arch had its fans. People who might as well have had TOURIST stamped all over them were lined up to enter the nearest leg. New York Police Commissioner Harley Renz, in his gray Joseph Abboud suit, white shirt, and polished black wingtip shoes, didn't seem to belong anywhere near this bunch.

But here he was, after a hurried flight from La-Guardia, following a lead on a New York killer. Might he gain national fame? He smiled. This was why he kept a suitcase packed.

Renz made his way toward the hotel entrance and air-conditioning. Quinn followed. "Some mess," Renz said, mopping his face with a white handkerchief.

Quinn didn't bother voicing his agreement. Though the identification of all the Adam Park victims was missing, doubtless removed by the killer, it was assumed that all three of them had been killed by the Gremlin. No one else was murdering people and then turning them into puppet pieces without strings. Not at the moment, anyway.

Quinn peered into the bathroom, where a female victim was sprawled in the tub. He stepped closer and saw that she'd been eviscerated, her internal organs stacked neatly beside her. Most of the blood had been washed from the tub and the pale dismembered corpse.

"There isn't any question about these victims being the work of the Gremlin," Quinn said. "I wonder if he knew we baited our trap at Faith Recovery Center, and that would occupy us while he committed his murders and mutilations here, in another city."

"Maybe," Renz said. "This doesn't seem at all unplanned."

Quinn looked around at the carnage and wondered what was wrong with the human race. With the Gremlin. He doubted if the killer himself could tell the real reasons for his murder spree.

"Sick, clever bastard," he said under his breath.

Renz stared at him. "You really think he's that smart? That he can move us around like chess pieces and commit murders without eventually being caught?"

Quinn said, "Exactly like chess pieces."

"Well, we're chess pieces that fight back," Renz said.

"Soon as we get some blood and fingerprints here, we're gonna run them through the national databases."

"I think we better concentrate on what's happening with Pearl and Weaver," Quinn said. He couldn't help it. He still wasn't comfortable with all the electronics taking over police work.

"I made sure there was plenty of protection at Faith Recovery," Renz said.

Quinn thought, Plenty of chess pieces, mostly pawns.

The techs arrived with their white gloves and medical equipment. Five minutes later the ME, a Dr. Nicholson, who looked amazingly like Nift, showed up, with his black leather case and cheerful, crude tactics.

He got to work immediately.

Renz appeared in the bedroom doorway. "Something odd about the toilet bowl," he said.

Quinn went over to the hall bathroom. Behind him, Nicholson continued tending to his work, seemingly uninterested in the bathroom and untouched by the gore. Seemingly. Quinn stopped his thoughts from going where rumor might rule.

He stood in the bathroom, staring at the conventional-looking white toilet bowl. Quinn hadn't heard it flush, and was glad Renz had thought to lower the seat.

When Quinn moved to flush the toilet, he couldn't find the handle. He examined the toilet more closely and encountered only its smooth white surface. No handle. He held his breath and carefully lifted the seat of the modern, streamlined commode.

It had flushed on its own. Must have been automatically and silently.

"Very impressive," Renz said.

Quinn waved a hand close to the top of the commode's tank. Two recessed rows of LED lights illuminated the smooth tank top. His fingers almost touched the tank, and silently the water in it swirled and disappeared.

"Very, very impressive," Renz said. "Can you do that with folding chairs?"

Quinn cocked his head to one side. A faint sound. He lifted the commode lid and a tiny whirlpool swirled steadily at the bottom of the bowl.

"It doesn't work right," Renz said. "Doesn't turn itself off."

Quinn smiled thinly, getting a mental image of two hardcase cops standing and discussing a futuristic porcelain commode in a hotel bathroom. Maybe they should be working for the Department of Sanitation. Maybe they should be plumbers. "We better not touch this thing," Quinn said. "My guess is that our Gremlin became intrigued by it. He had to take it apart and see how it worked, and how it didn't." Quinn let his eyes range over the gleaming fixtures and blue ceramic tile. "He cleaned the place pretty thoroughly, wiped it down. But things didn't go exactly as planned. That threw him. He couldn't be sure about where he might have left his own fingerprints."

Looking out the door into the bedroom, Renz pointed. "What the hell is that?" He was pointing to a metal object barely visible where the bed's comforter met the carpet.

Quinn went over and stooped down, feeling it in his legs. He used his ballpoint pen to ease out the object under the bed.

"Well?" Renz said, as they looked down at a strange metal contraption that faintly resembled an alligator with its mouth open wide.

"It's a wine-cork puller," Quinn said. "Taken apart. Looks like whoever did it had to use a screwdriver, then couldn't get it back together."

"Gee," Renz said. "Who do we know who'd do that?"

"Let's hope somebody who left a fingerprint," Quinn said. "And is rich, but not so sophisticated that he knows about self-flushing toilets."

Renz wrestled his cell phone from his pocket and used it to check the time. 11:45. The murders here were hours old. How many people had come and gone in the room since then? "The way this place has been wiped down, even if somebody's prints are on file from these murders, they probably won't match."

Quinn shook his head. "I say that the Gremlin either knows or is afraid there might be matching prints here, or he wouldn't have taken the chance and gone crazy trying to make sure he's wiped everything clean. And that commode . . ."

"What about it?" Renz asked.

"You tell me. You've had time to check on it."

"You're right. I used my iPhone."

"And?"

"The commode isn't broken—or if it is, the Gremlin broke it. It must have intrigued him because it doesn't have a flush handle and it's self cleaning."

Quinn was relieved. He was afraid Renz was going to tell him about how someone might have drowned via the toilet bowl, an ignoble death no one should be forced to endure.

Almost no one.

"I'm informed that the so called auto-flush feature is in a lot of swank hotels," Renz continued, "but none that our killer would have stayed in if he knew he wasn't going to pay the bill. This one tickled his fancy and he couldn't help taking it apart, or at least examining it to see how it worked. Gadgets are like porn for this guy. He couldn't get the thing back together and make it work, and he got flustered and had to rush to finish up here. That's why the place looks like it was given a once-over by a maid on speed."

"If there are prints that can be matched," Renz said, "the Crime Scene Unit will find them. They're a capable bunch, here in St. Louie."

"Notice that nobody here says 'St. Louie'?"

"I say it," Renz said. "But then I'm not one of the Millennials."

"Even if we don't have the killer's matching prints on file, he might think we have them," Quinn said. "That could work just as well. The clock is ticking. That should prompt the kind of response we want."

"I prefer being proactive," Renz said.

"What the hell does that mean?" Quinn asked.

"Means I have to wrap this up, then get back to New York and catch up playing commissioner. Seems we've got other problems in town there. Not just our dead-then-undead girl. Which isn't even a crime, as far as I know. How are Pearl and Weaver holding up?"

"Impatiently. They want action. Haven't had so much as a nibble from the Gremlin. He's cautious and he's smart," Quinn said. "You can bet he's at least mulling over going for the bait."

"Meanwhile we've got another death of note. A famous architect engineer."

"Victim or perpetrator?"

"Maybe both. I don't have the complete picture. It was a car accident but the police don't know whether it was an accident, suicide, or murder."

"Got a name on the victim?"

"Ethan Ellis," Renz said.

Quinn was surprised. "The guy who's designing the MOMA addition?"

"The same. I forgot you were a devotee of the arts."

"Any connection between that death and what we're doing here?"

"Only in the way everything is in some way connected with every other," Renz said. "Be sure to get in touch with me if there are any issues."

"Are issues something like problems?" Quinn asked.

Renz said, "Have a blessed day," and left to go to his car.

74

New York, the present

At Faith Recovery Center, Quinn stayed out of sight, behind the folding doors that partitioned Weaver's room from the adjoining one. In the monitor propped high in a corner, he could see Weaver with bandages over much of her face, lying beneath a thin white sheet that made her look all the worse. Her bullet-proof vest was completely covered by the sheet, as was the Ruger .25 semiautomatic handgun, within easy reach of her right hand. The plastic IV tube alongside her bed dripped only simple glucose.

A second monitor was trained on the door to the next room, so that anyone entering or leaving would be seen. Quinn knew that just outside the door was a uniformed cop in a chair borrowed from one of the small waiting areas. The uniform had a good view of the elevators from where he sat, as well as a view of anyone who might open the door to the fire stairs.

In the wall monitor, Quinn saw Fedderman pause outside in the hall, then enter Weaver's room. He was wearing a light raincoat and his hair looked damp. Fedderman took a quick glance at the tiny camera near the room's ceiling, disguised to look like one of the sprinkler heads of a fire-protection system. He walked over to the bed and leaned down, said something to Weaver that Quinn couldn't make out. Weaver seemed to nod.

As Quinn watched in the monitor, Fedderman walked toward the folding doors separating the two rooms. Then the doors parted near the wall and he appeared in the flesh and life-size.

"Watching old *Adam-12* reruns?" Fedderman asked.

Quinn thought about telling him ten-four, but he didn't want to start something. "Weaver still doing okay?" he asked instead.

"Says her flak jacket chafes. We both agreed that if that was our biggest problem we were doing okay."

"You're early if you're here to relieve me," Quinn said.

"I came in to show you these," Fedderman said. "Renz wanted me to make sure you saw them." He reached beneath his tan light raincoat and handed Quinn some printouts. "The police sketch artist aged these photos and they appear to be the older woman who was killed in St. Louis."

There were three copies of black-and-white photographs, front and profile views of a teenage girl. They weren't mug shots. She was wearing different blouses and might even have been older in one of the shots. In that one she had a more mature profile, and a different hairdo. It was cut short rather than shoulder length, as in the other photos.

The third printout wasn't a photo but an appeal to report the whereabouts of a missing sixteen-year-old girl named Jasmine. It was dated fifteen years ago. She had disappeared from the family farm one night and never been heard from again.

"Twenty-year-old Jordan Kray, a hired hand on the farm, disappeared at approximately the same time as Jasmine's sudden and unexpected departure."

"A connection?" Quinn asked.

"They might have been an item," Fedderman said. "A week after the disappearances, several people noticed half a dozen buzzards circling in the clear blue sky. Two men drove out to investigate.

"They saw more buzzards on the ground. Some of them were pecking and standing on something dark among the corn. One of the men got a shotgun from the truck's rear window rack and blasted away. Scared the birds, but they didn't go far.

"The man with the shotgun saw what interested the big birds. There was a man—or what used to be a man—barely visible in the rows of corn. His clothes were ripped and filthy, and birds and animals had gotten to him.

"There was an empty, worn, and weathered leather wallet near what was left of the dead man's body, Nothing in the wallet. No identification. The man who owned the farm kept asking the Highway Patrol troopers to remove the dead man from his field. He was informed that he was growing crops on a government easement.

"As the body was dragged a few feet closer to the tracks, onlookers saw that the victim was male and had on oversized Levi's that were reduced to rags that fell away when he was moved.

"The dead man was barefoot. Empty wallet, missing

shoes. No watch—wrist or pocket. He'd been picked clean."

More and more it looked to Quinn as if the dead man had been a train hopper. Maybe one who followed the simple philosophy of empathizing with losers, and then acting on what he'd seen or heard. What he'd learned. There were plenty of that kind around. Always they had ulterior motives. Always they were acting.

Sometimes they were lambs. Sometimes wolves. All the time they couldn't be trusted.

75

New York City, the present

In Faith Recovery Center, the uniform was seated in a chair outside where Officer Nancy Weaver lay in bed, where she was pretending to be Pearl pretending to be lost in a coma. Her protector was Sergeant Dave Gregg, three inches over six feet, and forty pounds over two hundred. He'd been with the NYPD over twenty years and had seen about everything that cops saw. He'd considered it an honor rather than duty when he'd been assigned this job. The two men running the show were fixtures in NYPD nobility. Renz, the commissioner who might someday become mayor. And Quinn, who was already a legend.

For the third time this evening Officer David Gregg braced with his arms and lifted his bulk up out of his chair. He hitched up his black uniform belt, yawned, and slowly strolled down to the waiting area near the end of the hall to get a candy bar out of one of the vending machines.

None of the nurses or occasional doctors seemed to

take the presence of the big uniformed cop as an indication that something might be wrong. Or, if not wrong, unusual. They were quick to return his smile, but always they hurried along. All that weaponry on his belt was made to inflict injury or death, the two things the doctors and nurses in the recovery center were trained to detest.

Gregg was glad to see there were still Zero bars in the machine. They were his favorite. They were delicious when washed down with a cheap red wine, but this wasn't the time or place for that. Maybe later.

A female doctor entered, recognized as such by Gregg because she was wearing pale blue scrubs, a matching skullcap, and floppy pull-on shoe covers. A crinkled cloth mask was still tied loosely around the doctor's neck. Coiled below the mask's tie strings were the twin tubes and earpieces of a stethoscope.

"Beautiful evening," Gregg said, and was answered with a smile. Everyone was so nice here it almost made you want to recover from something.

As the doctor eased around Gregg's bulk, it occurred to Gregg that he'd never seen anyone who looked more like a brilliant surgeon.

That was what alarmed him.

Still smiling, he reached out as if he were going to shake hands with the doctor. Instead he grabbed her wrist and held it in a powerful lock in one of his big hands.

This felt great to Gregg. He hadn't been fooled for long, and now he was making the collar. This was the kind of thing that might get him interviewed in the *Times*.

The play of strength in the doctor's arm prompted

Gregg's first misgiving. Something was wrong here. The doctor was strong as a man. *Was a man.* Not a large man, but strong out of proportion to his size.

The man's tightly fitted blue surgeon's cap had tilted and revealed a protruding ear, almost perfectly pointed. It gave him a constant appearance of alertness.

Gregg's smile faded as he said, "I think you'd better—"

He saw the stiletto-like knife in the doctor's right hand. The long pointed blade looked as if it were designed for taking and not saving lives.

It entered Gregg's corpulent body easily, angled upward tight to his sternum, and pierced his heart.

He couldn't cry out an alarm. Instead he made what sounded like a hopeless sob. No one had ever looked more like a real lady surgeon than his killer. Gregg knew he should have noticed that, acted on it, alerted the others . . . But he'd done his job. And now the light was fading.

He needed a doctor!

He didn't fall. The Gremlin supported Gregg and helped him to stumble over to a chair.

Gregg felt himself being eased down into the chair.

Once the brief struggle had begun, the whole thing hadn't taken half a minute. Gregg was having a hard time seeing now. He was too weak to move under his own power, and he knew he was dying.

He heard a distant, amused voice. "Take two aspirins and call me in the morning."

In some remote part of his brain, Gregg was glad somebody had a sense of humor.

Then the pain came.

* * *

When Gregg was dead, the Gremlin propped him firmly in the waiting room chair and arranged his arms and legs. Now he was posed looking like what he was, a cop taking a break. Arranging the body had gotten blood on the Gremlin's surgical scrubs, but that was okay. He knew that now he looked even more like a genuine doctor.

Or one from Central Casting.

He glanced at his watch. It was time to make the phone call. The one that would end the game with the winner not in doubt. Time for Quinn to learn his final and most important lesson: The winning game was not always the long game. Not even always the game you think you're playing.

He made his phone call.

And then another, that would change worlds and futures.

76

Weaver scratched beneath her left armpit where the bulletproof vest chafed. She tried to get something like comfortable. Her two-way produced nothing but static. She gave up for the moment. Probably some piece of medical equipment was running somewhere nearby, emitting rays that cured this or that, or displayed that or this, and interfered with communication. Weaver decided to give up for the time being and rest. A real coma wouldn't be bad right now. Except for the fact that she might not wake up.

Keeping that in mind, she tried to ignore her restlessness, and to resist scratching where the bulky vest itched.

Weaver's chief protector was now sitting dead near the other end of the hall. The killer had left a folded section of newspaper tented over the cop's ample midsection so the blood wouldn't seep through after a while and be noticed.

The Gremlin had scouted the territory, learning the layout of the rehab center. He knew the target's room number, and had even glanced into the room while making sure he knew where the clean laundry was stored.

It had all worked well, at least for a while.

It took the police less than ten minutes to get there. Sirens growled to silence as two NYPD radio cars pulled in at an angle to the curb in front of the Center.

Quinn was already, along with Fedderman, running toward the room where Weaver played the mystery woman who'd entered and then left the afterlife, and just a few seconds ago had almost lost her corporeal life.

He made it to room 409 just in time to watch the elevator doors close. But not before he caught a glimpse of Weaver inside. She wore a hospital gown stained with blood, probably from her nose, which appeared broken. The Gremlin was holding her with her arm bent behind her, in such a way that any upward pressure made her grimace in pain.

When she saw Quinn she smiled.

The subtle smile was brief and only at the corners of her lips, but it informed Quinn that the Gremlin had taken the bait. He had, ostensibly, Pearl, disguised as Weaver, playing the role of Pearl.

This was the kind of labyrinth the Gremlin wanted, or thought he wanted. Advanced chess.

More radio cars, sans sirens, arrived silently and were lined up outside the center. Both ends of the driveway were blocked.

The Gremlin slid behind Weaver, locked the double glass doors, and retreated into the maze of halls and rooms beneath the center.

Weaver felt around beneath her gown for her Ruger but couldn't find it. As they hurried down a hall lined with identical pea-green doors, the Gremlin removed the Ruger and held it up so she could see it.

Most of the rooms were unoccupied, but some of them sheltered recuperating patients. Now and then someone would glance at them from inside a room. If they had spotted something wrong, they didn't want to become involved. They didn't want to become dead.

The Gremlin needed one of those patients for a convincer. The woman who'd been dead but was somehow again alive had to know he would use the gun.

There was so much he wanted her to tell him.

A PA system clicked and buzzed. Then a woman's calm voice proclaimed that there were "difficulties being dealt with," and instructed patients and staff to remain behind the locked door of whichever room they were in until they heard the all clear. That was appropriately ambiguous, the killer thought. It carried exactly the right touch of controlled urgency. Panic was right around the corner.

Footfalls sounded ahead of them, and a uniformed cop and another nurse came into view. The cop had the woman by the elbow, hurrying her along. Suddenly they were face-to-face.

The Gremlin drew Weaver's gun and blasted away. The cop, who'd managed to get his gun halfway out of its holster, sat down and his eyes went blank. The nurse stared horrified at the Gremlin and started backing away.

The Gremlin bent down to get the cop's gun from its holster.

"You killed him!" the young nurse stammered, then she spun on her heel and ran down the hall to where it took a right turn.

"That was a bad idea," Weaver said, "killing a cop. Haven't you seen any of those old gangster movies?"

"All of them."

He made his way along the halls, tried some doors until he found an unlocked one, and slipped into an unoccupied room, pushing the supposedly injured Weaver ahead of him. It was cool in there, and quiet.

He was glad again to have studied the Center's floor plan, and thought he knew exactly where he was. If he made it about fifty feet to the next cross hall, dragging Weaver along with him, he should be able to turn right and use an exit.

Of course, the exit would be covered by the police, who by now must have surrounded the Center with much of their uniformed force, along with their teams of elite snipers.

The Gremlin went to the dim room's door and attempted to lock it, but discovered there was no lock. That was when, for some reason, an element of fear crept into his mind. It was a small thing, leaving him no more vulnerable, but it was like having a black cat cross your path. Nothing but superstition, but still . . .

Something else he should have thought of was the young nurse he had let run away after he'd shot, and surely killed, the uniformed cop. If he'd held her as a hostage, she could have become a valuable bargaining chip. Even though she was not the one he had come to collect.

The killer looked around but didn't see a phone. Probably the Center brought landline phones in and plugged them into wall outlets when new patients arrived.

He pulled his throwaway cell phone from his pocket and pecked out a number that was by now familiar. Quinn's cell phone's number. It could be traced to this area, but if he didn't keep the connection open for a while they wouldn't be able to pinpoint the room he was in.

There was no caller ID on Quinn's phone, only the number that had most recently called.

Quinn answered and identified himself.

"This will be a short conversation," the killer said. "It's time for me to have Pearl."

Quinn felt the anger grow in him. "I don't think there will ever be a time for that."

The Gremlin laughed. God, he enjoyed this! Whoever said victory was hollow didn't know what he was talking about.

When he heard the laugh, Quinn tightened his grip on the phone. "You're not going to get off the grounds here alive."

"After we trade, watch and see if I get off the ground."

Quinn knew the Gremlin might well have a way. He wasn't the sort who wouldn't have a plan B.

Then Quinn recalled Helen the profiler's words: "He doesn't want you; he wants what's yours. He wants Pearl." Helen had been right from the beginning. He'd been played for a fool. Weaver and her back-from-the-dead act hadn't fooled the Gremlin. The little bastard had guessed in the beginning that Weaver had only been an arrow pointing the way to Pearl.

"I have Weaver," the voice on the phone said. "She'll be actually and forever dead within an hour if you don't do as I say."

Quinn told himself that this was going at least somewhat as planned. But he didn't feel at all ahead in the game.

He wondered how Weaver felt. And the Gremlin.

He knew how Pearl felt, and he didn't like that, either.

The Gremlin surprised him again. "This place doesn't have a heliport," the Gremlin said, "but it does have a flat grassy area up front that will do for one."

Quinn was thrown by that. It was something he hadn't considered. "Are you telling me you want a helicopter?"

"Not for keeps," the Gremlin said.

Quinn thought it wasn't good that the killer still had a sense of humor. Some of the most vicious psychotic killers he'd encountered enjoyed a good laugh. It at least distracted them for the moment.

The Gremlin was using Weaver as the surest route to Pearl.

"Get me a police or hospital helicopter, and fast," the Gremlin said, "before it gets completely dark, or I'll shoot your policewoman, and then everybody will be shooting everybody else. You know how these things get out of hand. Some unlucky sap in the next block will be sitting watching crap on TV and a bullet will come in through a window and blow his brains out." He tightened his grip on Weaver and stuck the gun barrel under her right eye. "I'm waiting for your answer. You've got only so many seconds to make up your mind, and I'm counting."

Weaver said, "Don't bargain with the little prick."

Instead Quinn said, "What happens after you get your helicopter?"

"I guess that depends on what you and our phony, miraculously reborn girlfriend here decide. If she cooperates, the helicopter will simply drop down somewhere and let her out. If she doesn't cooperate, the same thing will happen, only from higher up." The Gremlin laughed. "I'll bet there'll be some TV copters, too. Recording everything. It will be immortal on the Internet."

Quinn stood thinking it over. At least the psychopath wouldn't be at the controls and wouldn't crash the helicopter.

"It isn't as if you have a choice," the killer said.

Quinn knew he was right.

"All right," he said. "I'll try to get you a helicopter. It won't be easy. I'll have to make some phone calls."

Quinn used his index finger to peck out Renz's number.

In the building's lobby, Renz answered a Center phone and listened to Quinn's concise request. Since all calls in or out of the Center were being monitored, he already knew the contents of Quinn and the killer's earlier conversation, so it didn't surprise him. Wouldn't have surprised him, anyway. Desperate people often viewed helicopters as if they were magic carpets that could swoop down and lift them out of trouble. It was wishful thinking.

Most of the time.

He said, "I can get us a helicopter."

"I need it fast, Harley."

"You'll get it."

Renz didn't bother telling Quinn that somewhere

along the line, probably in his brief stint in the army, the Gremlin had learned to fly a helicopter. That was only seven months before he went AWOL and was given a dishonorable discharge. What Quinn didn't know might not hurt him. Or Renz.

Quinn relayed Renz's answer. There were few people in the country who had the popular commissioner's push. A skillful social climber and de facto extortionist, he knew almost everyone connected to law enforcement. And not only in New York.

When he heard, the Gremlin grinned. The gun was still pointed at Weaver's head. She looked as if she'd just swallowed a smile.

People who lived on the edge, Quinn thought. Why did he understand them so well?

He caught a glimpse of himself reflected in a window.

It was subtle, but if he'd looked closely enough he might have noticed he was smiling.

It wasn't a nice smile.

Things got worse.

Renz called Quinn's cell phone and told him as much.

"We've got more information," Renz said. He sounded frazzled and desperate.

"Another phone call?"

"A letter, actually. Remember the Ethan Ellis death? Looked like suicide by car?"

"Of course." Quinn could feel everything enlarging, ‸‸ ‸ng more dangerous. "You saying murder now?"

‸‸ ‸e. Suicide by car. There was a suicide note in

an envelope stuck down between the seats. Had your name on it. From Ellis."

Now Quinn was dumbfounded. The possibilities his mind grasped were slippery and temporary.

"Note said he was being controlled by the Gremlin. Said we'd find out how. The thing is, we've gotta act fast. Ellis planted explosives in about a dozen buildings. He knew where and how to plant them. Not only will the buildings come down, but the *way* and sequence in which they fall will cause them to bring down strings of surrounding buildings, sometimes over a dozen at a time."

"Like dominos," Quinn said. He felt his heartbeat accelerate. Fear creeping in as he tried to grasp what he'd just heard. What it meant.

"But with people inside." Renz said. "Manhattan will be mostly debris when the chain reactions occur."

"What's supposed to detonate the explosives?"

"Timers that will activate sequentially so the most damage can be done. A car driven a route south to north, mostly along Broadway, is supposed to send out signals the length of the island that will activate the timers as it passes. That way the right buildings will come down in the right sequences." Renz's voice got heavy. "This will all happen within minutes after the first timer is activated."

"So somebody other than Ellis is supposed to drive the car and make the bombs live?"

"Nope. That's not our problem, now that we know their plan. Ordinarily we'd simply stop all north-south traffic, at least minimize the damage."

"Why can't you do that now?"

"We don't have to worry about a car or truck," Renz

said. "The killer wants a helicopter. The device used to signal all the detonator timers to start ticking is simply a bastardized cell phone. A brief helicopter flight over Manhattan with that thing broadcasting will cause approximately the same damage as a nuclear bomb."

"Is there a way to fly the same route and neutralize the timers or detonators by broadcasting a different signal?"

"That's what everyone here is trying to determine. We decided to talk to you about what we consider our only alternative."

"Which is?"

"Give the helicopter pilot what he wants."

"Which is?"

"Pearl."

As Quinn stood in the suddenly cold silence, he was sure he could hear the distant but persistent thrashing sound of an approaching helicopter.

77

It was dusk, and they heard the helicopter before they saw it. The engine itself wasn't that loud, but the air passing through the thrashing rotor blades as they provided lift and balance soon made conversation impossible unless it was shouted.

Downward-aimed lights illuminated the dimming landing area. The copter dropped to about twenty feet, toward the center of the circle of brilliant light. It rotated until its nose was pointed north and the craft was parallel to the building.

It settled in gradually, and the choppy, thrashing sound, the one from the Gremlin's nightmares, lost volume as the rotors and vertical tail propeller slowed and the engine idled.

The helicopter looked much larger on the ground. It was gray with a red cross and bore the lettering of one of the hospitals in the area, St. Andrew's. The killer had never heard of it. Didn't care.

A plainclothes cop came to the fore of the knot of people, then edged closer to Quinn and whispered, "Renz said to tell you the guy at the controls was a former attack helicopter pilot in Afghanistan. He volunteered for this job."

That was good to know. Confirmation. At least the Gremlin wouldn't be at the controls when the craft tried to take off.

"That's where they met," the cop said. "Both those guys can fly a chopper."

Great, Quinn thought. He could almost feel the odds shifting, and not in his favor.

With Quinn beside her, Pearl trudged toward the helicopter as if her feet were heavy.

The side door on the helicopter slid open.

Weaver stood leaning against it, the blasts of air from the rotors plastering her hair over her face. She was feigning a weakness she didn't feel. She was actually revved and ready for action. The pilot, a stocky guy with gray hair cut so close he was almost bald, slid over where he was visible and extended his hand to help Weaver climb inside. An encouraging signal that he was ready to get away from their exposed position fast. Another figure, no doubt the Gremlin, was barely visible seated in back

Weaver made a move as if to climb into the chopper, but Quinn squeezed her shoulder and she stopped.

"Wait," he said to her, "wait . . ."

"I'm no longer useful," she said, her head turned toward Quinn so the others couldn't read her lips. "He's sweeping up after himself."

He knew what she meant, and that she was right.

The look on the pilot's face was fear. The figure in back fired a small, silenced handgun.

Wearing an astounded expression, the pilot slumped forward. He scrambled to get out of the helicopter, fell to the ground, and died staring up at the slowly rotating blades.

While that occupied everyone's mind, the small nimble figure in the helicopter moved quickly to the front of the craft. He leaned forward, aiming the gun at Weaver. The helicopter's speaker system was on. "No one else has to die," the Gremlin said. "Quinn, give me Pearl and I spare the police lady. Disobey, and we'll see if she can come alive yet again."

Pearl had moved to the side of Quinn and now she edged forward and was standing beside him.

The Gremlin said, "Come forward, police lady."

Weaver, trembling, took a step toward him. He was seated in the helicopter, leaning slightly forward. Quinn knew the snipers had no clear shot at that angle. The Gremlin also would know it.

This kill-crazy little psycho is going to do this, get what he wants. We can't stop him.

"Police lady," the killer said, "step forward."

He grinned as she obeyed. "I no longer need you," he said with a twist of false regret.

That was when Quinn understood that the Gremlin had known from the beginning that he, Quinn, would make his double switch, sending Weaver to play herself, Weaver, playing Pearl. There had never been a dead woman whose heart had resumed beating.

As the Gremlin took aim at her, Weaver bolted. He shot her in the shoulder, and she fell.

Pearl had stepped around Quinn and was moving toward the helicopter.

"Pearl!" Quinn shouted behind her.

"Keep walking or I'll shoot him, darling." The Gremlin wore his grin like a mask.

Pearl kept walking toward him. When she was close enough, he leaned slightly farther to grab her and pull her the rest of the way inside the helicopter, still with the gun aimed at Quinn.

Quinn stood staring.

Quinn . . .

Pearl accepted the Gremlin's hand up. As she raised herself into the helicopter, she squared her body toward the Gremlin.

Quinn hadn't moved, except for extending his right arm slightly toward Pearl and . . . what? Pressing a key or button on his iPhone? Signaling?

In those last seconds, the Gremlin sensed that something was very wrong. His face twisted meanly. His eyes implored. "Quinn, you don't know—"

The blast was loud and sounded more than anything like a shotgun being fired. Its source was like something that used to be called a belly gun.

It was a shaped charge. The Gremlin would have appreciated that.

It wasn't just Weaver who'd been wearing a bullet-proof vest. Quinn had been sure that Helen the profiler was right when she said it was Pearl the killer wanted most of all. Given a choice, he would choose Pearl, who was the most important thing in the world to Quinn. Weaver had been wearing her unaltered vest. Let the killer think he was the one who'd decided on Pearl. Her vest had been altered in the front, and contained a small iron plate on which was a shaped charge aimed like a shotgun and full of nails and ball bearings. The explosive had been fitted to Pearl's midsection, outside the vest, and aimed straight forward. Her baggy hospital gown had covered the vest. Pearl had been instructed to aim her navel at the Gremlin.

It had worked.

Pearl had trusted Quinn and he'd come through. Weaver had suffered only a slight shoulder injury. She would live. Pearl, who had been target and become weapon, would live.

Pearl was sitting stunned and bent forward, and still had a stomachache, but the vest had diffused most of the pain of the charge's powerful kick. Her sore muscles would soon heal.

The Gremlin had taken the full force of the blast. It had been concentrated on him as planned. A shaped charge, directing its blast forward. The shrapnel of nails and ball bearings had blown him almost in half. He still looked astounded at having been killed by a woman.

Defeated by a gadget.

Pearl thought maybe they would bury the Gremlin with that same astounded expression on his face. She hoped so.

She hoped they would bury him deep.

Epilogue

Two weeks later, a man in a wrinkled gray suit and no neck came into Q&A, stood just inside the door, and glanced around. He was average height but broad, and had about him the look of a bill collector who loved his work. He walked directly to where Quinn was seated behind his desk. Fedderman stood up across the room, wondering.

But the broad man smiled and offered his hand to Quinn. "Frank Quinn." He said it as if he were telling Quinn and not asking him. "I'm Henry Safire."

"What can I do—"

"Listen," Henry Safire said. "That's all I want. Just . . . listen."

Quinn settled back in his chair. "You'd better not tell me I need insurance."

"There's something we thought you should know."

"You're off to a bad start. Who are 'we'?"

Safire drew a badge from his pocket and flashed it at Quinn. "I'm Homeland Security."

Quinn leaned forward and studied the ID and badge. He sat back. Said, "I'm listening."

"You might have some of this info," Safire said, "but I'm here to keep you up to date. We'll start with Ethan Ellis, the architect-engineer who died in that car accident. He committed suicide."

"Yes, I know that."

"You know about the envelope with your name on it tucked into his car's seat cushion," Safire said. "We read it and don't want anyone else to ever know about it. Ethan was into some pretty bad behavior. Compulsive. Illegal. Harmful. There is proof of that, but no point in letting the tiger out of the bag. Ethan Ellis was being extorted. Compromised. He had to obey orders, or some things harmful to him would have been given to the media and sensationalized. You were part of what Ethan planned in order to spare his family and reputation." Safire made a tent of his fingers. Looked at his nails, which were chewed almost to nonexistence.

"To be brief," Safire said, "someone owned and instructed Ethan Ellis. For several years Ethan studied the architecture and engineering of certain Manhattan buildings. He wanted to make sure that what was planned was possible. He chose buildings that could be brought down by explosives in such a way, and direction, that they would knock down adjacent buildings. So buildings could be destroyed in sequence, in strings of four or five, or more, like dominoes only messier."

"The Gremlin," Quinn said. "He was the architect's master. The Gremlin wanted those buildings destroyed, revealing what was inside. Everything exposed to his curiosity and compulsion. He could have been made to destroy some of the same buildings he'd designed."

Henry Safire seemed not to have heard. "Someone like Ethan Ellis could be made to determine exactly how the structures would fall, in strings of up to a dozen or more. Since he'd designed many of the buildings, he could also plant the explosives. Small, powerful charges, expertly applied, that could be detonated from a short distance. All that was needed was a driver to take a certain route at a certain speed through the city, sending out intermittent signals via a cell phone."

"What would keep this driver from being killed as half of Manhattan fell?" Quinn asked. As he spoke, he tried to imagine the island of Manhattan a jumble of wreckage north to south. Then he tried not to imagine it.

"The signals would activate timers on the bombs so they would detonate in precise sequences," Safire said. "This wouldn't happen until well after the driver, who activated the timers while keeping a constant speed, was far away."

Quinn pushed for more answers. "Why not simply use Ethan Ellis for the driver?"

"Let's face it, Quinn, some folks are squeamish about killing thousands, maybe millions, of people." Henry Safire shrugged. "Like you, Quinn."

Quinn said, "Thank God!"

"Besides," Safire said, "they had to have something profound on the driver. Something they could hold over his head that would scare the hell out of him. Something dearer to him than life itself. Even his own life."

"Then the car crash *was* suicide?"

"No doubt about it," Safire said. "We'll keep the motive under wraps as long as we can, but you know how it is with secrets."

"Secrets?" Quinn said. "There are none."

Postscript

Demolition experts, using information contained in Ethan Ellis's suicide note to Quinn, located and disarmed most of the planted bombs set to tick away to detonation when a certain code was broadcasted to them at a certain frequency. The chances of eventually finding and combining the code and frequency were practically nil.

Practically.

It shouldn't matter that a number of the bombs remained unfound, hidden away or concealed in cast concrete. Within a few years the explosive would become inert and a danger to no one.

In what used to be a car dealer's service center in Astoria, New York, the devoted son of Ethan Ellis worked assiduously, using mail-order parts and plans to rebuild a small, wrecked helicopter a Midwest TV station had given up on for weather and traffic reports. A home project, he called it, if anyone asked. When finished, it wouldn't lift or carry a lot of weight. Nor would it fly very fast, with a pilot and passenger limit of two people. But it could fly low enough to pass under radar, yet high enough so that its broadcast signals would reach receivers and detonators, even in buildings with higher floors.

That was enough. Even more than enough. For its final flight, the helicopter was only required to carry one passenger at a certain speed, along with a modem sending out a certain signal in a certain code.

Straight down Broadway.